CW01501524

YEARS BEFORE WHITECHAPEL - THE CHASE CONTINUES

INSANIA

BOOK TWO

MATT ROSS

For

Callum & Sam

When darkness devours all rational thought and all light is extinguished, the mind becomes a tormented vessel upon a raging sea where monsters live, deep within the murky waters of our consciousness. Waiting behind the shadows and nightmares of our worst fears, madness takes its hold and walks beside us.

Matt Ross, 2025.

The Surrey District Times

Obituary Announcements

Patterson James, Dr. *It is with deep regret and a solemn heart that we announce the passing of Dr James Patterson (57) at his home, Fox Hall. Dr Patterson was a well-known, much-admired, and respected member of the community. He had been a local GP for many years, serving the people of Surrey at his practice in Esher and surrounding hospitals and, for a time, advisor to Her Majesty The Queen. He held no distinction between the rich and poor, giving fair counsel to both equally, and will be remembered for his kindness, attentiveness, and patience. He will be greatly missed by all who knew him.*

He died surrounded by his family, leaving behind his wife Camilla and daughter Henrietta. A vigil and open casket will be held for four days at Fox Hall, commencing from 31st October, before a private interment to be held at the local church. If anyone from the community would care to come and pay their respects, the family would welcome your attendance.

CHAPTER 1

SURREY, ENGLAND, OCTOBER 1884

The mist sat low across the fields, clawing its way through hedgerows of hawthorn and blackthorn that bordered the road. From the window of his horse-drawn cab, he looked out at the barren landscape mirroring the cold grey blanket of sky above. The desolation was occasionally broken by clumps of evergreen bush sculptured flat by strong winds that whipped across their tops, as ornate houses rose from troughs in the stark countryside. Hidden from the world, they occasionally peeped through the weather like ghosts, homes built on money from the suffering and misfortune of others, the rich unashamedly displaying their power, status, and privilege.

The cab jolted roughly from side to side on the uneven surface, its wheels jumping in and out of the grooves carved over time into the frozen chalk. It swung through two large brick-built pillars with the name of the property, Fox Hall, mounted on an oak plaque. The driveway followed a gentle curve until the house came into view, an imposing structure dating from the Regency period. It was constructed from red brick and displayed two sash windows on either side of the ground floor, separated by a central door to the property. Stone pillars pitted by the wind and rain extended to a veranda and an oval window above the entrance. The second floor had two openings equally spaced on either side, with the final floor having two smaller casements inset into the black slate roof. Everything was positioned and aligned to show perfect balance.

He climbed down from his ride, instructing the driver to wait for his return. The driver, acknowledging the order, doffed his cap. Two mutes stood in front of a gloss black front door, with a large wreath of boxwood secured to the polished brass knocker. They were dressed in black, with matching top hats, each holding a staff covered in matching ribbon. It was their job to make sure people who wanted to pay their respects were greeted in the appropriate manner and, if required, escorted through the home to the room where the deceased lay.

He passed them without speaking, entering the house and sensing the pungent aroma of incense from handmade and ornate pastille burners to help mask the odour of the decaying body. But the smell of rotting flesh, evidence of death, had permeated its way throughout the house. The hallway was tastefully decorated and reminded him of his childhood home, which he had shared with his mother and father, who was also a doctor. However, his parents had not died peacefully with a loving family by their bedsides but by a series of savage, brutal blows—the images and screams he still treasured.

He entered the room where the wake and the open casket of the late Dr James Patterson had been placed. The room was still, the air rich with scent but empty of people, except for the man in the coffin, which was mounted on a large table with a tray underneath packed with ice to slow the putrefaction of the body. Six mahogany chairs upholstered in deep red satin with gold piping were positioned on one side of the room for contemplation, while the heavy drape curtains had been drawn across the large windows to keep the room private.

Illumination was provided by several candles placed carefully around the room, creating a respectful but sombre atmosphere. Mirrors once displayed had been covered in black cloth, following tradition, so the deceased spirit could not be trapped. A large grandfather clock in the corner of the room had been stopped, its hands positioned at three o'clock, the time death had come calling in the early morning, the Devil's hour, the opposite time that Jesus is said to have died on the cross, which he thought pertinent. He walked towards the casket, peering over, amused. James Patterson had been dressed and prepared, his eyes closed, his face painted with white pigment, and his lips coloured red to show that even after life had expired, it would appear to those of a more fragile disposition that he was only sleeping.

He removed his gloves, coveting the sensation of dead skin against his and slowly lowered his hand inside the coffin, brushing over the many flowers left by mourners, and gently stroked the cheek of the deceased, which felt clammy against the backs of his fingers. He wished he had been there to see this man's last moments. The clutching of hands with loved ones, the asking for redemption of past deeds done, the tightening of the chest, and the hanging on to the final breath as the Grim Reaper stepped forward to lay claim to the good doctor.

Although he would only have been a witness in this case, it reminded him of a more recent time. He missed the hunt, the pleasure of seeing his victims' eyes well up with fear as he savoured the last few seconds of their existence in his hands. He replayed that time, his thoughts lost in pure exaltation, blood racing, pumping through every capillary in his body; he was back there at that moment, aroused by the power, the climax of the kill, only for that special memory to be abruptly terminated by two people entering the room.

'Did you know my husband well?' a woman asked, walking

towards him. Her words were delivered with elegance and education but tinged with a touch of arrogance.

He placed his small black bag on the floor, quickly collecting himself. 'I had the privilege of meeting your husband professionally at various medical establishments. You should be in no doubt that his peers held him in the highest regard. I also understand he was in attendance at Buckingham Palace on more than one occasion to act as adviser to Her Majesty. So, I have to say it was an honour to have thought that he considered me both a colleague and a friend.'

'So, you're a doctor then, as my husband was?' she continued, looking interested, moving back her veil to reveal someone older than him. She was an attractive, slim woman in her early forties with streaks of grey hair coming through the dark. He noticed the soft scent of rose perfume followed her and that she had clearly enjoyed life's finer things, reflected in her poise and unblemished complexion.

'You don't *look* like a doctor,' a young freckle-faced girl remarked, appearing behind her mother. She was also clothed in a black mourning dress but without a veil.

'Please forgive my daughter's petulance. She has an inquisitive mind, like all children of her age.'

He looked over at the girl, who could not be more than thirteen years of age, his fist tightening by his side, and wondered how confident she would be after some time alone with him. 'Of course, I'm sure she meant no harm, considering the sad circumstances. It is a wonder she can converse at all, given that her father is lying dead not more than a few feet from us.' The daughter glared at him with disdain and hurt at his cold, blunt comment.

'But I felt it necessary to attend today and offer you my deepest sympathies and heartfelt condolences in person. I have endured the passing of relations myself and can assure you that the loss you *both* currently experience will—in time—lessen.' He paused.

'Thank you for your kind words and for taking the time to come to Fox Hall to pay your respects. It means so much to Henrietta and me that you made the effort, as indeed many have. It seems my husband was more popular than I imagined,' she said, almost raising a smile. 'Being his friend, you may have known my husband had reached an age where he was expected to have stopped working, but James was not the retiring type. He was just about to accept a new post as a medical consultant at a hospital for the mentally sick when the illness that was to take him from us struck him down,' she said, becoming slightly tearful as she remembered back to that time.

'How unfortunate for him, for you all.' He moved closer towards her. 'I have a private matter to settle locally that will take a little time, but I want you to know I am at your disposal at all times, night and day, should you require it.' He smiled, extending his hand.

'Please call me Camilla,' she replied, reciprocating, as he held the tops of her slender fingers slightly longer than necessary before releasing them. He noticed her delicate hand and the lightness of her touch, and the hand-embroidered lace mittens with a beautiful emerald ring encrusted with the finest diamonds sitting perfectly on her wedding finger. Her diction was flawless, and she had a natural air of self-entitlement that went with money and privilege, but he also saw a slight thaw in her deep blue eyes, which was enough to reveal that a crack had appeared in the wall she had built around herself.

'Have you travelled far?' she asked.

He sensed her curiosity grow. 'London. Which I will return to once matters here are concluded. But I have secured lodgings in the nearby village, which are sufficient for my purpose.'

'So, you won't be staying long, then?' Henrietta interrupted, her flame-red hair and dark eyes quite the opposite of her mother's demeanour. She glared expectantly at him.

He said nothing, knowing that she was being impertinent,

but in that moment, her fate had been decided, her destiny sealed.

'Henrietta, please go and see if there are other people wanting to pay their respects.' Henrietta reluctantly did as she was told and left the room, kicking the air as she went.

'As I have said, I must apologise for my daughter's rudeness she's...she is grieving. But maybe my daughter is correct, I'm sure a handsome young man like yourself has a number of engagements he needs to attend to. Perhaps more pressing interests elsewhere than to be here with a widow and her daughter?'

The comment intrigued him. 'No, madam, not at all you do yourself an injustice. Even under such difficult circumstances, you have made me feel most welcome, and other than one other engagement, I have put all other matters on hold. No, for me, bidding farewell to my esteemed colleague and friend for the last time must rightly take precedence over anything else.'

'Oh, I see,' she said, charmed by his candour, moving a lock of hair back slightly with one hand. 'Well, if that's the case, the funeral is soon, and as you and my husband were familiar, I'm sure he would more than approve of you attending the service. Maybe before you return to London, you will have supper at the house. To be honest, I could do with the company. James was older than me and made all the decisions in the family. I must confess it will be odd not to have him around for guidance.' She sighed, turning her head to one side, then back towards him. 'I think it best if I have my maid Annie prepare a room so you won't have to worry about making that arduous journey back to town.'

He grinned, calculating like a snake ready to bite that she was as vulnerable as a bird with a damaged wing, but a more profound, more satisfying thought washed over him: she was lonely and probably had been for some time. 'Of course,

I would be honoured to accompany you to his final resting place and look forward to dining with you and your *delightful* daughter. But now you must excuse me as I would not want to outstay my welcome.'

'Oh no, not at all. It has been a pleasure to make your acquaintance. Thank you again for coming. The ceremony is to be held at the local church, St John's, on Monday at 10 a.m. I must apologise...I didn't get your name.'

'My name...yes, of course; my name is Jack.'

Before she could question him further, he collected his possessions, turned, bid her farewell, and quickly left the house, making his way to the cab and instructing the driver to depart. He held his bag close, he would soon be back at work. As the carriage jolted forward, he rocked back and forth on the seat, laughing, talking to himself, shouting, mocking the dead, making stabbing motions with his hand. His eyes black, doll-like, and lifeless, he snarled, sniffing the air, sensing the prey like a jackal, circling before the kill.

CHAPTER 2

THREE MONTHS LATER

Dear Miss Hargreaves,

I write to you out of desperation and hope that you read this with the genuine intention it has been written. You have been highly recommended by a friend who once attended a séance at your home in Brighton. I am anxious that if I do not remove myself from my current situation, my daughter and I face great danger. I do not fear for myself as I have encouraged such recent events and no doubt deserve what fate holds in store for me. But my deep concern is for my daughter, who is still so young and should not come to harm because of the selfish and vain actions of her mother. To mitigate my predicament, I seek urgent guidance from the spirit world, specifically from my husband, who no longer walks on this earth. Only he can tell me how best to proceed under these difficult and dangerous circumstances.

You see, my husband died after a protracted illness, and I was facing the prospect of living in a large house with just my daughter Henrietta and our housemaid, Annie Crookshank. Henrietta shared a close bond with her father, and soon after his passing, she became reserved and withdrawn, which was quite unlike her natural self, and sadly, I was unable to console her. However, later, during the wake and burial, a man much younger than myself came into my life at a time when I was at a low point and almost certainly vulnerable.

He said he knew my late husband as a friend and in a professional capacity and felt compelled to pay his respects. We talked for some time, and I have to say I initially found his attentiveness intriguing, but then it became more pleasing as time passed. I suppose, in hindsight, I liked the attention of another adult to confide in, and it was not long before the relationship took a more, shall we say, intimate turn. After a time, I invited him to move into my home and share my life completely in every aspect.

However, my daughter did not take well to him and said there was something loathsome about him; a wolf in sheep's clothing is how she described him, and this was a position she steadfastly refused to change. Things carried on for a while, and despite my daughter's stance towards him, which I thought was ill-judged, I was happy, content to feel…alive again. I had opened my heart and my emotions and placed my trust in a man I barely knew. But then, without warning, he appeared to shift in character and mannerisms like a chameleon.

His moods became erratic and violent he seemed no longer to show affection and kindness but now appeared to despise—even— hate me. It was as if something had possessed him, something evil. It appears that my daughter was right about him all along, and I have been a fool, but I feel something else other than shame, something deeper; I feel scared.

I have become extremely worried about what to do and how to proceed. My daughter has now retreated into her room, and I have little contact with her, which deeply concerns me. The atmosphere in the house is heavy and dark, and I dread what might happen next. He has moved into my late husband's study, where he spends hours and hours pacing up and down, talking and shouting to himself. He has instructed us not to enter this room, or we will be punished harshly. It is his domain. I am at my wits' end, and the only person

I feel I can trust with any certainty as to what to do is my husband. He will advise me on the best course of action.

This is why I need your help resolving this situation quickly. I have included an advance for your services and travel. I beg of you to please come soon. You can stay at the house, we have plenty of room. Do not fear; this devil who persists in making my and my daughter's lives so desperate is set to leave on business and will not return for a few days. Please send urgent confirmation by return that you will be attending.

Yours sincerely,
Camilla Patterson

Elsbeth placed the letter on the table next to her and sat back, adjusting her dress and letting her black hair down over her slender shoulders. She considered for a while as the soft scent of lavender from her perfume filled the room. She felt the woman's torment, it was genuine and deep, and normally it would be a matter for the authorities, as it seemed the man was unpredictable and a threat to both her and her daughter. However, she knew how the police worked and the dismissive way they treated women, especially in a domestic situation.

The man of the house had absolute power and control, and his rule was seldom questioned. Finding a partner who respected or listened to a woman's view was rare, and it comforted her that she had secured financial independence when she was only in her thirties. She thought back to Inspector Abberline and the events that had unfolded in Brighton. She smiled, wondering how he was and what had become of him. She missed him.

She lit a candle on the table, its glow lighting up her deep green eyes and high cheekbones inherited from her Mediterranean lineage. She turned to the tarot cards for guidance, a gift passed down from her Nonna, who followed the old ways, and even though she had passed years ago, Elsbeth felt her warm, caring presence around her. Fanning the deck out, she put the pictures face down on the table and, placing her hand over them, let her mind concentrate on the letter she had received. She trusted her instinct and selected a card as she turned it over. A chill ran through her, and the room suddenly went icy cold. The candle flickered rapidly as if someone was blowing on it, followed by a foul smell like rotting flesh, and the sense that someone else was in the room.

She opened her eyes to find herself not in her house but somewhere cold and damp, like a cellar, small and claustrophobic, the sound of crows cawing outside circling above and the sweet smell of the dead lingering in the air. There was little light, but she felt herself moving towards a stone tomb on a plinth as sounds of scratching and muffled cries for help came from inside. She placed her hand on the lid as the panic within got louder. She wanted to help, but she couldn't as a hysterical, petrified scream filled the room. '*Help me!*'

The vision abruptly ended, and she was back in the comfort of her own home, her body shaking and beads of sweat forming on her forehead. She looked down at the card she had chosen and its image. It was a sign of things to come, a message from beyond, a warning, as a sudden rush of cold air filled the room and the table rocked violently from side to side, sending the cards across the room. Then, in a moment, everything stilled, but Elsbeth sensed a presence, something lurking hidden within the shadows, as goosebumps rose over her skin.

She stood up and slowly turned, checking around her, but there was nothing. The room was empty, and whatever it was had gone, but something stayed, the feeling burrowing deep into her bones. Only one card was left face up on the table. It was not one of change or new beginnings, as it could be interpreted. She knew this had another far darker message.

The cloaked figure stood on a pile of bleached bones, hunched over like a vulture, black storm clouds swirling above, its skeletal face peering out, its bony fingers wrapped tight around a scythe. The card of Death loomed back at her, waiting, ready to snatch life from this world into the next and down into the empty abyss of lost souls. She knew at that moment that she had no option but to make arrangements to leave immediately for Camilla Patterson's house. Someone was going to die.

CHAPTER 3

Camilla Patterson crept down the stairs to the hallway and the room where he had shut himself away for the last few days. Night had pulled its inky cloak of darkness over Fox Hall, only shadows bouncing off the walls, the crackling from the log fire in the main room, and the movement of a grandfather clock indicated life in the house. Camilla held onto the bannister with one hand and a small candle mounted in a pewter dish in the other, her bare feet moulding into the carpet pile. She descended each step cautiously, her breath fast, her mouth dry.

The last thing she wanted was to alert him, as he had become unpredictable and his character had changed so much since moving in with her and her daughter, he had become something sinister. The sounds emanating behind the locked door of the study over the past few nights reminded her of something untamed. Clawing at walls, footsteps heavy and quick as if he were caged, pacing up and down, snarling, gnawing noises like bone being splintered and chewed.

Her daughter, who stayed in her bedroom on the first floor, lay on her bed, gaunt from not eating. The skin on her face had grown to be pale and blotchy, and she had become even more distant, hardly speaking, no longer the confident, questioning child but now just morose and isolated. Camilla blamed herself, but she was still her mother, with a mother's instinct to protect, so she had to do this, she had to find out what he was doing in the study and what secrets he was keeping behind the door.

She reached the bottom step, gently placing her foot on the tiled floor as if it were a thin crust of ice, looking towards the study door. She hesitated for a moment, not knowing what to do *he could be in there, or he might not.* She felt her chest tighten, the anxiety rising in her like a red-hot flame, the fear of the consequences of her actions. Gradually, stealthily, she moved towards the study until she stood outside. She leaned in, pressing her right ear to the grainy wood panel. She listened intently, but there was nothing. *Maybe he's gone, just left. Please, God, just let it be true…let this nightmare end.*

She wrapped her shaking fingers around the doorknob, wrestling with even the thought of turning it, but she knew there was no other way. She paused, her heart beating like the wings of a small bird, tears clouding her vision, her eyes now dulled, red veins spidering across the whites of her eyes from absolute terror. She held her breath and twisted the handle—it creaked.

She felt her legs buckle and a feeling of sickness in the pit of her stomach as a hand reached out from behind her and touched her shoulder. She stood back from the door and froze, the scent of danger in the air, the smell of death even closer. *Should she beg, plead for forgiveness, or throw herself at his mercy?* A thousand scenarios tore through her mind. The hairs on the back of her neck stood proud. She waited for that voice, that terrible, awful voice that had become synonymous with misery and pain.

Then it came from behind. '*Shhhhhh.*'

CHAPTER 4

'...I'm sure I heard him in there earlier, something being dragged across the floor, somethin heavy like.' Annie spoke as quietly as she could into her mistress's ear.

Camilla jumped back, keeping her voice as slow and controlled as she could. 'My God, Annie, you nearly gave me a heart attack.' Each woman looked as frightened as the other.

'Sorry, my lady,' Annie said, taking a spare key out of the front pocket of her white apron. She stepped in front of Camilla, slowly bent down, and looked through the keyhole. 'There ain't no key in the lock. It's dark...I can't see much at all,' Annie whispered back, pressing her eye as close as she could to the opening.' I'm not sure...he could be in there.'

Camilla touched Annie lightly on her back. 'Alright, very, very quietly, stand back up. I'm going to have to go inside. I have no choice. Give me the key, I have to see what he's been doing.' Her voice still hushed and knowing she would need both hands, she passed Annie the candle. 'Hold this, and don't let go, whatever you do' Camilla, petrified, her hand trembling, started to slide the key into the lock. Just as she did, the Grandfather clock in the other room struck the hour. A loud gong went off, the sound carried throughout the house, echoing in the silence. Her grip slipped, and the key fell out of the keyhole, clanging as it hit the tiles.

Both Annie and Camilla stood still, almost paralysed with fear. Camilla looked over at Annie. 'Get ready to run.' Camilla instinctively grabbed hold of the doorknob to stop it from being opened. Only her breathing cut through the silence as she prayed to herself for a few seconds, then sighed with relief as nothing happened, looking over to Annie, who stood beside her. She slowly released her grip, bent down, picked up the key and put it back in the lock, turning it twice, *click, click*. Holding her breath, she inched the door to the study open. It was pitch black and stank of decaying meat, the atmosphere foreboding, heavy like the promise of a storm rumbling in the distance.

Their warm breath mixed and spiralled in the gloomy light of the candle as Annie nervously held the only illumination they had high above her head. Camilla knew it as a large square room, but it felt small and claustrophobic in the dark, with heavy drapes pulled across the only window at the far end. She felt her body stiffen and tingle. The yellow flame danced, reflecting off the walls, revealing strips of wallpaper that had been torn away, like skin. Drawings of stick people hanging from gallows, some with limbs missing and strange symbols above them, had been etched into the surface of the plaster, and large holes were gouged out of the wall in places, chunks lying on the floor and trodden into the carpet. Camilla felt a chill run down her spine. Her husband's writing desk sat centrally, with a leather couch cloaked in darkness against a wall on the opposite side.

'He's not here, my lady—best be quick, though he could come back any minute,' Annie, worried, her breathing short, started to panic that she had never heard the master leave.

Camilla strolled around the desk, running her fingers over the top, remembering happier times. 'Annie, bring the candle closer, please, so I can see over here,' still keeping her voice low. The drawers had been pulled out and some were thrown on the floor, while others were left hanging half in and half out, their contents removed. Annie did as asked and went over to join her mistress, treading carefully, trying not to make any sound. Camilla sifted through some of the private correspondence addressed to her late husband. One stood out, the address ringed around in thick black ink.

Lidgate Manor Asylum Re: Position of Resident Physician/Doctor

She read further, confirming an offer of employment for the position to commence early next month. The hospital was unaware of her husband's passing. In the meantime, Annie kept looking skittishly about, not wanting to be in the room longer than she had to be. 'I'm worried, ma'am, if he finds me in 'ere going through his stuff …there'll be hell to pay.'

Camilla ignored the comment. She knew the risks, he had warned her, but this had to be done as she continued to look through scraps of paper and correspondence with her husband's signature, which had been repeatedly copied. 'Keep searching, Annie.' Then, deep under a pile, she found something even more concerning: a letter addressed back to the Asylum Governor accepting the position, dated after her husband's death. Camilla paused for a moment in thought. 'He's pretending to be my husband.' Before she could say another word, a terrible scream came from upstairs in the house—from her daughter's bedroom.

'Listen to me, Annie. You must leave now. Run as fast as possible to The Poacher Inn at Coldharbour and ask the landlord for help. Do you understand?'

Annie nodded nervously. 'But what about you, ma'am?'

'I'll…we'll be fine. I have to get my daughter, please, you must hasten,' Camilla shouted, her face white with shock—a parent's worst fear—her child was in danger. She wasted no more time and rushed out of the room, disappearing upstairs and heading towards her child's shriek.

Annie was suddenly left alone in the study, only the candlelight swayed in silence. She looked about, turning one way, then the next, her eyes squinting, trying to fix on points, but the dulled light played tricks, shadows appearing on the walls and ceiling, shapes forming in dark corners. Her ears pricked, listening for the slightest sound. She felt nauseous her chest ached, and her stomach muscles tightened bending over for a second, she wanted to vomit. *I'm being stupid. He's not here. As ma'am said, I need to get out, get help.*

She righted herself, gently placing the candle on the desk behind her, and made her way across to the exit. She felt wrong for leaving Camilla and her daughter to the mercy of this monster, but she knew she had no choice if she was to be of any use to them. Hearing the panicked footsteps of her mistress above echoing off the wax-polished floorboards, Annie Crookshank gathered up her black dress and white apron to her ankles and ran out of the house, down the drive across a field, and disappeared into the dense, dark wood.

CHAPTER 5

A dark moon sailed silently behind scudding clouds, silhouetting its transit across the thick forest below. It was night, a time of shadows and strange sounds that carried on the cold air for miles, a time for the strong to hunt the weak, a time to kill. Bracken and twigs snapped and cracked underfoot as he tracked her through the sea of ferns, stopping now and then to examine the area, looking out for signs of her passage.

Fallen leaves had turned to mulch, adding to the rich, musty, earthy aroma of a midwinter evening. He knew the girl would panic, as they all do, leaving a trodden path to hide amongst the trees, thinking she would be safe. He smirked at the pathetic attempt and that this lowly house skivvy could somehow outthink him—he smiled. It was only a matter of time. *Then, I will introduce you to how real pain feels.*

He snarled, jaws snapping at the chilled air, leaning his head back with his face to the sky, and he let out a primaeval howl like a wolf. The canopy above shook, a thunderous sound of branches bending and swaying echoed as a huge flock of starlings took flight, vacating the sanctity of their nests, hundreds twisting one way then the next, the harsh chatter and trills warning others of danger while making good their escape. It made him smile that she would have seen the display and heard the commotion as the murmuration dispersed across the sky. It was a message: *I'm coming for you.*

He wanted her to feel his grip tighten, he wanted her to experience every morsel of panic and fear. He tasted the air for her scent, confident she would soon break out from the thick bracken like a hunted animal and make a run for it, scared witless but still somehow believing she had a chance, thinking she could get away and find sanctuary. He sniggered at the pointlessness of it.

He waited, eyes fixed. She was getting nearer, her pace quickened. He could hear her breathing becoming erratic and deep, gulping the air down to feed her lungs, the fabric of her dress tearing against brambles, giving her position away. He could hear her weeping, begging for help, she was petrified. It brought a warm feeling he hadn't felt for a while: pleasure. He crouched down, masked by the undergrowth, the dark wrapped around him, he grinned. He remained still, the frantic footsteps darting one way, then the other, getting closer and closer, the prey now within reach, *not long now*, his back arched, his heart raced.

Like a beast, he pounced.

CHAPTER 6

Camilla discovered her daughter cowering in the corner of her bedroom, kneeling to her level. She spoke calmly but firmly. 'Henrietta, listen. We need to leave your room, it's the first place he will look. Don't make a sound.' Camilla stood back up, gently lifting her daughter by her arm.

Henrietta moved closer to her mother, her body shaking. 'I'm sorry, I didn't mean to scream, but I'm frightened. What are we to do?' Her face was pale, contorted with fear. 'Please…I'm so scared, I don't want to die…he hates me.'

'Shhh, I think he could still be here…in the house,' Camilla said, gently, placing a finger on her lips and keeping her voice to a whisper.

Henrietta always found comfort in her mother's words, even now when she was in danger, it made her feel safe to have her mother by her side. Camilla eased the door open a bit at a time, until it was wide enough for them to slip through. Clasping her daughter's hand, they slid along the hallway with their backs to the wall, past two dimly lit lamps and then the stairs, which were bathed in darkness. Camilla knew it was too dangerous to venture down, as he could be waiting at the bottom or making his way up. She knew she had to hide, to choose her time.

The next door belonged to a spare room that hadn't been used for some time, as *he* did not allow visitors. Nobody ever came to see them anymore since *he* had moved into the house. Camilla guided Henrietta into the room, closing the door quietly, thinking he would go first to her daughter's bedroom. If she were right, it might just give them a window of opportunity to escape. She realised it was risky, but she had little choice their lives depended on it.

The room was cold and dark, the curtains drawn it smelled musty and unlived-in as Camilla took Henrietta around a four-poster bed, past a large wardrobe and to the other side, where they knelt in a corner. 'Now Henrietta, listen carefully to me when I tell you I want you to run as fast as you can… don't look back get away from this place as quickly as possible. I've sent Annie ahead to get help and bring the police, so don't worry about me she'll be back soon. I promise it will be fine, everything will be back to normal, back to the way it was… before he came into our lives.' Camilla looked at the pained expression on her daughter's face, the tears forming in her eyes, and knew she didn't believe her. She placed her hand on the side of Henrietta's face. 'Please, my darling, you have to go, you have to get to safety.'

'But Mummy. I don't want to leave you. I'm so scared, Mummy…please,' Henrietta pleaded, her eyes red from crying, shaking, she grabbed her mother's hand.

'You have to be brave…you have to…' Camilla's attention suddenly turned to the hallway outside, as a telltale creak of the stairs turned her skin cold. She looked into her daughter's face and kissed her on the forehead. 'I love you, I always have,' she said, cradling her sobbing face against her chest. 'You have one chance,' she said, whispering, as Henrietta nodded through the tears to show she understood.

The door to the room groaned open, the air was stuffy and dank as a dark figure stood silently for a moment. Camilla's heart skipped a beat as she recognised his silhouetted outline by the hallway light, her attention quickly drawn to something clasped tightly in one hand and glinting in the luminescence, something long and thin. *Oh my God, it's a knife*—her gut tightened, she felt sick. He advanced slowly towards them, with each step getting closer and closer.

Camilla put her hand on the small of her daughter's back, feeling her breathing was deep and rapid, her heart pounding through her body like a drum. She kissed her head, waiting until he was almost upon them, then thrust her forward and to the side of him. Henrietta staggered to her feet, hearing her mother's frantic scream from behind her.

'*RUN!*'

CHAPTER 7

Inspector Frederick Abberline stood in front of the mirror at Notting Dale Police Station, adjusting his tie. His china-blue eyes peered out from behind his glasses, which were sitting precisely in the position he liked. His black suit and white shirt were always pressed, his black shoes polished, and his laces neatly tied. At forty-two years of age, he stood six feet tall, was of a slim build, had a full head of blond hair, and had been married twice. He looked forward to years as a detective at Scotland Yard, and yet now, in this posting, he felt as if life was passing him by, and he might as well be on the other side of the world. Looking at the calendar on the wall, with the days neatly crossed out in earnest, he wondered how much longer he would have to endure this humiliation.

Notting Dale was a small building with just two floors. A set of steps from the outside reached the ground floor, which served as the reception area, featuring a desk and a bench for the public to wait on. The basement had a large cell which was used for prisoners, mainly low-level criminals such as pickpockets or drunks, waiting for their day in court.

The station's decor was spartan, with plain plaster walls that had yellowed and cracked over time from water damage caused by a leaking roof. An open area behind the front desk

26

had furniture strategically positioned in the centre of the room with several rusting filing cabinets lining the walls, and posters of those wanted above. It served as a space for conducting administrative tasks and also for interviewing suspects. It was also used as a restroom, with a coat and hatstand for the staff, and a makeshift office for Abberline. Given his rank, he was provided with a shabby wooden screen for privacy, as well as a desk and chair that were both extremely uncomfortable. It was a long way from the warm and opulent conditions he was more accustomed to at Scotland Yard.

He had been at the station for what seemed like an eternity, and it was very different from what he was used to. After the Brighton murders and the escape of their prime suspect, immediate action was taken to quash any mention of the incident in the media. A deal was made with the press, and the reputations of Scotland Yard, its Police Commissioner, and Abberline's direct boss, Head of CID James Monro, were unaffected and internally cleared of any association with the operation.

Abberline, who had been ordered down to Brighton to take charge and oversee the investigation, was made the scapegoat and quickly dispatched for an indeterminate amount of time to a small local police station, where he was now, with all the excitement of a blocked drain. He despised every minute and longed for the day to return to central London to investigate what he termed '*real*' crimes.

He felt annoyed, but he knew that politics and reputations lay at the centre of it. Unpopular with his boss, Monro, he was the sacrificial lamb, served up on a silver platter to pacify those in power, but he knew he would find a way one day to get back to The Yard where he belonged. However, he was pleased that Elsbeth had been kept out of the firing line, she had suffered enough as a spiritualist and psychic nearly paying the ultimate price. He had thought about writing to her but had decided against it. It never seemed to be the right time, or maybe deep down, he just felt it was better to leave things as they were; he didn't know.

An uneventful few weeks passed until he received the communication he had been waiting for. He had been summoned to a meeting at Scotland Yard and was to report immediately. There was no further explanation about why or what the meeting was for, but Abberline took this as a sign that they needed his assistance, and that gave him one thing back he dearly needed: hope.

He quickly gathered his things in a neat, orderly pile, mentioning to the desk sergeant, who was half asleep, that he had to go to headquarters, and promptly left the building for the train station to take him into central London. The journey didn't take long, and he was soon walking down familiar pavements. The city growled with life, the smells, noise, and streets teeming with all kinds he loved it and wanted to be reinstated with immediate effect. *Maybe this is it, they want me back.*

The large oval clock outside Monro's office still ran slow. Nothing had changed; the smell of wax polish on the dark wood parquet flooring, people hurrying up and down past him, too busy to ask who he was or what he was doing there. It filled him with dread and excitement as he waited for the familiar shout through the opaque glass door of his superior's office. Abberline knew Monro disliked him and would keep him waiting longer than necessary to remind him of his place. He didn't care. If he was being taken back into the fold and given his old job back, it would be worth it. Nothing mattered more to him than returning to The Yard, where he belonged. Then came the bellowing sound of his boss.

'Abberline, get in here.'

Abberline shot up and went into Monro's office. It was as chaotic as he had remembered it, files and folders strewn across the desk and a small man of five feet two, balding, a pot

28

belly and a large handle moustache, sitting behind it. He felt an overriding compulsion to tidy the folders up, but he knew this would antagonise Monro even more, so he had to resist the urge however strongly his affliction pulled him. If he were here to mend bridges, it would be best not to annoy the one person who had his fate in his hands.

'Sit, sit, Abberline. I don't have long,' Monro impatiently gestured to Abberline as if he were a dog. 'The Commissioner is due here soon, and you're the last person he wants to see.'

Abberline noticed Monro's irritation towards him hadn't improved, and his expectations about maybe getting his position back and any forgive-and-forget exchanges were beginning to fade. 'Yes, sir, but it was you who wanted to see me, and I can assure you it is not my intention to cause you any distress or displeasure.'

Monro examined Abberline with a cold stare. He didn't like him, his mere presence exasperated him like an annoying scratch you couldn't get to.

'You were transferred to er where…um', he riffled through some papers on his desk.

'Notting Dale,' Abberline replied before Monro could locate the information.

'Yes…indeed, that is correct. Well, you know why you were sent there, don't you, man? We can't have you back here going about your usual duties as if nothing happened. It's just as well that the Commissioner settled the matter quietly. You did yourself no favours down there in Brighton, Abberline. You had a chance to show what you could do, to prove everybody wrong, but you failed, and you let the killer run amok, then escape.'

'It wasn't quite as simple as that, sir.'

'Well, from where I'm sitting, you're lucky even to have a job. Maybe don't rely on women with crystal balls, inspector. Leave that for the fools prepared to pay for such fairground trickery. Good old-fashioned police work alone would have caught him.'

Abberline knew that Elsbeth Hargreaves was no fraud, even if he didn't understand or agree with her gift. She had been of great use to him in Brighton, and the investigation would have been more challenging without her intervention, even though they worked in very different ways. Nevertheless, this wasn't the time to disagree, he knew only too well that Monro was not a man to be argued with.

'I've called you back, Abberline, because of a case, and I can't spare anyone else, and to be honest, given your new posting, you're the nearest to the scene. Get down to Surrey, review the situation, and report back to me, and *only me*, you understand. I don't want you talking to anyone about this. Just go there, get the facts, and report back to me. Is that clear? This is not your case, you are *not* in charge. It's a simple task; I would have passed it to a constable if I could spare one.'

Abberline realised that his hope of returning was all but gone, he was being used as a messenger boy, yet there was something else Abberline felt Monro wasn't telling him.

'Where is the crime scene, and what crime has been committed, sir?'

'Surrey Hills, a woman has been murdered, and as I said, not far from your new station, inspector.'

'That's across the border, sir, with respect, isn't that something Surrey Police should be handling?'

Monro sat back in his chair, mulling over how to respond. 'In normal circumstances, this would be a local matter…but this is to go no further than this room. It turns out that the murdered woman worked as a housemaid for a prominent doctor who was an advisor to Her Majesty the Queen. I understand the doctor has passed on, although the woman in question was still employed at the home. We received a report that she had gone missing, then a little while later, a local dog walker, unfortunately, came across a body in the Surrey Hills. She had been murdered. Some identification, a letter with her name, Annie Crookshank, and her address, Fox Hall, was found about her person, so it wasn't hard for us to link the two. I have a file here, read it on your way. Given the sensitive nature of this, I had the information sent directly to me as urgently as possible. Everything is there, some photographs taken at the scene and documentation about who to talk to regarding the body, etc. Your contact down there is Detective Collins. They have moved the victim to the local morgue, so make sure you also talk to the coroner.'

Abberline opened the folder to read the short paragraph about the deceased, then looked carefully at the images provided. She had been found in woodland sitting down, legs apart, tied to a tree and some rope wound around her neck.

'I don't know if she was strangled with it as well, you will have to ask the coroner about that. She had also been stabbed multiple times, her face disfigured, her nose and ears removed, and her private parts heavily bloodied.' Monro interrupted.

Abberline stopped reading and looked back up at Monro. He had seen this before; they both had.

'I know what you are thinking, Abberline, the wounds, the ferocity of the attack, however, the killer you let escape in Brighton is long gone by now, probably across the water. He won't do it again and risk getting caught a second time. No, I am confident this is something else altogether, and the likelihood that we are dealing with the same maniac is so remote that I have trouble even saying it. And why dump the body away from where she worked?'

'I don't believe she was dumped there, sir. It is my opinion that she was hunted and killed at the place where we found the body. Notice here.' Abberline held up one of the photographs of the deceased, pointing at a certain area. 'She has deep scratches and abrasions on the lower part of her legs and ankles. Logic informs us that these injuries were most likely caused by her lifting her skirt so she could run at speed through the bracken and nettles of the wood. She was scared, sir, and whoever she was running from caught up with her.' Abberline waited for his answer, monitoring him closely. He had a feeling Monro was trying to play this down, but for what purpose was unclear.

'Well, maybe Abberline, but no, I have to say, as I have already stated, this murder has all the hallmarks of a domestic nature.'

And yet your first thought was to send me. You want me to make sure this monster has not returned to haunt us all again, Abberline pondered.

'May I ask if the victim's employer has been informed of the discovery?'

'No, not as yet. I want to make our preliminary enquiries first, then we'll approach the employer, Mrs Patterson. As I said, this is to be kept strictly on a need-to-know basis. The Patterson woman is connected, albeit by her late husband's profession, but we don't want another scandal on our hands, *do we*, Inspector?' Monro's tone was terse.

Abberline looked down at the preliminary crime report again, seeing the savage and brutal footprint of a killer with no remorse, no feeling. He was certain this was not a simple task, he sensed there was more to this than he was being told, and he recognised the butchery, the relentless rage, behind the hands that delivered the blows to this poor woman. He didn't believe this was just some random killer, but he had to be sure, he had to be certain beyond all doubt that the evil he faced in Brighton had not returned.

As he left Monro's office and returned to the streets of London and the sounds of the city, he pulled his coat collar up as a cold wind whipped around the corner of the building. Yet there was something else, a notion, a feeling that someone was watching, eyes burrowing into the back of his head as if his grave had been walked over. His body shivered, and his blood suddenly ran cold, an emotion he thought was buried had returned—fear.

CHAPTER 8

Abberline arrived at Coldharbour, a small hamlet nestled in the Surrey Hills comprising of a few small cottages dotted along the road. He thought the place strange and was at odds with its name as there was no river, inlet, or moored vessels anywhere to be seen. Or maybe it was a lost reference to the gate at the Tower of London where Queen Anne Boleyn walked under to reach the inner ward where she was executed. He thought this mirrored the savage and unnecessary killing that had occurred close by, whatever the origin of the name, it resonated with him.

The road led into the centre, where a large public house, The Poacher Inn, stood prominently, its thatched roof, white plaster walls, and timber construction indicating that it was old and had been here for some considerable time. He had booked a room in advance of his stay and mused to himself that the establishment was most likely the only source of entertainment for the locals for miles.

Abberline disembarked from his ride, paid the driver, and entered the premises. The landlord, George Lamb, a small, stout man in his fifties with a ruddy complexion and head of greying red hair, greeted him and listened as Abberline informed him of the official and, at the moment, confidential nature of his visit. However, any aspiration that this was news to the landlord was quickly snatched away, to his annoyance, as knowledge of the murder in the woods had already reached George Lamb.

Abberline, clearly irritated by this fact, made it clear to him that he had to be discreet and not add fuel to the fire but keep his ears open for any local gossip regarding the crime and, more importantly, any potential witnesses. 'Anything you might hear, I want to know about, is that understood. However small or irrelevant you may assume it to be. I want to be informed,' Abberline said, signing the register, knowing the local pub was often a good repository for gossip.

'Yes, sir, of course. Never had trouble like this down these parts before. Now, if what I've been hearing is true, it's simply terrible. What sort of man does that to a woman, eh? I know what I would do to him if I were given half the chance.' George cocked his head expectantly, waiting for more information, but to his disappointment, Abberline didn't take the bait.

Abberline put the pen down, staring directly at George. 'This is a police matter, make no mistake, and if anyone should hamper my investigation or try to take matters into their own hands, they will feel the full force of the law. Is that understood?'

George said nothing, nodding in a submissive manner he knew his place and didn't want any trouble, realising that Abberline was not a man to be trifled with. A tall lady with threadlike grey hair tied back in a neat bun with a tired expression and hollow cheeks appeared from behind a wooden partition and handed over his room key. 'Whoever is responsible, just make sure you lot get him. Just cos we ain't livin' in no big city don't mean we matter any less.' Her tone was not quite rude but abrupt and, in a way, appealed to Abberline as he loathed small talk.

'Sorry, inspector, where's my manners?' George interrupted.

'I must introduce you to the wife, Ethel. We run the place together. She knows everyone around here, not much she don't know about, ain't that right, luv?' George Lamb looked at his wife, trying to extract a smile from her, but was soon cut dead by a look that could kill a man at ten feet.

Ethel turned her attention towards Abberline. 'Don't concern yourself, inspector, it's me that runs the place, other than boozing with his mates in the bar, I'm not sure my husband will be of much use to you. I will have my ear to the ground, of that you can be assured, and I will let you know if anything is said regarding the crime. Now if there's nothing more, inspector, some of us 'ave work to do,' she said, glaring back at her husband while slamming the register shut with a loud thud. Before Abberline could reply, she disappeared behind the divide, leaving George looking embarrassed and bruised.

There was a silence between them that was suddenly broken as the door to the inn groaned open, bringing a welcome reprieve for both men and, with it, a rush of cold air, followed by a local policeman. The constable stood in front of Abberline, giving a slight bow with respect to his rank and then went on to inform him that the inspector was to accompany him to meet with the local detective in charge and the coroner at the scene. Abberline instructed the landlord to put his things in his room and followed the policeman out of the inn into a cab.

The horse waiting for the command to proceed, chewed on the metal bit between its front and back teeth as warm breath shot out of its nostrils. The animal pawed impatiently at the solid ground, finally getting the order to *git up*, followed by a slight snap of the reins from the driver, who was perched on a platform on the back of the cab, wrapped in a thick coat and scarf. The cab jolted forward, shunting the passengers from side to side within the carriage as the wheels slowly turned, churning the snow as they made their way out of Coldharbour.

They followed the road, climbing through the densely

wooded area of oaks, beeches, yew, and ash, making up some of the many species that hugged their route as the smell of fallen damp leaves, nature's aroma, scented the air. Abberline stayed quiet during the journey, preferring to keep his conversation for later. He wasn't one for idle chatter but instead looked out of the window, noticing the higher they got, the more the woods seemed to close in. Tall trees, some with silver bark, cracked and scarred from the winter, arched and swayed, their branches gnarled and bare, tangled and embraced, protecting each other from the harsh weather.

They stole the sky above, blotting out the light, giving an eerie feeling of secrets left untold, hidden, and woven into the bramble and ferns that covered the ground below. Abberline shivered. It was an eerie and uneasy place, and one he found difficult to adjust to coming from the city, but he knew it provided the perfect cover to be watched and followed.

After a while, they arrived at the murder scene and alighted from their ride. Abberline noticed two men standing by a large oak tree. One of them was tall and portly, he guessed, in his mid-forties, dressed in a suit and bowler hat, the telltale regulated dress code of an officer of the law. The other was smaller in stature and notably thinner, with silver hair, and was pointing to an area at the base of a large tree with a wide girth, gesticulating as if trying to give some demonstration or explanation.

'Ah, Inspector Abberline, I believe?' The taller individual turned to greet the new arrival, extending his hand out. 'I'm Detective Collins, Surrey Police.'

'Yes, thank you both for meeting me here. I thought it wise to see the spot where this occurred firsthand and to get a feel for what I'm dealing with,' Abberline replied, shaking the man's hand.

The other man quickly followed, introducing himself as Arthur Bates, County Coroner for Surrey.

Abberline forced a smile. 'Well, that's the formalities over, please tell me what you understand to have occurred here. As I'm to report back to Scotland Yard with any new or relevant information.'

Coroner Bates took the lead and explained the details as best he could. 'The body is of a woman, thought to be Annie Crookshank, the housemaid in employment at Fox Hall, not far from here. She was found tied to this tree with some kind of twine, probably rope. As my report has recorded, the deceased was found to have multiple stab and slash wounds to the torso, some delivered with such force that they have penetrated the bone. The face was disfigured, with the nose and ears having been sliced off. Finally, she was impaled with the murder weapon, an extremely sharp, thin blade six to eight inches long.

The final blow, I believe, severed the costal cartilage, sternum and spine, exiting the body into the tree. You can see the mark here,' Bates said, pointing to the damaged bark. 'The force required to deliver such a strike would be, in my opinion, immense, so in all likelihood, a man is the perpetrator.'

Abberline's discomfort and concern were growing. 'The weapon used was one you might find…for example, amongst a doctor's or surgeon's equipment?'

'It's possible. The blade used has a serrated edge, but it's anybody's guess where someone would get such an implement. It's highly specialised and wouldn't be easy to come across, especially around this area.'

Abberline's blood ran cold as he was told the blade was serrated, another detail that brought traumatic flashbacks. It made him anxious, but he tried to avoid giving too much away. 'The wounds inflicted on the victim, I've seen similar before during the course of my duties. As a coroner, can you say the loss of blood was the primary cause of death?'

'Well, there was also some attempt at strangulation as

some rope was also found about her neck, and I can show this more clearly back at the morgue. I don't believe this was meant to kill her, but it would have disabled her and indeed rendered the victim unable to call for help. However, to answer your question, the other injuries and the massive loss of blood ultimately were the cause of her death,' Bates replied.

Abberline remembered the victims in Brighton who had all suffered the same method. But he was duty-bound not to discuss that case or the possible ramifications if his suspicions were correct. Even so, he needed conclusive evidence as there was still the outside chance that this could be unrelated and that this was the work of just an extremely violent individual with a personal grudge. But the rage and the weapon both made him feel uneasy.

'We should go back to the morgue.' Bates remarked. 'If you have further questions, I can show you the condition she was found in, and you can see for yourself the ferocity of the assault.'

Abberline moved closer to the tree, looking around its base. 'Yes, that would be most helpful. Do you recall seeing any footprints or anything out of the ordinary, anything out of place?'

Detective Collins looked as bemused as the coroner at the question. 'Footprints? What on earth do you mean?'

Abberline was irked by the response. He knew how important it was to preserve the scene, especially one where someone had lost their life. Yet convincing the police force to take him seriously and of the importance of this process was an uphill struggle. 'What I mean, Detective Collins, is that it is clear the victim, given her injuries, didn't do this to herself, so the person who committed the crime may have inadvertently left something behind that can further assist us in forming a description of the perpetrator.'

'I'll tell you, inspector, you don't need footprints to know what this…what this animal did to the woman was nothing short of madness,' Detective Collins, clearly annoyed, snapped back.

Abberline knew he was already on the back foot with Collins. It had been tough enough back at Scotland Yard, trying to convert his boss, Monro, to his way of thinking, but it was proving even more difficult out here in the back and beyond. 'I appreciate emotions are running high, but these details are important. You see, just from a simple footprint, I have devised a method to calculate and measure the size and depth of the imprint. This then provides not only the height but also the weight of the individual, thereby bringing us closer to understanding who we are looking for. Or, more importantly, ruling out those it could not be, saving a considerable amount of time.'

Detective Collins looked even less impressed than he had before. 'Really?' he said unconvincingly. 'Well, I'm not familiar with these new-fangled things. All I know is that good old-fashioned police work has never failed me yet in all my years doing this job, and I doubt it ever will.' He didn't like someone just turning up like this and telling him how to do his job. He wanted to know more about Abberline's intentions while on his patch. 'Why is Scotland Yard so involved in this? Surely, it's a local matter? I'm not happy with them getting involved, and I want that on the record?'

Abberline considered his answer before responding. 'Yes, I would agree with you under normal circumstances. However, the victim worked for an employer with important connections, and The Yard want to be sure there is nothing more to this.'

Detective Collins was not entirely convinced by the explanation, but he knew of the family and their importance in the area and had little option but to accept it. Abberline outranked him, and he didn't want this London Inspector with his new ideas in his county any longer than necessary.

'Have you contacted her employers? The Pattersons at Fox Hall, Detective?' Abberline asked.

'No, I was informed to leave this for London to follow up. It's all very odd if you ask me. Fox Hall is not far from here, and I could have easily made the trip to notify them. They must be concerned about why someone they see every day is missing.'

Abberline knew that his boss, Monro, was orchestrating the investigation, and he wanted a tight rein on how much was known until he decided to impart any facts regarding the case.

'Thank you for your diligence, detective. However, I will now return with the coroner, Mr Bates, to see the body...' Abberline looked over to Bates, making him aware of his intentions. 'Before making my report back to The Yard, who will no doubt then take the appropriate action to contact her employers. You can consider your involvement in this matter at an end now.'

Detective Collins was taken aback by Abberline's directness but followed his instructions, speaking privately to Bates for a short while before leaving. Abberline walked back to the tree one last time, noting in his pocketbook that blood had soaked into the bark and had sustained deep lacerations where the rope had been fastened tightly around its circumference, disfiguring the surface. He reached out, touching the area, the residue smudging, filling the contours of his fingertips. He began to realise that this was no ordinary killing, it was ritualistic in its execution and bore all the hallmarks of something far darker.

A terrible high-pitched scream like a woman being attacked rang out from the woods, followed by a flock of nesting birds squawking and flying up from the trees. Their wings beating the air, and spreading like a vast net across the sky, startling Abberline, who quickly turned on his heels.

'Don't worry, inspector, you pavement people don't understand the way of the country. It's just a vixen calling for its dog,' Detective Collins shouted across to him. Then, a crack and snap of wood in the forest echoed like a gunshot. Abberline squinted his eyes to see better, but nothing was obvious, just an uneasy feeling of being watched.

He thought back to Annie Crookshank and why she had been left at this precise spot. Was it a display? Was the killer announcing his return, maybe his sick way of saying *I'm back*, leaving this poor woman to die an agonising death alone, petrified and in a place where there was no one to save her, no one to hear her cries for help. The killer knew that out in the woods, it would be very unlikely he would be disturbed, free to let loose his most depraved desires, hidden within an untamed landscape of shadows and ghosts.

CHAPTER 9

Detective Collins was taken back to the police station whilst Abberline and the coroner continued to the county morgue. As they arrived, Arthur Bates opened the doors. The first thing that hit Abberline was the strong smell of almonds, the sweet embalming fluid used on the deceased. It reminded him of The Death House in Brighton. Bates appeared to be a decent and competent man, and Abberline had dismissed making comparisons to Cripps, the Brighton Coroner—a repulsive individual driven by greed and responsible for the death of Detective Rawlings.

They walked down a corridor and entered the examination room with white tiles from the ground to the ceiling and a red concrete floor to hide the blood. The room had a layout similar to Brighton, with several tables centrally positioned and above a water pipe running across the roof, spurring off over each table, with a shower head to wash away any residue left after an autopsy had been completed. Bates fetched the remains of Annie Crookshank from a separate storage area towards the back of the room, wheeling a familiar double-lined lead casket packed with ice to help preserve the cadaver with a small glass window at the top to assist recognition. He undid the latches on the casket and lifted back the lid.

Bates placed some round spectacles on the bridge of his nose, picked up his notes and commenced reading from them out loud. 'So, our victim is a young female, roughly in her early to mid-twenties, as I mentioned at the scene where the poor wretch was found, she had been strangled with the rope found around her neck. I'm not sure this would have been sufficient to end life, or was intended to. We can see the ligature marks on the skin and some bruising to the soft tissue, which is consistent with such an attack. But to my mind, insufficient pressure was applied to the larynx or the cartilage, where one would expect to see more damage. As a result it would have incapacitated her, which would have then given him the time to inflict the other injuries. This, I believe, was the most likely scenario.'

'So this was about getting control quickly?' Abberline asked.

'Yes, one could make that presumption, but of course, we have no idea what was going through the mind of this maniac,' Bates replied.

'Do you have the rope?'

'Yes, of course it's here.' Bates collected it from the table beside him and handed it to Abberline, who studied it carefully.

'This knot I've seen it somewhere before, but...I can't quite remember where,' Abberline said, turning it over in his hands, trying to recall.

'Well, it's commonly known as a love knot. But why use that type, especially after what he did to this poor girl, God only knows,' Bates replied.

Abberline was sure it was not left to symbolise any affection the murderer may have had for the victim. 'No...the killer left this for another reason, and I know I have seen it elsewhere, however, at present I have to admit my memory evades me.'

Bates, unsure what else to add, continued with his report. 'This killer wanted the victim to feel as much pain as possible.

As you can see, her body has received several punctures, wounds or cuts, if you like, to the upper and lower parts of the body, in particular the privy parts, which would typically indicate a sexual motive. Again, the incisions were not so deep as to cause immediate death, so to my mind, these were inflicted as a form of torture.'

'Was she interfered with?' Abberline asked.

'If you are asking if she was raped...' he paused. 'It's difficult to ascertain, as the genital area has been badly mutilated, but I would say...no. This was motivated more by anger than lust, in my view.'

'The cuts and abrasions to her lower legs and ankles have come from running through thick bracken?'

'Yes, those lacerations have been caused by the flesh tearing against thorns commonly found in wooded areas around here and were most likely sustained during flight, some are still embedded in the skin. Then there is this stab wound here,' Bates pointed to the exact area on the body. 'This was delivered with great force, probably the death blow. It passed through the sternum or front of the chest, ending in the spinal column, which would have also penetrated the heart. As if that was not enough, finally, her face has been disfigured by the removal of the nasal part of the repository system and the cartilage and skin of both ears.' He removed his glasses, his hands shaking. He reached for a glass of water to suppress the need to vomit, wiping his brow, looking away to the floor for a moment's respite.

Abberline looked at the torn, lifeless body of this naked individual before him, once a young girl endowed with the carefree spirit of youth with dreams and aspirations of her own, now a frigid corpse lying in a mortuary, butchered like an animal. There were some alarming coincidences here with this murder and the ones in Brighton last year: the same anger, similar dismemberment of the body. The same surgical knife with a serrated blade was used on the three women he killed.

Still, Abberline didn't entertain the falsehood of coincidences. This was the only other case like it since Brighton, so the likelihood that they were connected was high. *Maybe he was leaving a sign, his mark, for me.* Something else surfaced, a moment he still could not explain. 'I wonder, Mr Bates, if you could be so kind as to answer a question for me?'

Bates, now slightly recovered, answered. 'Yes…yes, of course, if I can, inspector.'

Abberline thought back to Brighton and the incident where he thought he had shot the killer, possibly the same killer responsible for the murder of Annie Crookshank. 'If a man is shot at least twice at close range, would it be possible for him to make good an escape still?'

Bates looked puzzled. 'I'm sorry, inspector. I'm a little confused. How does your question relate to this poor soul lying here?' he said, gesturing his hand back towards the corpse.

Abberline didn't want to give any more information away than he had to. 'Is it possible?'

Bates shook his head. 'It might be, but I would have thought any escape was unlikely if you fired at short range. But I can't be sure as I wasn't there, and in the heat of the moment, you may have thought you hit the target but didn't. The only other explanation is that they were only flesh wounds, which would not necessarily affect his ability to flee, and that could be how he managed to evade capture. These are the only two likely scenarios I can think of inspector that are plausible.'

Abberline had to admit that maybe Bates was right, but something about that time still bothered him.

'Did you ever get the man you thought you shot in the end?' Bates asked.

Abberline thought for a little while before answering. 'No…No, we didn't. He got away. We can only hope he died from his wounds.'

Bates took a deep breath. 'Well, if it's any consolation, if he didn't get the wounds treated, infection such as gangrene would undoubtedly set in, and in most cases, death would follow, and a painful one at that.'

Abberline thanked Bates for his assistance and moved the discussion forward to the present case. 'How far is Fox Hall from where she was murdered, Mr Bates?'

'Not too far at all, if you took a shortcut through the woods, if you had a mind to,' Bates replied.

Abberline thought for a while. 'Hmm, I need to go to Fox Hall.'

'Didn't Detective Collins say Scotland Yard would inform the victim's employer?' Bates asked.

'This is too serious to wait, and anyway, this girl's employer has a right to know what became of her, obviously omitting the gruesome details of her demise. Maybe they can shed some light on why she came to be in the hills, away from her work. More importantly, they need to know for their safety that the killer is still at large, and if my thinking is correct, they could also be under threat.'

'Have you ever known of such a crime, inspector? I have to say I'm at a loss as to why anyone would want to commit such an atrocity upon another human being. I've never seen anything like it. It makes one think about what could drive a person to engage in such an abomination. Where could such a person come from?' He stared over at Abberline, shaking his head in disbelief.

Abberline looked down at Annie Crookshank's broken and ripped body and into her milky, dulled eyes as he replied.

'Yes, I can tell you where he's come from—straight from hell.'

CHAPTER 10

Abberline returned to his lodgings, taking a cab back to The Poacher Inn at Coldharbour, where he planned to stay at least the night depending on how tomorrow's events transpired, he would have to consider extending his time. His mind was consumed by what he had seen at the murder scene and later at the morgue. Flashbacks to Brighton and the killings flooded his thoughts, and the carnage he witnessed at the hands of a maniac who got away, something he still blamed himself for.

As he entered the reception, the smell of beer and tobacco hit his senses. The bar area was packed with what he presumed were locals, mainly men drinking, laughing, and singing. Some sat at tables alone, minding their own business, while others played card games like whist or were engaged in the game of Knucklebones, where dice would be thrown into the air and caught on the back of the hand in a particular way so that the highest number won the round, with sudden cries of excitement often following.

But it was loud and raucous, as with most public houses, fuelled by cheap beer. Abberline was used to this and ignored the noise for the best part, turning his attention to the landlord, George Lamb, who went to a small cupboard behind him where the room keys were stored. George turned to greet

Abberline, almost standing to attention, pre-empting the conversation.

'Nothing yet, inspector. As you asked, I've been keeping me ear pressed to the ground,' he said, reaching up with his thumb and forefinger and tugging on his right ear lobe as if to reaffirm the statement. 'Do you expect to stay long, inspector?' George asked inquisitively in an attempt to thaw the cold between them.

Abberline knew the landlord was being nosy and replied in his usual curt manner: 'I'll let you know if my requirements change. I'll have supper in my room this evening and a glass of cold milk.'

'Ah, right you are, then.' George replied. 'Er… would you like to partake in something a bit stronger, like maybe some of our local ale, sir? Consider it on the house, of course.' George rubbed his hands slowly together like Uriah Heep.

Abberline looked at the landlord with contempt. 'No, not at the moment. You should also be aware that as an officer of the law, it would be inappropriate for me to take anything without paying for it. If, and when I want any refreshment, I will let you know. Now, to make it clear as I have already said, if there is anything you might hear regarding the murder while serving your customers, I want to know, is that understood?'

'Oh yes, sir, inspector, I understand completely, you can count on George Lamb to do his duty, so to speak. You know, I had an inkling to join the force meself when I were a young'un like, you know, do my bit.' George glanced over at Abberline for a morsel of approval but didn't get it.

'Hmmm, indeed…Just bring my food up to my room when ready.'

'Yes, of course, sir, as you like.' George replied, wearing a slight look of disappointment on his face.

Abberline climbed the stairs to his small room, which had a bed, a writing desk, a classic blue-and-white pattern wash basin with a jug for shaving, and a large window overlooking the front of the inn. It was clean and suited his purpose, but he missed the comfort of home and his wife, Emma, the daughter of a local merchant from Hoxton and a year younger than he was. His first wife, Martha, died just two months into their marriage, something he never quite got over but kept very much to himself, still keeping the engagement ring he gave her in his waistcoat pocket. He took his overcoat and jacket off, hanging them on the back of the door, and sat on the edge of the bed, contemplating his next move.

The injuries sustained by Annie Crookshank still troubled him, there was no denying it. They were very much like the ones inflicted on the three women in Brighton. They displayed the same savagery and anger. More importantly, it appeared that the same or similar weapon had been used, a long, thin knife with a serrated edge, one that a surgeon might use. He felt nauseous even thinking about the awful consequences if they were linked. Holding his arm where he had received the deep laceration from the escaping killer, the scar it left was a permanent reminder of what the case nearly cost him and how close he came to losing his life.

He got up, walked over to the desk, sat down, pulled out some paper and a pen from the drawer underneath, and started writing a letter to his wife. It was a way of forgetting the day and the darkness as he wrote, telling her of his hopes and plans for the future and how much he missed her. After finishing it, he folded it neatly into an envelope, took his glasses off, placed them on the table next to the letter, and returned to the bed. He lay down and closed his eyes, drifting off to another time. A warm summer's day, the sound of two larks floating high in a clear blue sky and the warmth of his wife's smile, and slowly went to sleep.

CHAPTER 11

The road to Fox Hall had forged its way into the countryside with a blanket of rumbling grey skies above. The smell of salt air brought on the wind from the coast reminded him of Brighton. Abberline recalled the sombre days in the town and the hunt for The Ripper, how close they had come, and how certain he was that two of his shots had struck the target, but then questioned himself if it was more wishful thinking and he had just missed.

He wondered how Elsbeth Hargreaves was, if she had recovered from the ordeal and returned to her life in Brighton, holding her séances for those who could not let go and needed closure. He felt guilty about not making contact, but he had his career to try and salvage, and being posted to a backwater station in the suburbs of London was far from ideal. He knew it would take some time to re-establish his reputation if he was ever to return to The Yard.

The murders of Mary Quinn, an eighteen-year-old prostitute, Rosie Meeks, a shop worker, and Amelia Stanton, the wife of the local MP, were loathsome and beyond anything anyone had ever witnessed before. The mutilation and savagery of the attacks were incomprehensible, and Elsbeth was lucky to escape with her life. If it had not been for the bravery of Detective Rawlings, who was killed, she would have held hands with death.

That time, he knew, had damaged them both in different ways. His physical injury to his arm from a knife wielded by The Ripper had taken time to heal, but the fall from grace was, in many ways, more challenging to recover from. He hoped Elsbeth had been able to return to everyday life without too many repercussions, but he knew she was strong, independent, and resilient.

He had stood alone before his peers to receive judgment, knowing Elsbeth's involvement had brought heavy criticism from Scotland Yard, who made it clear they were vehemently against a renowned spiritualist participating in the pursuit of a homicidal maniac. To their thinking, this was undermining their authority, and the very thought of asking someone who spoke to the dead called into question the professionalism of the police and made a mockery out of the whole investigation. Yet his boss, Monro, had actively encouraged it at the time, something he later intensely denied.

Abberline knew ultimately that he would be accountable for the escape of their prime suspect. His bosses covered up the trail leading back to Scotland Yard, making a pact with the press not to publish anything more about the Brighton slayings in return for complete access to future crimes. Abberline was hung out to dry and made the scapegoat, but he knew that without Elsbeth Hargreaves, a lot more women would have lost their lives.

He still fought with his version of logic and couldn't quite countenance a total acceptance of her spiritualist world, but he had witnessed with his own eyes phenomenon he couldn't explain; *there are more things in heaven and earth,* as Shakespeare had once written. If there was any good to come out of the experience personally, it was to face his prejudice and endeavour to keep a more open mind on the subject, even though he found it at odds with everything he believed.

The carriage trundled and bumped along an empty, harsh landscape, clumps of hard grass peeking through the broken flint and chalk stone track as it passed furrowed fields bordered by stone walls fractured with age and cold. Men and women worked the land, heads down, toiling until supper. Only the mewing of a single red kite that hovered high above averted Abberline's attention as he entered through the main gates of Fox Hall. The horse slowed as the house grew closer. He knew that informing people about a death required tact and diplomacy, particularly in cases of murder where the victim had met with a violent end.

However, he felt he was duty-bound to inform the employers of the murder and the current situation, to a point. He didn't want to go into too much detail about the injuries inflicted on the victim. As he questioned how it would help to know that a person they saw every day had been found tied to a tree, stabbed multiple times, and had their nose and ears sliced off. Some things were better left unsaid, as they would only bring unnecessary distress if known.

As the cab stopped outside the entrance, he noticed he was not alone. Another carriage was parked just the other side of the drive. He paid his driver and asked him to wait, as he didn't expect to be long. He suspected the other vehicle contained Detective Collins, who would have wanted to be present when he told Camilla Patterson the news about Annie Crookshank. After all, Camilla Patterson was the wealthy elite, and Abberline felt sure Collins wished to show he was in charge, not this outsider from London. He walked over ready for a confrontation, his shoes crunching on the loose gravel, but the person emerged before he could reach the carriage window.

'Inspector Abberline, as I live and breathe, what on earth are you doing here…'

Abberline stood facing the last person he thought to see, a smile slowly forming.

'I could ask the same, Elsbeth.'

CHAPTER 12

Elsbeth greeted Abberline in a warm yet respectful manner, reflecting a friendship that had been formed and tested. 'How are you, Abberline? I trust now fully recovered from your wounds?'

'Yes, better now. It's left a scar, my penance and a permanent reminder for allowing that maniac to escape.'

'We did everything we could, and I saw you shoot him, I saw the bullets rip through the clothing, so I don't understand how he could have got away,' she looked bemused. 'You know I asked after you at Brighton Police Station, I wanted to see if you had settled back into your old life at The Yard in London. They told me you had been reassigned, but that's all. There was still the same hostility towards me, the same looking down at me because of my gender, but there was also something more profound. It was as if they despised me, and held me responsible for the death of one of their own. I felt I was being judged, holding the guilt box with Detective Rawling's name inside.'

'No, Elsbeth, *you didn't* kill Rawlings, and this was not your fault, Rawlings was doing his job, for which he paid the ultimate price. You could not have done anything to prevent his murder, you were still suffering from the chloroform that was given to you by his accomplice, Cripps, so there was nothing you could do. Rawlings was a police officer, and he knew the risk, we all do. I was sent there to catch that lunatic, I was in charge, and believe me, no one holds themselves more accountable than me.'

Elsbeth thought back to that time when she was trapped and then taken by the killer deep inside the sewer system, thinking that her time had come. 'If it were not for you, I would not be here today. I doubt anyone could have accomplished anything more than you did to try and stop him. No one was responsible, Abberline, least of all you.'

Abberline thanked Elsbeth for her reassuring comments, but it did little to alter his perspective on the matter. 'Anyway, Scotland Yard made sure it was me who was to be served up as the sacrifice, and the price was my head on a plate, and willingly, my boss provided it, shifting any attention away from him. The press was told to back off and forget about what happened in Brighton. Then I found myself posted to a small station outside central London for the foreseeable future. Out of sight, out of mind, I suppose.'

Elsbeth, annoyed by the injustice of it all for him, sighed and continued. 'So, what brings you to Fox Hall?'

'The murder of a woman, her body was found in the woods near here. There was some information on her revealing that she worked for the family that owns this place, the Pattersons. The victim was Annie Crookshank, who was employed as a housemaid to Camilla Patterson. Mrs Patterson's late husband was a doctor of some prominence and had been an adviser, I'm told, to the royal household, Her Majesty at some point. So, the murder of an employee in a home where the owner worked at Buckingham Place has raised more than a few eyebrows, and my boss has been told in no uncertain terms to find out what happened. Seeing he had no one else to send, not even the Scotland Yard cat, he ended up reluctantly giving me the task of attending the scene and gathering all the material relevant to the case.'

Elsbeth leaned over and touched Abberline's arm, her deep mauve velvet glove matching her long crimson day dress. Like most women of means, Elsbeth dressed well and followed fashion from Paris and London, preferring garments with a lightweight cage under the dress that gave volume and was made from cane or baleen, replacing the heavy, multi-layered crinolines. Her hemline was just above the floor, showing her black leather boots with a French heel, the laces tied around a series of small buttons and pulled tight. She wore a number of petticoats and a corset, not that she needed it as her waist was naturally slim, finished off with a matching bonnet and cloak to keep the cold at bay.

'Ah, well, as I'm sure you know, the good Dr Patterson is no longer with us and died some time ago. So, is this police interest more about a connected dead man's reputation than the poor woman who worked for him, who has ended up murdered?' Elsbeth showed that her cutting sarcasm was still razor sharp. She respected him and his abilities, but she always put the woman first, knowing they were generally treated like second-class citizens. 'And did it cross your mind *why* they dispatched you? I thought you had been sent to the back and beyond?'

'Monro, my boss at Scotland Yard, couldn't or wouldn't spare anyone else, but I noted something deeper behind the request. Elsbeth, there is more to this than you know. This murder has similar hallmarks to Brighton, and I believe I was sent here because The Yard wants reassurance that the madman who killed those women in Brighton has not returned.'

'And is he back? Is this the work of The Ripper?'

'Annie Crookshank had been disfigured and stabbed multiple times, including her privy parts. On balance, I would have to say yes, the level of violence and body mutilation all point to it. It's the staging that's different. The way he left the body is almost as if he wants to fashion or frame it somehow.'

'Had any of her internal organs been removed?' Elsbeth asked, which was a fact she knew from her previous experience with The Ripper.

'No, but both ears and the nose were cut away and not found near the body and are still missing. So, Elsbeth, how do you come to be here? I have to say I didn't expect to see you for some time. And why here, of all places?'

Elsbeth took a letter from her bag and handed it to Abberline, who read it while listening to her. 'I received this from Camilla Patterson, asking me to conduct a séance here at Fox Hall to contact her dead husband. Camilla wanted advice on a personal matter. A relationship she had formed with another man that had soured and had become toxic, and reading between the lines, I believe had become dangerous. She was concerned not only for herself but also for the welfare of her teenage daughter, Henrietta. She was frightened and needed to know what to do by taking advice from the one person she trusted, but who was sadly no longer alive. And, that inspector, is why I am here, to do what I do: commune with the dead. I've already knocked at the house, but nobody answered, so I was about to depart and return later when I saw a carriage arrive, and I have to say curiosity got the better of me. I always trust my instinct, and it was telling me to stay and wait to see who this was, and that proved the correct decision, as here you are.' Elsbeth smiled.

Abberline knew he still had to put logic before Elsbeth's gift of intuition and suggested they try again, proposing they go around the back as the house no longer had a servant to attend to callers. 'Maybe if anyone is inside, they didn't hear you calling, it's such a big place.'

The Hall had a substantial garden behind it, mainly laid to lawn with a beautiful white marble water feature situated in the centre of the garden. The running water brought peace and tranquillity to the surroundings, which Elsbeth took some comfort in as she followed Abberline through a set of double doors leading into the house that had been left ajar, which was strange given that it was cold outside.

'There's a way through here.' Abberline noticed. Elsbeth kept close as they went into one of the back rooms of the house. It was quiet and dimly lit inside, with a bouquet of flowers starting to wilt and die on a sideboard. At first, little seemed untoward, but it was quiet, too quiet there should be signs of life. The large rectangular room appeared to be intact, there was no debris, which might be expected if there had been a burglary. The furniture and paintings on the wall were all untouched. Abberline looked round to Elsbeth. 'Be careful, something's not right here.'

Elsbeth knew enough to trust his experience and slowly followed him out of the room into what appeared to be the main hallway, which was rich and heavy with the smell of beeswax used for polish which reminded her of her school-days. To the right of them was a door, and in the centre of the hallway sat a magnificent stairway that led up to the other floors. It was carpeted in a deep blood red and black pattern, handmade from a blend of wool and cotton, kept in position by brass rods fixed to the treads. A grandfather clock in another room on the other side could be heard ticking while the door they moved towards appeared locked. Abberline placed his shoulder gently against it, applying his weight to try and force it open.

The wood creaked and strained, but still, it wouldn't budge. 'We're going to have to force this open,' he murmured. 'But it will announce our presence, so we'll return later.' Abberline's voice was low and measured as Elsbeth nodded in agreement. He pointed over at the stairs and the floors above, slowly moving towards them. As they started the ascent, the air was electric and heavy, the tension fraught, weighing down on them both. Abberline was just ahead, testing each tread carefully to ensure it didn't groan under his weight, his eyes narrowed and strained as he watched every shadow. Elsbeth brought up the rear, now and then checking behind her just in case. Her heart beating and breath short she clung onto the dark oak bannister like it was the side of a lifeboat, anxious, her palms sticky from sweat.

When they reached the first floor, a narrow hallway, they were greeted by the same heavy carpet that led down from the right to what appeared to be three rooms with their doors closed – *Keep out.* Two wall gas lights, set on a low flame, had been left on, revealing the way with a dull, yellow, dreamlike haze as Abberline and Elsbeth moved gradually along the corridor. The first door opened to a dark space; long curtains covering a window had been drawn, shutting out any light, and it smelled old and musty, abandoned and cold, not even a memory lingered. Nothing else could be seen except the faint outline of a bed and an empty wardrobe, its doors gaping open, with a number of wooden coat hangers hanging bare, like stripped bones.

Abberline whispered. 'We need to keep going, we need to find Mrs Patterson.'

'They knew I was coming,' Elsbeth said as she followed him out of the room. She was conscious of a bad feeling in the house, a depression that seemed to breathe from every corner, room, and wall, destroying any good that once inhabited it. Now, it was a place that harboured anger and fear. Abberline put his hand on the doorknob of the second door to the next room, the cold brass pinching his skin as it turned.

Elsbeth stood right behind him, without warning, the image of the tarot card she had selected before her journey engulfed her mind. 'The Card of Death', suspended in front of her, spun clockwise with a deep crimson background, then stopped. She stood frozen to the spot, unable to move. The skeleton face leered out at her, the two spaces where the eyes would be now black holes, sinking into oblivion. This portal to the future was bound tight, like the root of a tree, around her soul in this decaying house of death.

Abberline pushed the door open, the stale air slithering out of the crack, hissing like a coiled snake, bringing Elsbeth out of her state and back into reality. Together, they stepped into the unknown.

CHAPTER 13

Camilla Patterson's naked body loomed out from the wall above her bed like a ship's figurehead. Her feet had been bound and nailed to the wall above the headboard, and a series of ropes suspended her body. Her arms stretched out like wings of a bird tied at her wrists and secured to each side of the room. It was as if she were in flight, looking outward towards the thin line of the horizon, but this was not a mariner's guide sent to protect the vessel from the perils of the oceans; this was intended to deliver another message.

Her eyes and tongue had been cut out, and her stomach slashed open. The reek of death was overpowering, like rotting meat. Abberline and Elsbeth stood silent, finding it difficult to speak trying to comprehend the horror that was displayed before them. The victim's mouth appeared grotesquely stretched across her grey marbled skin, giving the appearance of a smile, making the sight even more disturbing.

Elsbeth felt sick to her stomach, turning her head away for a moment. She then moved reverently towards Camilla, a tear slowly descending her cheek. She spoke softly to her soul. 'I'm so sorry.'

Abberline was also clearly shocked at the level of violence, walking around, studying the body and taking notes, his instinct as a policeman to record everything to examine the scene, took over, helping him cope with the carnage. Camilla's face was ashen and drained, and her mottled skin akin to the patina of cemetery stone. He held a quizzing glass to his eye, inspecting the cut to the abdomen. 'I'm no coroner, but this incision to her stomach validates our recent discussion. Look here, at the evidence, it's like footprints in the sand. Was it left by mistake? I don't believe so. I think it was here for us to find.'

Elsbeth went over to join Abberline, who passed her the magnifying glass and told her to look carefully at the skin where the laceration had been made and pay particular attention to the edges. She wanted to retch, the sweet, sickly smell of decomposing tissue and the sight of this woman's stomach contents was overwhelming. 'What am I looking for, Abberline?' she asked, coughing into a lace handkerchief she had taken from her cuff while trying to divert her gaze from the body.

'Let your eyes do the work, hold the glass just far enough away from the surface so it enhances the area you are examining.'

Elsbeth moved the implement back and forth until the image suddenly came into focus. The unmistakable pattern of a jagged edge on both sides of the skin was enough for her to feel a strong sense of having been here before, an emotion she would often experience as a psychic, but she wished she hadn't this time. 'It's him. The Ripper, the knife that's been used, has left the exact markings as the one used on the victims in Brighton, something I'll never forget,' Elsbeth said while shifting herself away from the abomination in front of her.

Abberline could see she was shaken but continued with his reasoning. 'Yes, the same is true for Annie Crookshank and Camilla Patterson. The question is, have we found him by chance or by design? As I said, my thinking is the latter. He knew I would be sent down to investigate the missing servant because of the unusual and savage injuries inflicted on the victim. The Ripper knew it would be moved up the chain of command to Scotland Yard, and because Annie worked for a family where the husband was connected to the royal household and even Her Majesty, it gained even more importance.'

Now angry, Elsbeth paced around the room as she recalled the correspondence that had brought her to this place. 'The letter Camilla Patterson sent to me, the one I showed you, she said he was dangerous, and she was in fear for her and her daughter's life, and now...and now she's dead.' She stopped as the full weight of what had happened in this room to desperate and frightened women who had reached out to her for help dawned on her. 'I should have come sooner...maybe then...' her words tailing off as the emotion became too much.

'You can't take a wild beast like The Ripper and tame it. This would have always happened. You could not have prevented it. In the end, he's returned to form, a deranged, sadistic killer, and left us two defiled, dead women to show a very clear message that he's back and dare I say it, even more empowered than before,' Abberline pronounced.

Elsbeth thought for a moment, turning her head slightly. 'Camilla Patterson also said that he had locked himself away in her husband's study for days on end. She had no idea what he was doing there and didn't dare disturb him. But maybe we will find something in there.'

'Yes, you're probably right. We'll go downstairs next as I suspect it was the door we found locked, and if I'm right, that's exactly where we will find what else he was up to.'

Elsbeth looked up at Camilla, her eyes reflecting the pain and compassion for the dead woman. 'What about her? We can't just leave her like this?'

'Of course not, but the murder requires proper documentation, and we need to retain the scene as it is until Surrey Police get here. This is how we build on cases in the future by detailing everything, not just the victim, but the room and how it was found. Every piece of information could prove to be important. I'll go down to the local station and tell them what I expect them to do.'

'No, Abberline, we'll go together. You're not leaving me on my own here to be fish bait. I made that mistake before, which nearly cost my life,' Elsbeth said in a determined manner.

'As I remember it, Elsbeth, you took it upon yourself to go alone, but it's fine we'll go together, all right,' Abberline said confidently as Elsbeth looked over at him with a knowing smirk.

'But the daughter Henrietta is still missing,' Elsbeth exclaimed. 'We have to check the rest of the house first. She could be hiding anywhere.' Then a thought entered her mind, a terrible, awful possibility that she didn't want to think was possible, but she had to know if Abberline had also considered it. 'There is also another…' Elsbeth couldn't bring herself to say the words, so Abberline finished them for her, his expression grim.

'You're trying to ask, is this monster capable of killing a child? I believe he has no boundaries, no rules, and is just as likely to take the life of one as young as Henrietta as he is an adult.'

Elsbeth's face went as white as a sheet. 'I…I can't, will not accept that, it's too much we have to find her,' but the thought slowly took hold in her mind.

'Hang on a second, there's…' Abberline looked closer at the victim's face.

Elsbeth looked on, horrified. 'Surely, there is nothing more to be gained from this. Hasn't she suffered enough? We must now concentrate all our efforts and find Henrietta.'

Abberline ignored Elsbeth's pleas. 'It's her expression, don't you see it's not right, it has been made to look like this.' He moved closer and reached up with his right hand, gently touching Camilla's left cheek, feeling something under the skin. Elsbeth turned her head away, finding it hard to look. 'There is something wedged across both cheeks inside her mouth, forcing her hideous grin.' He moved his hand from her face and towards her mouth, placing his fingers inside the stump of what was left of her tongue, still warm and wet, and slid against his skin as he gradually removed a piece of paper that had been rolled up. It was soggy from blood and saliva. Little by little, he undid it and read the contents.

CHAPTER 14

Elsbeth waited to hear what the note had said. 'It's not good news,' Abberline reported.

To Inspector Abberline and Elsbeth Hargreaves
    So sorry to have missed you, but I'm sure you've had time to admire the work. As for the little bitch daughter, that will keep you busy for a while, don't bother searching the house. She is not there. But time is running out, so you had better hurry, or she's going to meet a very grave end indeed, and it will be another corpse for you to bury and have on your conscience.
    Regards
    Jack

Elsbeth gathered her thoughts as Abberline handed the note to her to see for herself. 'If she's not in the house, where is she? He's using her to his advantage, he knows our priority will be to find her, giving him time to slip away.'

'Yes, and it's working. We can't leave a girl to die. He knows that,' Abberline said. A loud bang got their attention, followed by many heavy footsteps running into the house and up the stairs. Detective Collins appeared at the top of the landing with four other officers.

'Didn't you say you were reporting back to The Yard after seeing the coroner, eh? Call it a policeman's nose, but I had an inkling you were going to make ya way here, inspector, and I ain't wrong, am I?'

'Detective Collins, it's good that I did, as this is now a crime scene. Camilla Patterson has been murdered.'

'Murdered!' Collins replied, shocked.

'Yes, I'm afraid so, you'll find her, or what's left of her, in here,' he pointed towards Camilla's bedroom. 'But let me warn you, it's not a pretty sight. Also, we have a more pressing issue: the daughter is still missing, and we need to pool our resources to find her. If she's not in the house, there's the study downstairs, and we know he used it exclusively, so he might have been careless and left something about where she might be, but one thing is for certain, we have little time to waste.'

Collins nodded in agreement as Abberline and Elsbeth left and quickly sped down the stairs to the room in question, leaving the detective and his men to take their first look at the murder scene.

As they reached the bottom, Elsbeth thought about the note. She suddenly realised she didn't have it and thought she must have dropped it, so she started to return to the landing, but Abberline caught her arm. 'I have it, don't worry,' he said, patting his jacket pocket. 'I don't want to have to answer any awkward questions, not at the moment, I'm treating this very much on a need-to-know basis, and the less Collins and his men are aware of it, the better at this stage.'

'What motivates someone to do this? What possible advantage can they gain from inflicting so much pain on an-other?' Elsbeth knew these acts of rage of such violence could only come from one source—evil.

'I've been working on a theory since our last case together that some murderers are like hunters. They kill to satisfy a need, an urge within them. The Ripper enjoys the selection process if you think about it all of his victims so far have been women, and that itself tells us something. It tells us he has a deep-seated hatred for the female gender, maybe something that he's had for a long time, and we can see that in the method he uses to unleash that pent-up anger by mutilating the bodies.

It's not just enough to kill them he has to do more to satisfy his lust for pain and suffering, and I believe that he sees this as a natural expression, but of course, to any sane person, it is nothing short of abhorrent.' Abberline paused momentarily, letting the gravity of what he had just explained to Elsbeth take hold. 'To my mind, he has a taste for it. He enjoys seeing them beg for mercy, having power over them, it's an addiction, and he's not going to stop.'

Elsbeth thought carefully about what he was saying. As a woman, she felt the same vulnerability and bond to those who had been slain.' So, when you mean 'selecting', how does that work?' She wanted and needed to understand something that made sense from the madness.

'In a way, like an animal hunts, or, if you like, stalks its prey, that's what our killer is doing. He's carefully choosing them, separating vulnerable women, and then, when they are at their most exposed, he strikes.'

'You mean he's behaving like a predator.' Elsbeth asked, wanting to understand more.

'Yes, Elsbeth…he's what I'm calling predatorial, like any wild beast would be, and if my theory is correct, we can use this to our advantage, and it might give us an edge in catching him.' As they reached the locked room in the hallway, Elsbeth was still mulling over his hypothesis, as Abberline wasted no time and kicked the door hard with his right foot. It sprang open, slamming back against the wooden panel wall behind.

Abberline immediately went to the windows and drew back the heavy, dust-filled curtains to let in the light as dirt from the material clouded the stale, musty air. The room was a mess of paper and bits of broken furniture everywhere. One of the walls had been painted with a number of strange symbols and half-complete sentences scribbled randomly without any context. 'We need to look for any evidence in here that might lead us to where he has taken the daughter.'

Elsbeth felt the room was full of negative dark energy, his energy. She was feeling dizzy as Abberline came over to help her, taking her arm to steady her. 'Do you need to sit down?' he asked.

'No, I'm fine. I'm sensing someone's fear…something awful.' Closing her eyes, she emptied her mind of all thoughts, waited for a connection, and then spoke.

'Abberline, it's someone…I can't see their face, but it's a woman—a young woman.' Elsbeth moved her head from side to side, slowly trying to focus on the grainy images that were fading in and out. 'She can't…she can't breathe…she's outside, a place with lots of trees, running for her life.' Elsbeth felt a tightening in her lungs, heat rising through her hands. 'The woman wants to scream, but…she can't.' Elsbeth's airway constricted as she felt a sharp, agonising stabbing pain in the small of her back, then another and another.

CHAPTER 15

'Are you sure you are alright?' Abberline asked.

Elsbeth, still in shock from what she had seen, held onto his arm, shaking a little from the ordeal. 'I observed absolute fear, panic. That the woman was being hunted down like an animal, she was petrified, desperate to escape,' she paused, 'from something evil.'

'Was it the daughter, Henrietta?' Abberline asked against his better judgment, preferring to put his faith in cold, hard facts, but he had seen Elsbeth's ability before, and it wasn't the first time it made him question his firmly held beliefs.

Elsbeth thought for a short while before answering. 'No—the energy was not that of a child…it was female but older, but someone still connected to this house. Maybe a person who works here.'

Abberline made sure Elsbeth was steady before letting go. 'If you're right, it has to be the murdered housemaid. He's taunting us while showing us what he can do. This is about theatre. Look at how he left Camilla Patterson. He's evolving and becoming more inventive. The murders in Brighton were pure butchery, nothing more, nothing less, that's his base nature. But here we see him shift, and now he wants to frame his work as if he is…proud of it. I'm not saying he won't revert to self, I'm sure he will, but it's as if he's playing a game with us.'

Elsbeth's expression changed to one of concern, there was a slight upturn of the mouth, and her eyes had a watery glaze. 'We need to find Henrietta, she is the only person left who has seen what he looks like—the only one left alive, well at least we hope so.'

'Yes, but he would have factored that in. He may well be mad, but he's not stupid. This is perverted amusement for him, and I believe he has kept her living as part of his sick thinking to see if we can get to her in time.'

'But where could she be?' Elsbeth asked as Detective Collins appeared, slumped against the door to the study, his head bowed, trembling with a mixture of indignation and repulsion after seeing the body of Camilla Patterson.

'What kind of sick twisted bastard does that to another person. I thought I'd seen it all doing this job for the years I 'ave. What happened to their maid was bad enough, but what he's done to that poor woman up there, it's the Devil's work. Two of my men, just youngsters, both new to the job, had to get outside. Been sick as dogs.' Detective Collins was pale and grey from witnessing the crime.

'I know, Detective,' Abberline said. 'I'm sorry they had to experience that. Maybe now you comprehend the situation's urgency and why this couldn't wait for Scotland Yard to get involved?'

Detective Collins rolled his shoulders over, heavy in defeat, his voice low and fraught as he turned to walk away. 'I need to get back to the station and organise the coroner to come by and have her...what's left of her, taken back. I'll leave one of me men here just in case he decides to return.'

Abberline and Elsbeth watched Detective Collins leave, his steps slow and plodding; they both knew there was little chance that the killer would risk returning. His work at Fox

Hall was complete, and he most likely would be making good his escape as Abberline's attention was drawn back to the mound of papers across the late Doctor's desk.

'Help me go through this shambles, Elsbeth we might find something to indicate where he has the daughter.' Abberline hated the disorder, it irritated him and his natural compulsion for neatness grated on him as he fumbled through the stack of correspondence. Seeing his frustration, Elsbeth went to assist and carefully went through the notes and letters, picking each one up, studying the contents, who it was to, and what it said.

'Abberline, look at this. It's a letter addressed to Dr James Patterson confirming his appointment as a medical doctor at an asylum in Surrey. And here is another where Patterson accepts the position, but the date is wrong, he can't have…'

'What do you mean, Elsbeth?' Abberline asked.

'He can't have written this; he was dead. It's dated after he passed.'

Abberline examined it carefully. 'This is not one you would send to someone. It's a draft; look, there's no address and all these scraps of paper with Patterson's signature on them. The Ripper has forged the letter back to the asylum, posing as the late doctor. He must have known that Patterson, and the hospital staff never actually met. The asylum would jump at the chance to have someone of his medical pedigree, a highly skilled and qualified medical man who had once worked at the royal palace, advising, possibly even treating Her Majesty. They would take his arm off —pardon the expression, Elsbeth—to have a person like that on the staff.'

'That's all well and good; we know where he's headed, but it doesn't help now. We need to find the daughter and fast. But she's not in the house; he's already told us that in his note…'

Abberline took out the scrawled message from his pocket, examining it again. 'The answer is in here. I'm sure. He's testing us.' He read through it line by line, word by word, until it clicked.

'Elsbeth, it's here written in plain sight. *You had better hurry, or she's going to meet a very **grave** end indeed, and it will be another **corpse for you to bury** and have on your conscience.*'

Elsbeth listened as the words once more transported her back to her home and her vision before leaving for Fox Hall, the damp, cold air, the scratching and muffled calls for help. She snatched the note from Abberline, her heart beating in her mouth, her hand shaking with dread, as she read it herself to be sure. 'My God, the poor girl, she's underground. He's buried her alive.'

CHAPTER 16

Abberline crumpled the note back in his pocket and, with Elsbeth, left the study. 'I know where she is,' Elsbeth exclaimed, rushing as she took the lead, exiting from the front of the house.

'You don't have to say, I've worked it out. There's only one place she could be', Abberline replied, right behind her.

Elsbeth stopped as they got outside, the bleakness of winter matching her mood as she turned and answered anxiously. 'The graveyard where her father is buried.'

'Exactly,' Abberline said, equally horrified. 'We'll take my cab. I'll be there in a second. I have to quickly speak with Collins before we leave.'

'Abberline, we don't have much time. We have no idea how long she has been underground.'

'I know, I know, but I have to see him, I'll be as fast as possible. You get ready to leave, tell the driver where we need to go, and there'll be something extra for him if he gets us there quickly.'

Elsbeth lifted her long black dress above her boots and rushed in the direction of the waiting carriage as Abberline ran towards Collins, who was outside talking to one of the officers.

'Detective, this has to be quick, so just listen. I think I know where the daughter might be. I need you to stay here and check the house for me, search every nook and cranny just in case I'm wrong.' His voice was sure but stressed as he wanted to convey the urgency of his feelings.

Collins nodded in reply and shouted after Abberline as he took off towards the waiting carriage, 'I've dispatched one of my men to fetch the coroner here to clean up this bloody mess and remove the body of Mrs Patterson.'

Abberline looked back over his shoulder as he ran. 'Okay, thank you. If I find her, I will bring her back here. Wait for my return.'

Detective Collins watched as the cab with Abberline and Elsbeth pulled away along the drive towards the gates, talking out loud to himself as he turned around towards the house. 'Christ, I hope that poor girl isn't in here she would have heard the whole thing, every scream her mother made during that ordeal.'

Elsbeth stayed silent for the first part of the trip, adjusting her dress and position to be more comfortable. The green and black leather upholstery provided some cushioning, but the ride across the county roads was tiring. As the cab rocked her from side to side, she clasped her gloved hands tightly, her thoughts returning to the sight at Fox Hall. A deep, dark, foreboding filled her with dread as she thought about the daughter who had been taken by the same monster. Time was fast running out. Henrietta was just a child alone, scared and with no one to protect her. She had to know. 'How much air would the girl have if you're right and he's buried her?'

'I am not sure. It depends on factors such as her height, weight, and age. Also, her mental capacity to deal with the situation. Imagine being trapped underground, all alone. Nobody can hear you scream. Cold, frightened, with no light at all, unable to move your body, and worse, no way out. It's a lot to ask of anyone to keep calm. However, that issue alone could determine how long anyone can survive in such conditions.'

'How come?' Elsbeth anxiously asked.

'Well, the more a person panics in a confined area, the quicker they breathe, thus the more oxygen they use and in a finite space, which is not good.'

Elsbeth looked even more concerned. 'Well, we better pray we find her, and soon.'

* * *

It was pitch black when she came round, her eyes squinting in the dark. Her body shuddered as she took a deep breath, the air stale and damp. She gulped it down, finding it hard to swallow. Still drowsy from the cloth he had wrapped around her face, the sweet, ether-like odour lodged firmly in the back of her throat, she felt trapped, unable to move her arms or legs.

She brushed the stone sides of the tomb with her fingers. The material felt pitted, hard, and cold. Turning her head from side to side, she tried twisting her body but couldn't. Her heart raced, beating faster and faster. Her breathing became shallow. Her shoulders were wedged in tight, the lid pressing down on her face; she couldn't move an inch, she was sealed in, entombed.

Warm, salty tears trailed across her young cheeks, as absolute panic took hold. She shrieked as loud as she could. 'Mummy, where are you…help me!' A moist, slimy sensation beneath her made the skin on her back wet from something congealed and dead below. Sweat formed on her brow as her mouth went dry she started to tremble, every fibre in her body tensed, every muscle cramped up she began to shake hysterically. She wanted to vomit. Her nails snapped as she desperately clawed at the sides of the stone coffin. 'Please let me out…please.' She stopped and listened, thinking she heard movement, the shuffling of feet. *Maybe someone was there, someone heard me.*

Her heart raced. She kicked her feet out towards the bottom, tearing the skin on her heels, but she couldn't reach. She yelled again. 'Oh God, please save me. I'm in here, please, can't you hear me? Please help me, please God… help me, why won't you help me?' She screamed over and over again until she could do no more, sobbing uncontrollably, mucus running out from her nose as she realised. There was no one there. She was alone and forgotten. Her chest tightened, it was becoming hard to breathe, her lungs burned with pain. She was petrified. Then, like a flame being snuffed out, her mind shut down, and darkness engulfed her.

CHAPTER 17

The cab halted just outside the church. Elsbeth and Abberline hurried out and stood looking over towards the gravestones that stretched around both sides and far into the distance, where the grass was uncut and had become buckled in the cold. Records of those who had passed, names etched into the surface, were said by some to be a means by which God would identify the dead and make judgment against their soul. Abberline and Elsbeth hurried towards the entrance, opening one side of the double gate and entering the grounds.

The church, a typical twelfth-century building constructed from local light-yellow limestone, sat in an east-west elevation in the middle of the grounds, capable of holding a congregation of around three hundred people. It served the villages and towns in the surrounding area. Weddings, marriages and, of course, burials were performed here regularly. Luckily, on this day, the church was shut and locked, so Abberline and Elsbeth felt they had some anonymity to conduct their search for the missing daughter.

A path of large grey stone slabs snaked around the church's circumference, kissed with a frost that also touched the headstones. Some stones came right up to the border, standing erect while others, over time, had cracked, leaning back or to one side, with a patchwork of moss eaten into them. A large black crow perched on top of one, its beady black eyes suspiciously following the pair, cawing into the air—a gatekeeper for the dead.

'I suggest we split up so we can cover a larger area in less time, as we have no idea how long she's got, so we need to be quick. You take one side, I the other,' Abberline said while weighing up the job before them and any signs of recent activity.

'Agreed, we should look for anything related to the Pattersons. My feeling is that they have more than just one member of the household buried here. Families of this size and wealth often have reserved plots, unlike the poor, who were lucky to be granted an unmarked ditch somewhere.'

They met at the back of the church a short while later, both out of breath from rushing around, but none the wiser and still without finding anything.

'Maybe we're looking at this in the wrong way,' Abberline said breathing heavily.

'What do you mean?'

'Well, your point about the husband, James Patterson, not being the only one of the family laid to rest here is probably correct. The Pattersons are rich and have lived in that house for generations, so it stands to reason, as you say, that they would have some church land put aside.' Abberline stood looking towards the number of graves stretching back towards the furthest point of the grounds. 'But there's absolutely nothing to indicate a recent ceremony. If there were, the ground would be disturbed, and time is running out.'

Elsbeth could see what he was saying. 'But who said it had to be a plot of land? Why not a family plot inside their *own* mausoleum? Isn't that what the wealthy do? They have it built so that when one of them dies, they get to be put to rest in the family crypt.'

Abberline looked over towards the east side of the church, where a row of white structures sat next to each other. 'Let's hope you're right because we're out of options if we don't find her very soon...' Elsbeth didn't need him to complete the sentence, she knew just how urgent the situation was, they both did.

Abberline and Elsbeth headed at speed to the private tombs, each made from grey granite with ornate Roman-Grecian-style decoration. Large, heavy wrought-iron ornamental gates, stained with orange rust, protected the peace of the departed. On the outside of the structure, the family name was etched and mounted on a brass plaque, so it wasn't long before they located what they were looking for.

'Here it is!' Abberline announced. The metal had turned a blue-green by the weather, but had the family name of Patterson on it. The gates were shut tight by a heavy chain that had been looped through the bars and secured with a padlock. Abberline looked for something to prise it free, noticing a spade left by the side of the building nestled in the undergrowth. He picked it up and struck the padlock.

The lock broke off, the chain slid away, and the gates creaked steadily open, revealing a gloomy, cold room. Four caskets were lined up in a row. Rainwater had leaked through the roof over the years, staining the lids and making the writing hard to decipher. The sides warped, cracked, and decayed like the bodies inside. Pieces of broken limestone from the walls and ceiling were scattered like confetti over the ground, yellowed from time, mixed with dried leaves blown in from outside and crunched underfoot.

Abberline reached into this pocket, took out a small box, and struck a match. 'These graves are too old and have been here for decades. I can see stairs at the back; they must lead down to another level.'

They rushed over, knowing they needed to hasten but

apprehensive at the same time, this could be a trap. At the top of the stairway, Abberline lit another match, looking for something better to use, his hands shaking. He found a small plate with a half-used candle inside a ledge to his left. He lit the wick, and they moved swiftly down the narrow stairway into the crypt below.

The chamber felt oppressive, heavy, and smelt dank and mouldy. It was smaller than the one above, with little light; the air even colder as it burrowed through their clothes, stinging their skin. In the centre of the room, the eerie outline of two caskets was positioned side by side. The room was still, and only their breathing filled the space around them.

Abberline held the light over the first coffin as Elsbeth read the inscription, her words slow and reverent. 'This is his mother. It reads *Mary Patterson, wife of Peter Patterson, beloved mother to James, died this day, 1827;* Elsbeth traced the letters with her index finger on the cold stone as she spoke. 'She passed nearly sixty years ago, she died young, in childbirth most likely.' Abberline moved the candle over the next tomb, the text revealing it belonged to the husband, Peter Patterson. Then, the last. *James Patterson, the beloved son of Mary and Peter, died this day, 13th October 1884.'* Elsbeth instinctively put both hands on top of the tomb. 'We need to open this.'

Abberline paused for a moment, knowing that if she were wrong, the consequences of this action would be all his boss would need to terminate his career permanently. Even if he had almost hit bottom, the last few feet before the drop into oblivion were all he had left to cling onto, so they were precious.

But life came before pride and his job, and he quickly dismissed any thoughts of concern. Without saying a word, they started to push on the solid slab lid with all their might, sliding it inch by inch. It grated and groaned stone against stone, gradually moving. Then, without warning, a sigh of stale air breathed out from a crack, like a mummy's sarcophagus, the seal was broken—the dark within opened up like the gates of Hades, revealing its dreadful secrets.

CHAPTER 18

The body of Henrietta Patterson lay lifeless and still, her face pale blue with the effects of pallor mortis—twisted, contoured, and terrified. Her mouth stretched open wide in a final scream, frozen in time, that unique moment when she realised all hope was lost had somehow been preserved, moulded into her death mask. The body of her father was beneath her. The repulsive odour of his rotting corpse made both Elsbeth and Abberline turn momentarily, the fumes scraping the back of their throats.

'Can you imagine being that young, trapped and sealed up inside this stone box, unable to move, unable to be heard, dark, alone, with the body of her dead father? It must have been the worst death imaginable, she must have gone insane,' Elsbeth said, wiping a tear away.

Abberline was silent, peering down at the young girl they were too late to save. 'No…No, I can't. I thought I had seen his worst…this monster is beyond reproach. Her distress must have been at the extremities of what anyone could endure and in ways I cannot even begin to comprehend. She was just a child. I only hope that I can repay the deed he has done here, and I can assure you I intend to make certain he feels every bit of pain this poor innocent girl had to go through.'

Elsbeth reached inside and cradled the limp hand of the child in hers, stiff and cold to the touch, the nails blackened and shredded to the skin. She sent thoughts of peace for her spirit to be free of pain and fear. To be allowed to pass over without wandering this earth for eternity as a restless, haunted soul. As she placed Henrietta's hand back on her other one, she noticed a small slip of neatly folded paper by her side. Elsbeth carefully removed it, read its contents, and then handed it to Abberline. 'You might want to listen to this. He's left us a message.'

Dear Abberline and Elsbeth

Oh dear, it appears that you always turn up late for the party, thus, unable to save yet another poor soul. She screamed for hours, you know. I sat here listening to her begging and crying and the sounds of her nails snapping as she tried to claw her way out. It was...unique. Understand this, try to find me, and I will dance in the blood of your torn and ripped bodies. Let this be a warning to you both: do not follow; leave well alone.

I am everywhere, I am watching. I am death.

Jack

Abberline let the note drop down by his side and looked at Elsbeth. 'We need to go back to Fox Hall so I can inform Detective Collins that there will be one more body for the coroner to take back to the morgue.'

'Then what? You return to Scotland Yard and tell your spineless boss that their worst nightmare has come true. The bogeyman is back.' Elsbeth said.

Abberline didn't have to think about that prospect long before answering. 'No, they had their chance. They covered up the mess in Brighton, hoping, like me, it would all just go away. But they were wrong. Someone like this, someone as vile and insane as this, can't stop. He is feeding off what he does, it's an addiction, and if left to do what and where he wants, he will become worse than we can ever imagine.'

Elsbeth raised her arms in frustration and anger. 'So, my question still stands, Abberline, what next?'

'Remember the forged document we found in the study at Fox Hall? We go to where we know he is, we track him, and this time, we destroy him. Send him back to the vile creature who gave birth to him. The Devil.'

CHAPTER 19

Lidgate Manor was one of the largest private asylums in the Home Counties and had the harshest reputation. It was originally constructed during the Georgian period from hand-crafted bricks moulded in wooden blocks from locally sourced clay as a private residence for wealthy shipping merchant Lord John Barnstable of Lidgate, his wife Isabella, and their three children. No expense was spared, a folly in the form of a Bell Tower was built, and rang out over the hills and fields every time there was to be an event at the manor.

The home's interior was filled with the finest carpets and furniture money could buy. It was packed top to bottom with works of art from all over the world, and they would often hold wild, hedonistic parties with fires lit in metal cages mounted high on wooden poles that could be seen for miles. However, it was said locally that the property had been built on *dark earth*, known to be cursed, and anyone who lived on it would pay the price.

All appeared to be well for a few years until one day, a servant found Lady Barnstable hanging from a large oak tree in the grounds, taking her life for no apparent reason. There were no more parties after the suicide of his wife, and Lord Barnstable became a recluse with his three remaining children. Poachers reported tormented screams and cries in the dead of night coming from the manor house and it was not until some months later that the local vicar from Shere, a small village nearby, went calling to find his lordship had drowned the staff in the lake then killed his children and himself in ways the vicar said only a man possessed by Satan could have undertaken.

As there was no one to stand to gain from the inheritance, the bank quickly secured the building, and the artworks were sold off to pay for the considerable gambling debts run up by the owner. The manor then stood empty and derelict for a number of years until 1847, when a group of investors secured the sale for a modest sum. They then began construction, transforming it into a privately run asylum, a business that would generate a substantial profit with the right management in place.

By this time, building practices had changed, and bricks were now being produced by mechanical means, so everything became far quicker and cheaper. The main house was gutted, and internal wings were built for the inmates. Additional areas were constructed, along with a gatehouse for security and a few more outhouses. The large lake at the back of the property was filled in and left as open ground, later to be used for more grisly purposes.

The main building and its surrounding walls stood tall, a foreboding landmark that made a statement. At the entrance to the asylum was a guardhouse with two massive black wrought-iron gates that required the strength of two men to open and close. They were designed to keep the unwanted out but also served as a stark warning to the inmates that there was no way out unless it was in a box. There were several outbuildings, but the main block consisted of two wings, constructed primarily from red brick that had become pitted with age, housing male and female patients who, for the most part, were kept separated. Male and female inmates were contained in large, overcrowded, and unsanitary wards with iron bars fixed to the windows to prevent escape. The sweet tar-like smell of carbolic acid used to disinfect the floors, along with body odour, was always present, staining the air.

Those small amounts of inmates considered low risk were sometimes allowed to wander within the confines of the ward, while others were secured to their beds by leather or metal restraints. Some patients were criminally insane, while others with a lesser form of mental illness had been committed to a life of incarceration, depravity and degradation by the judicial system, based purely on hearsay.

Many people had been misdiagnosed, either due to poor practice or ignorance, and, worse still, in some cases, by design. It was not uncommon for a controlling husband who wanted to marry another or to profit in some way from the estate to have his wife sent to an asylum without any questions and removed from the marital home on medical grounds. There were many immoral officials who would be only too happy to take a financial incentive for such a transaction.

All patients at the asylum were exposed to the same brutal system operated by the governor and his sister. Treatment was harsh, cruel and mostly undocumented, with most, if not all, resulting in deep trauma or loss of life. The day-to-day oper-ation of the place was managed by guards who also served as security, along with a pack of dogs bred for their viciousness and tracking abilities in case anyone was stupid enough to try and escape. There was a separate medical wing comprising a consulting room, separate living accommodation for the resident doctor, and a dormitory for the small contingent of female nursing staff.

It was all overseen by Governor Ignatius Crane, a cruel and sadistic man in his fifties, and his younger sister, Maude, a small, thin spinster with short grey hair cut harshly across her forehead in a straight line like Richard III, hollow cheeks, and bright amber eyes. A stern and equally abhorrent person, who administered the accounts while also metering out discipline, which she *so* enjoyed.

Crane, a man prone to sporadic violent acts, sat back in his office chair, the rusty springs creaking, as he contemplated the arrival of the new doctor. He wore a black suit with a white-winged collar shirt that clung to the sweat of his overweight body. His eyes were piggish in size and washed-out blue, his skin pale and offset by a flash of white hair and eyebrows. He was an anomaly suffering from a severe case of albinism, which gave him his ghost-like complexion. A condition that was not understood, which caused him to be bullied and labelled a freak in his younger years. Now older, he preferred a solitary existence within the confines of the asylum, where daylight was limited, allowing him to slip unnoticed among the shadows.

Ignatius and his sister were answerable only to the board of trustees, which comprised of wealthy men in prominent positions who convened twice a year to review the accounts. Provided the establishment was returning a healthy profit, a blind eye was turned. Crane was given free rein to run the place as he saw fit without any inquisition. Pain, humiliation, and the removal of human dignity were prerequisites for Crane's rule, and he expected all his employees to follow his orders without exception. He believed that if you enforced these things, and crushed any thought of hope, you could rule them with minimal staff because they had lost the will to fight or contemplate ever getting out. Complete obedience was his mantra for both inmates and staff. Any misconduct or be-havioural issues from a patient would be met with immediate punishment, which was swift, merciless, and meted out with unconditional ferocity. Crane ran the hospital for financial benefit. *'Be a nice little nest egg, my dear,'* he would often say to his sister, rubbing his hands together.

The few guards employed were male, some coming from the village of Shere, and were of different ages. They were responsible for discipline, order, and security and were given complete authority to do as they pleased to anyone at any time. The patients feared them; some worse than others had a particular reputation for savagery, mocking the sick and beating them so severely that some inmates died from their injuries and were taken out of the block under the cover of night and buried in shallow, unmarked graves where a lake once stood. During their time at the asylum, patients were confined to cramped, cold, rat-infested conditions, long forgotten by the courts or families who had had them committed. The bell in the tower was rung for only two reasons: a death or an attempted escape.

Ignatius Crane sat behind his large oak desk with Maude in front of him. The desk had been made from the large tree that once stood within the grounds where Lady Barnstable hanged herself. He often wondered what the tree would have been like in the day with her body swinging from it and the crows picking at her flesh. Crane looked over to his sister, his eyes fixed and cold. 'Now that we have a new doctor for the hospital wing, we can get back to more important matters.'

'Do you think he will be a good fit for the position? We have not even met the man, and yet you employed him,' Maude asked her brother, her voice terse and tinged with irritation.

'He comes highly qualified and could prove to be most useful brother. I doubt he will pose any issues for us. If he does…well, his time here will be short-lived.'

'As with the other one,' Maude sniggered, looking out of the window towards the makeshift graveyard. She moved back towards her brother, planting both hands firmly on top of the desk, arching forward. 'The last one was soft, giving out pills and whatnot, costing us money. This is no place for sentimentality. 'We can't have that happen again, so this one had better toe the line and not query our methods.'

'As I have said, I'm sure he will be accommodating, and if not, well...' Crane, accustomed to his sister's temper, stroked the top of his desk, his fingers following the contours. 'This is a dangerous place, and accidents can and do happen, my dear, as you may recall.' The moment was disturbed by a respectful knock at the door, followed by a young guard entering the room.

'Sorry to disturb you, Governor, Ma'am, but we've had word of a visitor at the front guardhouse. He says he's here to see you, sir. Said he's the new doctor.' The guard, who was not more than eighteen years of age, stood erect and nervous, waiting.

'All right, boy, don't just stand there. Go to the reception, he will have to sign in then, make sure there is someone to bring him down, and be quick about it,' Crane bellowed.

'Yes, sir...right away, sir,' the lad replied, visibly shaken, leaving immediately.

'Now, my dear, we will soon find out what this doctor is made of,' Crane said, getting up to join his sister. He gently touched the side of her face as she held his hand close to her skin, caressing it.

CHAPTER 20

The visitor alighted from the cab, clutching a small black bag tightly in one hand, and looked up at his new place of employment. He made his way up the steps, noticing two or three people wearing all-white clothing as they tended to the grass and shrubs along the border. He was greeted at the top by a woman, a nurse wearing a white cap and a long, grey cotton dress, in her late twenties, with auburn hair and a rather tired and pale complexion. As he approached, she shuffled her feet nervously back and forth, her leather boots scuffed from age. 'Dr Patterson, I presume,' she nodded respectfully. 'Governor Crane has been expecting you. After signing our register, I will take you directly to his office, where he is waiting.'

The visitor said nothing, passing by her as if she didn't exist, through two enormous wooden doors and into the building, where he stopped. It was a large area with high ceilings, the walls covered in portraits of past and present investors and previous governors, all looking down onto the wooden waxed floor, their gazes cold and stern. A desk sat in the middle, with a guard sitting behind it who waved the nurse impatiently over.

'He'll have to sign in. You know the rules.' The guard snapped at the nurse, his head buried, not acknowledging either of them.

She looked over at her guest. 'Er…if you don't mind, Doctor, it's the governor's instructions. So we know who is on the premises, who they are visiting, and why.'

He stayed silent, picking up the pen and completing the details as requested.

Dr James Patterson, newly appointed Resident Physician of the Lidgate Manor Asylum, to see Governor Crane.

The guard turned the ledger around and read the entry. 'Hmm, right, you can go through now, sir. The nurse will guide you if you don't mind.' His attitude suddenly changed, giving the doctor the rightful respect that came with his position.

They continued down a long, narrow hallway, dimly lit by lamps fixed to the white-painted walls. Towards the end, another set of stairs with a gate padlocked with a heavy chain led down to another level, swallowed by darkness. He paused, looking into the silent abyss.

'What is down here?' he questioned, arching his body slightly to get a better view.

The nurse thought for a moment before replying. 'It's where we place those inmates who have not responded well to treatment and have continued to be more troublesome. The governor has them separated from the general population for an indeterminate period of time. For their welfare, and the good of everyone, you understand.'

He stood listening, his grip tightened on the handle of his bag, his head cocked to one side as a cold wind raced up from the bottom. The eerie stillness was broken by the sound of high-pitched shrieks and screams from below. Metal bars rattling, growing louder and louder, like caged animals, petrified by something desperate to escape, sensing danger, sensing death.

CHAPTER 21

Shere was a small, delightful village on the river Tillingbourne, nestled within the arms of the Surrey countryside, a few miles from Guildford, which served as the main town of the area. It contained a few houses, farm cottages, and an inn which bore the same name as the village. There was also a church dating back to 1190, which provided worship and bible classes on Sundays for the local children and surrounding towns. Most villagers worked for farms, which were deeply ingrained in the wool and sheep industry, with several mills situated on the banks of the river.

A few men were employed at Lidgate Manor, located a few miles northeast of the village, out of sight and away from prying eyes. Abberline had arranged for himself and Elsbeth to stay in separate rooms at the inn, where they would discuss how best to proceed. There was much to discuss, and they needed a way to get access to make those in charge aware of this dangerous impostor.

Abberline was the first to arrive and left instructions with the innkeeper to be contacted when Elsbeth Hargreaves had booked in. In the meantime, he went to his room and un-packed a small overnight bag he had brought with him from Coldharbour. He folded his shirts, socks, and underwear in the pine chest of drawers provided, making sure to arrange everything with precision. He unpacked his cut-throat razor, shaving brush, and cream onto a shelf above a small sink and mirror that was on a stand, which he adjusted until it was aligned and arranged just the way he wanted it.

Abberline knew his boss at Scotland Yard, Monro, would be growing increasingly impatient and would be expecting him back to deliver his report on the Surrey Hills murder, which is why he was dispatched there in the first place. If Monro found out that he had ignored instructions and travelled to Fox Hall with the express idea of informing the employer of the death of their servant, he would be incandescent with rage. But Abberline did things very much his way and had a strong sense of moral duty. He would argue that telling the employer of the murder of one of their staff, who no doubt had been in service with the family for some time was, in his opinion, the decent thing to do. They had a right to know.

He also justified his actions by logic. He knew that if he had obeyed orders, the bodies of Camilla Patterson and her daughter would not have been discovered for some considerable time. The killer would have had a significant advantage and, more importantly, he would not have learned where this monster was headed, and why. Witnessing the mutilation of Camilla, and later finding the note where her daughter had been entombed, made it certain that this carnage was the signature of The Ripper.

Abberline had little faith in the hierarchy. It was always more about politics, public image, and budgets than actually keeping the streets safe. So, for now, he decided to keep this to himself and find out more before reporting back to headquarters. He required a plan of action and a way to stop the slaughter that would follow, as sure as day followed night. Abberline had seen firsthand the handiwork of this lunatic and the damage he had inflicted. After recent events, it was now beyond question that his worst nightmare had become a reality. His nemesis was back.

He went over to the small window of his room, which looked out onto the front, as a carriage drew up and a woman of some distinction stepped down into the moonlight. Her slim build, dark hair, and confident manner made him smile as he instantly recognised Elsbeth. He collected a notepad and pen, ready to meet her. As he made his way to leave the room, his attention was drawn by a slip of paper that had been slid under the door.

Bending down, he picked it up, adjusted his glasses, and opened it to read. There were no words, just a pair of eyes with a straight line below for a mouth staring out from the paper. It was basic, almost childlike, but had an intensity to it that made it feel alive, as if the eyes were watching and following him. He moved the drawing up closer to examine it in more detail, noticing long, fine strands of hair mixed in with the ink. Human hair. A chill ran down the length of his spine as he suddenly realised the dark, rusty brown liquid that had soaked into the fibre of the paper was not ink but something else: blood.

CHAPTER 22

Abberline took the drawing as he went downstairs to meet Elsbeth. She stood at the bar in a deep mauve dress and matching hat with a small light netting that hung over the brim just enough to disguise her face. As she signed the registry that the landlord had put before her, she noticed out of the corner of her eye that Abberline was approaching her.

'Good day to you, Inspector Abberline. I have asked for some tea to be served here at one of the tables. The landlord has assured me that this establishment would not open its doors to the public for another hour or so, so we should have enough time to discuss our business without interruption.'

'Shutterwitch,' the landlord blurted out.

Elsbeth looked up at a shabbily dressed, small, balding man of about sixty years of age who had an exceptionally rounded head and face, which reminded Elsbeth of a cannonball, and wondered what on earth he was talking about.

'Shutterwitch ma'am, that's me name, Jonas Shutterwitch. See it says so above the bar like.' He pointed to a plaque with his name embossed on it as the current landlord of the inn. 'Ave to say, not often we get a lady of your refinement travelling here on her own. Er, will your husband be joining you later, ma'am, if I may be so bold as to ask?'

Elsbeth stood glaring back at him, her skin bristling with irritation at his all-too-common presumption. Elsbeth calmly put the pen back on top of the register, picked up her room key, and placed it in a small reticule bag made from the same fabric and colour as her dress. 'Let me make something very clear to you, Mr Shutterwitch, women like me can and often do travel by themselves for all manner of reasons, which obviously comes as a cultural shock to you, so I will mark this down to your lack of education and being stuck out here in the middle of nowhere. It should not be a prerequisite to be shackled in marriage for a woman to have freedom of movement.'

I am here on business, and that is all, is that simple enough for you to understand? I am here to meet with this man who is an Inspector from Scotland Yard on official business.' Elsbeth turned, pointing towards Abberline. Jonas Shutterwitch, taken aback by her directness, searched for the correct response, not wanting to antagonise the lady any further. Before the landlord could dig an even deeper hole to fall into, Abberline stepped in to save him from further mauling.

'I should have declared who I was when I booked to stay here, but it is most definitely true. I am a police officer here on active duty, and this is Miss Elsbeth Hargreaves, who is also here to assist me with my enquiries. Now, I would like some tea brought to the table, and I can confirm we will be dining here tonight.'

The landlord looked over at Abberline, appearing slightly sheepish as Elsbeth had already left to find some seating. 'Er, yes, right you are sir, no harm meant nor done I'm sure, eh. She's a feisty one, sir, that's no mistakin be a brave man who was to take issue with her.' He made a small attempt to laugh at his own words, but could see that Abberline remained un-impressed. 'Right well, I'll get on like. Cook's making mutton pie tonight, all local, sir, if that's agreeable to you and…and Miss Hargreaves?'

'That will be fine. We will dine at seven and have a table reserved for us, preferably at the back, out of the way of the rabble who will no doubt be in here en masse.'

He sat opposite Elsbeth at a small, round oak table that was still sticky and stained with beer from the previous night. 'This was slipped under my door, and I believe it's clear who it's from,' he said, taking the neatly folded paper from his pocket.

Elsbeth took hold of the paper and stared at the image, tracing around the blood-soaked lines that made up the drawing of the face with her right index finger. Flashbacks of her running through a thick forest, breathing scared, petrified for life, falling and pain shooting through the knees, Abberline watched as the display unfolded in front of him. Elsbeth turned her head from side to side, feeling an acute, sharp stabbing pain in her side.

She was seeing and feeling everything through the eyes of another, Annie Crookshank. She felt a coarse, rough material like rope around her neck, burning her skin. Then something else tied around her chest, pulled so tight she felt her ribs crack, followed by a face peering down at her, eyes cold with nothing behind them, tall, dark-cloaked, he opened a small black bag on the ground in front of her and…then she screamed for mercy, feeling warm salty tears pouring down her face. As the stranger got closer standing over her, she felt his rage, his excitement, his lust. He raised his arms above his head, his hands clasped together, holding something, then a flash of steel followed by blackness.

CHAPTER 23

The nurse opened the door to Governor Crane's office, allowing the doctor to enter the inner sanctum first.

Crane sat back in his chair, deciding not to get up and greet the man, which was the usual fashion. Instead, he remained seated, wanting his visitor to know that he had to earn his respect, it was not just given. Maude, stood in the corner of the room, remaining silent, cautious, and untrusting of this new person, watching, observing, and waiting.

The office was formal and functional, containing a desk, three basic wooden chairs, a metal filing cabinet, and tiled terracotta floors. But it had a strong smell of damp and decay about it. The walls and ceiling were plain and painted white, with a large picture of the manor before it was an asylum hung on the wall, and a photograph of Queen Victoria next to it. A small coal-burning grate provided the heating, but little else was in the room. Ignatius Crane didn't like spending money on anything.

'Doctor Patterson, I hope your journey here was a pleasant one. Please take a seat and make yourself comfortable. This is my sister, Maude, she is in charge of the accounts and, of course, is invaluable in assisting with the day-to-day functioning of the place.' Crane looked over at his sister, who stood still and emotionless, just nodding. 'Can I get you any refreshments?'

'No, thank you.' The Ripper carefully surveyed the room, thinking how pleased he was with himself for making it this far and carrying off the deception of forging documents that altered his identity to that of the deceased Dr Patterson. Now, all he had to do was convince these two he was who they thought he was, and all would be well. This was to be a new chapter for him. He sniffed the air slightly as he sat opposite Crane's desk, which was free of any paperwork other than a plain brown folder, which he assumed contained the correspondence between them. Crane then opened the folder, removed some papers, put on his glasses, and began to read the contents as a deliberate ploy to keep the new employee waiting and affirm his authority.

Crane briefly looked up and noticed the nurse who had escorted the doctor was still in the room. Irritated by her presence, he snapped at her to leave and finish her other duties, which she duly did. 'Now, Doctor, I have read through your credentials, and I must say they are most impressive. I see you have attended Her Majesty on occasion, which has to be the highest point of anyone's career. May I ask, having not had the pleasure of meeting our beloved and most gracious Queen, how is she in person, and what is it like to be in her presence?' Crane always had aspirations of being summoned to the royal palace, but so far, this was nothing more than a fantasy and had no bearing on reality.

'She's charming, intelligent, and delightful and does not suffer fools gladly. However, to get back to your question, it is an honour and a pleasure to serve the monarch. I can only hope that I have gained her trust and that she sees me as a confidant and a trusted physician.' He knew that by saying such a statement it elevated his standing more. He watched Crane's reaction and enjoyed putting this little man in his place.

Crane felt annoyed at the doctor's pomposity and apparent

closeness to The Crown, but he also knew that was in the past and that now he was a long way from London and would be dealing with a vastly different type of patient. 'Well, indeed, but you are still young so I have to confess I see this as a rather odd choice, I would have thought you more suited to a city hospital, but I see from your letter to us that you wish to learn more about the mentally ill, so you applied for the position of Resident Physician at Lidgate Manor. Well, you have come to the right place for that, I can assure you,' Crane grinned. 'The board has approved your position, and all that remains after our little chat will be for you to be shown to your medical room, its facilities and, of course, living quarters. I might ask, did your wife have objections to you staying away from home for long periods of time?'

He waited for a moment, remembering the wife of the real Doctor Patterson, splayed out above her bed as if in flight, her lacerated torso covered in blood, her face wearing a sickly smile that he staged by pressing a rolled-up note inside her mouth. 'No, Camilla had little issue with me being absent. In fact, it was she who insisted that I apply for the position. To be honest, my wife does not have much to be concerned about anymore, she is as free as a bird, you might say.'

'Lucky then, having a woman so understanding,' Maude snarled.

'Don't mind my sister, Doctor, she speaks her mind, and working here, you will come to appreciate that.'

The doctor felt a bond with Maude. Something about her resonated with him, the coldness and cruelty in her tone were admirable. She was a kindred spirit, one to be developed, he mused, as Maude spoke again.

'What is your position on treatment for these…these irritants, doctor? The last resident physician was far too concerned with what he called rehabilitation, and that cost us money. We don't have the time or the resources to try and cure the sickness they have. They are all beyond help and don't know any different, locking them up day and night is better for them and us. Follow the rules, Patterson, don't question, and you will have no recourse from us and be free to ply your trade however you see fit.'

Crane sat up in his chair. 'My sister is, of course, correct, we can't have any more of this so-called new treatment, trying to get these lunatics better. They have been sent here in most cases by a judge, and if the law has deemed it necessary to have them incarcerated for their own good, then who are we to argue? No, as my mother used to say, spare the rod…'

He couldn't have wished in his wildest dreams that he would end up working for people who share the same values as he does. This was too good to be true; he was unconstrained, free, and there was no longer the need to hide in the shadows. 'I can only assure you both that my way of thinking aligns with your expectations—perfectly. I have little time for these new theories, in my professional opinion, they are a total waste of time. Order and authority are key in letting them know who is in charge and ensuring they do not forget that. We are not dealing with normal criminals, these people, as you have so correctly pointed out, are insane, and the only method of dealing with such affliction is strict discipline. My role here is to administer medical assistance if and only where it is deemed necessary. I certainly do not agree with any unregulated expense.' He could see that Crane was finding it hard to contain his excitement. Even his sister, the ice queen, seemed to thaw a little towards him.

'This is precisely required: a common-sense approach to the task at hand. I think you will fit in here very well, indeed.' With that, he lifted a small brass bell out of his drawer and rang it loudly. Some barking in the distance followed, catching The Ripper's attention.

'That sound you hear is the dogs,' Ignatius said, his eyes

gleaming. We had a pack of them brought in from Germany. We leave a couple to roam the grounds at all hours as you can see they can hear a pin drop.' He paused as if to labour the point, 'and will tear a person to pieces.'

After a short while, there was a knock, and one of the guards stood at the door. Harker had been at the asylum for some time. A local man of limited intelligence and not known for his bedside manner, he preferred a more physical approach.

'Take the doctor to the medical unit and show him his living quarters, and be on hand to assist the doctor in any request,' Crane scowled.

Harker stood waiting for the doctor as Maude spoke, observing the doctor rise from his chair. 'One of us will be along later to see how you have settled in. If, in the meantime, there is anything else you need, please don't hesitate to ask a member of staff, who I am sure will be happy to oblige.'

The doctor collected his small black bag, thanked Crane and his sister for their time, and stepped out into the narrow hallway, following Harker. He found it hard to contain his joy being in such an environment. He recalled the words that had been said in the meeting, *however you see fit*. That statement changed everything! As they turned a corner, they went through two sets of locked double doors, then eventually into an area painted white with a large red cross on the wall, which was a symbol of humanitarian aid widely used after 1870 and the formation of the British Red Cross.

They went through one last secured area that led into a small room with several wooden trolleys, each topped with metal trays and featuring an array of sharp and ominous surgical instruments. In the middle of the room, a large chair was mounted on a swivel base, allowing the person seated to be examined at various angles. It was not dissimilar to a dentist's chair, and he thought of many inmates here and the hours of amusement he would have with it.

'This is your consulting room, with separate sleeping accommodation, which hopefully, will be satisfactory for your purposes. It's where the previous physician saw his patients and performed any necessary procedures. The recovery ward is just through the next set of doors,' Harker said, pointing in the direction. 'I will leave you a set of keys so you can move about the building as you like,' he said, removing a bunch from his coat pocket and placing them on a small white desk. 'I'm here for you, whatever you need, as the governor requests, so you only have to ask. Any of them nutters give you trouble, you let me know. The governors had me doing the rounds on the wards at night until you arrived, so I know how to deal with them.'

The Ripper thanked him and then dismissed him, while inwardly laughing at the thought of anyone giving *him* trouble. He continued looking about his new abode, then back at the many instruments, brushing his fingers over them. *So many to choose from, what fun we will have,* he thought. A scream filled with pain echoed out from the ward he smiled, recognising the sound placed his black bag on the side of the desk, and walked out of the office to where the sick were. A line of twenty beds, ten on each side of the room, greeted him, all filled with men and women of all ages, most sleeping, some awake.

An old woman, emaciated and reeling in agony, secured by a leather restraint to her bed, looked over towards him and appeared to be trying to say something. He slowly moved towards her, watching her, intrigued as to what might be ailing her. She raised her gnarled hand. Wrinkled skin covered with brown spots, stretched across fragile bones, was waving him closer. As he approached she tried to speak, but only a whisper emerged; she appeared to be fading in and out of consciousness.

'Please.' She gulped what little air she could. 'Help me, water, please…please, I beg of you, water.'

'Of course,' he replied in a calm and reassuring manner, pouring some into a large glass from the jug on the sideboard next to the bed. 'I'm the new doctor, don't worry, you'll feel better soon.'

She smiled up at him, her soft brown eyes, once full of life and hope, now dulled and filled with suffering. 'Thank you, Doctor, you are a good man…God will smile down on you.'

He sat down on the bed, gently placing his hand behind her head and tipping it slightly forward so she could sip slowly from the glass beaker, watching the relief on her face as she did so. Then, he increased the pressure harder against her mouth, forcing more and more liquid down her throat. Her feet kicked out, and her body began to shake violently, turning and twisting, the leather strap around her waist tearing into her linen nightgown as she choked, unable to swallow fast enough. She grabbed at him, trying to free herself from his grip, but he was too strong.

Some of the other patients woke up laughing, pointing, grabbing the side of the bed, rocking from side to side, hollering and squealing, like wild beasts. The moment was reaching its climax he could sense it, her face was a perfect picture of panic and fear in a last, futile attempt to cling onto life. Then her frail arm fell back onto the bed with the lightest of touches, like an autumn leaf from a high branch. Her bloodshot eyes, wide open, reflecting the horror of her last seconds, were still and empty of life, staring up at him as water dribbled gently from her mouth and over her cracked lips.

CHAPTER 24

Elsbeth recovered from the vision of Annie Crookshanks's murder in Surrey Hills and sat back in her chair her hand shaking from the ordeal, took a sip of water. Abberline had witnessed this before, and although still shocked and not quite able to believe it, he had to admit that there were details about the killing that only he knew and had not divulged to Elsbeth. Yet, she was accurately able to recount them as if she were present at the scene at the time of the murder.

'I was her for that time; I was that poor innocent girl Annie, running through the trees and bracken feeling an overriding need to get help…but not for herself but for someone else—her mistress. But she was being followed, stalked all the time, by the killer who waited until he thought she was at her wits' end crippled with fear. Then he snatched her. Dragged and bound her to a tree, and slaughtered her like she was nothing more than a piece of meat.'

'Look, Elsbeth, I don't confess to understanding this gift you have, but I have to admit, since Brighton, I have tried to keep a more open mind on the subject and what you have just told me somehow fits with the facts of the case as far as we know it. The housemaid was most likely sent out from Fox Hall to raise the alarm, but her fate, along with her employer and daughter, was already sealed the day The Ripper met them. They were all going to die. It wasn't a matter of if, so much as when, it would happen.'

'You mean after he had got what he wanted, to take on a dead man's identity?' Elsbeth said.

'Yes, after escaping from Brighton, The Ripper could not have known that Scotland Yard wasn't hot on his heels and still searching for him. So he had to disappear, but his true nature got the better of him, and he struck again. But this time he finds out a way to completely vanish, steal an identity and become someone else. However, the reality was that my boss, Monro, and the Commissioner wanted Brighton and The Ripper to go away.

They wanted it hushed up, as it would have brought too much unwanted attention to them and The Police Force. The Commissioner is all about self-preservation. He is a politician and has connections and personally knows the owners of all the newspapers. So it wasn't hard for him to intervene and shut off any embarrassing and potentially damaging publicity about the three women who were butchered at the hands of this maniac.'

'Why women, Abberline? What is it that makes him want to hunt and mutilate women? I'm trying to understand what motivates someone to do such horrific things.'

'As I said in Brighton, this is a new type of killer we are dealing with here, an evolution of violence, specifically targeted towards women. I believe he has a deep-seated hatred towards them, something maybe in his past, his childhood, possibly, that triggered this, I'm not sure, but there has to be a reason behind this madness.'

'Or it could be he's just insane, born that way. Women are not aggressive and are not usually physically strong enough to fight off a male attacker. So he picks on women because they are an easy target and put up the least resistance.'

'I agree with you, Elsbeth, wholeheartedly, on everything you say. But it's not as simple as that if we are ever going to catch The Ripper, we must try to understand what motivates him to select women in the first place.'

'What are you looking for, Abberline? There is some thought process behind this, some logic, because how can there be any intelligence in what he does?' Elsbeth sat back in her chair, exasperated.

'No, I'm not saying that. He is clearly mad, but I'm trying to find a pattern for his kills. If we can see that, we might just be able to predict where he could strike next and prevent a death. He is also good at wearing masks, being different and manipulating people to get what he wants, which he has learnt to do. I believe he does have a need, a thirst for this, and I don't think any of these murders, starting with the very first in Brighton, are random. I think he has thought about them, planned them. I don't know how else to say this, but it's chilling if I'm right. It makes him a very dangerous and different type or category of killer than anyone has ever seen before.'

'Well, if you're correct, how are you going to convince your boss and Scotland Yard of this theory, as last time they did everything they could to sweep it under the carpet. They don't care who the victims are as long as it goes away. One of the women was the wife of an MP. How did they manage to conceal that?'

'It's not what you know, it's who you know, Elsbeth, and it's an old-school network at play here, a close circle of rich, powerful men who would have their way at any cost. Until, or more importantly, *if* public opinion should ever turn against them, they will continue to do this and protect their interests. It's politics, everything is politics, Elsbeth.'

Amelia Stanton was indeed the wife of Joseph Stanton MP, who served as a member of parliament for the area. However, more importantly, Stanton was a military man, where duty and honour were everything, and this code meant more to him than his marriage and a woman who he said would still be alive if she had not made public and derogatory remarks in the local paper about the killer. I'm sure the Commissioner would have reminded Stanton of his service to Crown and Country, and this would have been a deciding factor in Stanton agreeing to stay silent on the matter and go along with the whole conspiracy.'

'So politics and men's egos are more important than the lives of innocent women is that what you're saying?' Elsbeth snapped at Abberline. 'Stanton was a vile, obnoxious man and a bigot, and Amelia deserved better than ending up another victim of The Ripper, but I've seen the corruption and self-serving interests in men like Monro and the commissioner before and what they're capable of. Look at what happened to you; you paid the price for their failure and incompetence.'

Abberline agreed but thought it best to move the conversation back to the case, as he knew it would be some time before he could have enough information to understand the killer and his motivation. 'We need to go back and draw on everything we know about The Ripper from Brighton and these recent killings and formulate a strategy. We know what he's capable of, what he's done, and more importantly, where he's hiding, and that's where we get him.

'And how do you propose we do this?' Elsbeth asked.

'The only way we can, devise a plan to break into an insane asylum.'

CHAPTER 25

Elsbeth and Abberline spoke for some time about how best to infiltrate the Lidgate Manor and how likely any scenario was to succeed. It was a complex and dangerous undertaking, one that required thoughtful and careful planning at every stage of the operation. However, what they both had to admit to was their lack of insider knowledge. The place was shut tighter than a drum. There was a rumour that all employees were required to sign a document stating that whatever they saw, or thought they saw, inside the asylum would remain within the confines of the institution. Nothing was to be repeated outside, or it was quite likely they would find themselves as one of the patients, which in itself was a death sentence.

Abberline and Elsbeth pondered on this, thinking through various ways to better understand how the place operated, as without this, the mission was doomed from the start. As they sat over dinner consuming their supper, the landlord, Jonas Shutterwitch, sauntered over to the table. 'Good evening, sir, madam, and might I say how delightful you look, Miss Hargreaves.'

'I look exactly the same as when you first met me, Mr Shutterwitch,' Elsbeth snapped back.

The Landlord stood speechless for a second, expressing a

forced smile. His yellowed teeth closely matched the colour of the pastry on the mutton pie they were eating. Abberline, seeing the similarity, smiled to himself before placing his napkin down to question the landlord.

'Now, Jonas, as you know, I'm an officer in the police, an Inspector. And as you are, the landlord of this establishment, and no doubt the eyes and ears of the village and surrounding area, I would like to know what you can tell us about Lidgate Manor.'

Jonas pulled up a chair from a nearby vacant table and sat down. The strong smell of beer and sweat followed him, as his face quickly changed from an appeasing one to one exhibiting a deep concern. By this time, the pub was full of locals at one end of the bar, their voices raised with laughter and singing. Jonas Shutterwitch didn't want to be heard, so it was good as they were at the other end of the room.

He knew only too well how dangerous it was to talk about Lidgate Manor. He huddled in closer, speaking in a soft, subdued tone. 'I dunno what your business is at Lidgate, inspector, nor do I want to know. All I can tell you is that anyone who goes in there don't come out. Governor Crane and his sister run it, and there is plenty that goes on you wouldn't wish on your worst enemy. And one things for sure they don't like anyone poking about asking questions.'

Elsbeth intervened, wanting to get to the point. 'We need to know how easy it is to access the institution.'

Jonas looked even more worried at the prospect of what he was hearing and even more at the information he was being asked to give. 'Look, my advice is to forget it, you can't just wander up there, knock on the door, and expect to be let in, it doesn't work like that. Crane and his sister rule that place with an iron fist, and God help you if one of you gets caught… People tell of awful sounds from that place, like the noises you hear in your worst nightmares.' He shook his head, turning around to make sure no one was listening.

'You seem very nervous,' Abberline remarked.

'I am, and so should you be! It's an evil, wicked place gives me the shivers just thinking about it, it does.'

Elsbeth leaned over towards Jonas. 'Is there anything more you can tell us about it?'

Jonas replied quickly. 'I can't…can't tell you nothin more. I don't want no trouble, understand.' Elsbeth noticed him rubbing his large hands together, the skin hard with calluses and stained by years of moving heavy oak kegs.

'We understand your position, but do you know someone who is employed there? Possibly one of the men from the village? I can assure you that we will make it worthwhile for them.'

Jonas thought for a while. 'Most will not speak of it, but I know one man who might be prepared he worked there as a guard until they caught him thieving. But because you're police, and given his present occupation he might not be so accommodating.'

'I am assuming that this man is involved in some illegal activity, such as poaching, as this seems prevalent in these parts and would explain his reluctance to speak with me. But tell him I'm not here for that. I don't care if he provides you with stolen meat I just want some insider details about the asylum, that's all,' Abberline said.

'Can you please at least just ask him?' Elsbeth implored.

Jonas looked at them both, said nothing more, stood up, and walked towards the bar through the crowd of revellers. A few minutes later, he returned with a tall man, about six feet in height, slim, wearing a long raincoat and a wide-brimmed hat pulled down, obscuring his face. 'I need to get back to me customers, but this man can tell you what you need to know, and I've told him you'll pay him as agreed. He worked there, at Lidgate, for a while before…'

Abberline gestured for the stranger to join them at the table as he took his place. Elsbeth didn't get a good feeling from him, but she knew they had little choice if they were to gain any insight.

'My name is Inspector Abberline of Scotland Yard, and this is Miss Elsbeth Hargreaves, who is assisting me. We are trying to find any information regarding Lidgate Manor Asylum, and as I understand, you once worked there. Any information you can provide would be greatly appreciated and well compensated.

The man appeared restless, agitated and on edge, looking about him all the time as Elsbeth spoke.' I assure you, the inspector is not interested in any activity you may or may not be involved in, such as poaching. We are not here for that, we just want to put your mind at ease on that point. It's information we seek that is all. It might be easier if we knew your name,' she said, hoping to form a bond.

'No names, dearie, here, and let's get one thing straight: I don't like the police, and they don't like me. So what if I do a bit of poaching here and there? A man's got to eat, don't he? Anyway it ain't none of your business, I don't trust you lot, never ave, never will.' The man folded his arms across his chest in a defensive manner.

Abberline reached into his coat pocket and placed two gold sovereigns on the table. They were shiny, with the young Queen Victoria's head on one side and St. George and the Dragon on the reverse. 'But you believe in these, don't you? They were struck by the Royal Mint two years ago, so genuine enough,' Abberline said, moving them across the table.

Before the poacher could swipe them off the table, Abberline took one back. 'You'll get the other *only* after I hear what you have to say.'

The poacher not trusting anyone, took the remaining coin and bit down on it to test if the metal was genuine. It left a slight indentation proving it was real after which he quickly placed it in his waistcoat pocket. 'I'll tell you what I know, Peeler, then I'm gone, understand, but I want the rest of me money.' The man's voice was gravelly and hoarse as if he had been shouting a lot.

'Done,' Elsbeth said before Abberline could get a word in.

'But show yourself first, and take off that hat. I want to see who I'm dealing with; I don't like it when I can't see a person.' Abberline employed several techniques to detect whether someone was telling the truth or not, including their tone of voice, whether they avoided questions, their body language, or lack of eye contact, for these were the mirrors to the soul.

The poacher slowly removed his hat and placed it on the table. 'I don't hide myself because I don't want to be recognised. I do it because of this.' He lifted his head to reveal the left side of his face, horribly burnt and disfigured, the skin dry, cracked, and covered in blisters. The entire side had drooped, with no expression at all. The left ear was shrivelled up into a small ball of flesh, the nose collapsed, and the left eye was only a slit with just the white flicking from side to side like a lizard. 'This is what happens to you at Lidgate Manor if you steal from them, and I was one of the lucky ones.'

It was both sickening and shocking to Abberline and Elsbeth, and it was hard for them not to show their revulsion at the sight before them. 'You're saying this happened to you at the asylum. Governor Crane did this to you?' Abberline asked.

The poacher looked over at Elsbeth, his only working eye fixed on her. 'Him and his sister. Crane held me down while his sister, Maude, threw paraffin at me, getting me on the side of my head, then lit it. She laughed, watchin me burn, and screaming in agony. Some people don't believe in evil, so I show them this, then they believe evil is real enough, and it lives and breathes at Lidgate Manor.'

CHAPTER 26

Maude Crane unlocked the door to her brother's office. She had decided to visit the new doctor later, giving him time to get his bearings on the place. The meeting with him had gone as well as expected, but she didn't trust him; besides her brother Ignatius, she didn't trust anyone. There was something the doctor was hiding; she could feel it, a woman's intuition that made her want to discover more. And yet, strangely, she found herself drawn to him; there was an underlying intensity about him like a river of molten lava. He disguised it well, but beneath that cold, calm exterior, she felt there was an inferno, and it intrigued her. She wanted to know more.

Perhaps it was because he represented something new, as not much ever changed at the asylum, or could it be that he was tall, young, and handsome and held her attention in a fashion she was not accustomed to? She didn't know. Maude would not be fooled by such trickery, reminding herself of who she was, her position, and her past, as well as the one person with whom she shared a history, hidden and unspoken things buried deep within their memories like the cold, damp earth.

She had grown up in a middle-class family in West London with her brother Ignatius, who was five years her senior. Her father worked as a bank clerk, and her mother was a seamstress at a well-known Savile Row tailor, who had tried to pass on her skills to her daughter, but Maude wasn't interested, preferring to spend all her time with her brother. Ignatius who was an albino, which meant it was difficult for him to go out in the daytime as he found the sunlight hurt his eyes.

When he did venture out, people would stop and stare at him, pointing and shielding their children from him. Street kids would shout abuse at him, calling him a circus freak and worse, when one day he and his sister went to the shop to buy some sweets, and they were set upon. Ignatius received such a beating that he never left the confines of his house again. It was at that moment, when fists and boots rained down on her brother's body, standing watching, that she discovered she didn't feel any sense of remorse or protection. Instead, she felt something entirely unexpected she felt—excited.

The curtains were always drawn in the family home, making it dark and uninviting for anyone who ever came calling, which was seldom. They were both home-schooled and went through a number of teachers, who left after a short while, unable to deal with Ignatius and his violent mood swings and Maude's disturbing nature. Over time, Maude and her brother became more and more inseparable, spending long hours sitting in their gloomy rooms whispering, planning, and reading medieval accounts of instruments of torture. A few years later, in their late teens, the family suddenly sold their home and moved to Surrey. The reason behind the immediate relocation was never spoken about, even up to their parents' deaths. Maude and Ignatius knew, it was *their* secret.

CHAPTER 27

Elsbeth and Abberline listened intently as the poacher told them about Lidgate Manor, the way Crane and his sister ran the asylum, and how obsessed they were about security, employing local labour who had a leaning towards violence. Guards were posted at the front gates, which was the only way in or out of the institution, and were under strict instructions not to let anyone enter the premises without the correct official paperwork. Any visitor who failed to produce this on request would be summarily refused entry.

Once inside, there would be additional guards regularly walking the perimeter, night and day, constantly checking for anything out of the ordinary or suspicious. Most inmates were confined to their cells, but some who had become trusted to carry out manual work around the buildings were allowed out under supervision for a few hours at a time. Others may attend medical treatment, but generally, any movement was kept to a minimum. The only other time when a possible infringement of the rules could occur was during feeding times. Men and women sat separately for breakfast, lunch, and dinner in the main dining area. The food, which never changed, was unrecognisable and unfit for human consumption, dished out cold on filthy, rusting metal trays.

'You wouldn't serve that slop to a dying dog,' the poacher said, wiping his mouth with his sleeve.

Abberline wanted to know about any weaknesses in the system. There was usually something, a fault in the security, that would allow them access, but the place was locked down tight, and there was no easy way in.

'What you want to get into that shit hole for anyway? What you after ain't nothing in there but death, pain, and misery,' the poacher said.

'Never mind, that's an official matter, and as you said, you don't care much for the police, so let's move on.' Abberline was getting frustrated.

'Look, the only way you two are ever going to get in there is if one of you is committed, that's the only way I knows, but if you do that, whatever it is you want, you ain't coming back out cos if they find out, you're as good as dead and believe me it won't be pleasant.'

'You worked there as a guard for a while, is that not correct?' Elsbeth said, ignoring the man's deliberate attempt to unsettle her.

'Yeh, so what of it?'

'So, you were presumably issued a uniform?' Elsbeth continued.

The poacher thought for a while before answering, guessing what was coming next. 'No, no, if they find out I gave you that, they will kill me. You ave no idea who you are dealing with ere.'

'No, *you* have no idea who you're dealing with here. I assure you, if you don't hand it over, I'll inform the Governor just how cooperative you have been.' Abberline waited for the threat to sink in.

'You lot are all the same. How do you think you're going to get away with it, eh? They'll smell you're a wrong-un in a heartbeat.'

'That's not your concern, is it?' Abberline snapped back. 'I'm a police officer. 'I've been in and out of prisons, so if anyone can convince them otherwise, it's me.'

The poacher grunted. 'I want the rest of me coin you promised, tis me that's takin all the risk.'

'You get the rest when you bring the uniform here tonight and no later,' Elsbeth said,

The poacher stood up from his seat and placed his hat back on his head, pulling the brim down to cover his disfigured face. You just make sure you pay me the rest of my money.' With that, he left, making his way through the crowded bar and out the door into the night.

Elsbeth sat back in her chair. 'He's right, you know, we can't just walk up and hope they let you in, even if you're wearing a uniform. We're going to need more than that.'

Abberline paused. 'He also said something else. The only way to get inside is for one of us to be committed.'

'Abberline, you are not seriously thinking what I think you are; please tell me I'm wrong?'

'It's the only way, Elsbeth. If we're going to catch this maniac, this is our best shot. You won't be alone, I'll be coming in with you. With both of us on the inside, we can work together, find The Ripper, and finally deal with him once and for all.'

Elsbeth thought back to the poacher, remembering the horrific facial injuries inflicted on him by the Governor and his sister. She shivered as her blood ran cold, realising that Abberline was right. They were entering one of the darkest hell holes in all of England, and it was clear that Lidgate Manor was home to more than one monster.

CHAPTER 28

Abberline charged a jug of beer to his account for both of them as they started planning a way into the asylum. There was only so much preparation they could do, the rest would be down to luck, and luck was something that didn't register with Abberline. In his mind, he was safe dealing with logic, facts, and certainties, but he also knew that, in this instance, there were numerous variables, and any one of them could go wrong.

Elsbeth toyed with her hair, as she thought through the problems. 'If I'm to be committed to Lidgate, it will need to be convincing. We will require the official paperwork and have it approved by two independent professionals, a doctor and a judge. We could use a forgery, but we have no idea what the documentation looks like. Don't forget the guards see this every day, and if they catch us out, it's over before it's started.'

Abberline considered the points carefully, pouring some beer into two glasses. 'I would have thought you would prefer wine, being half Italian.'

'Well, as they say, when in Rome.' Elsbeth smiled, taking a large gulp from her glass to prove a point.

Abberline was no longer surprised by this many-faceted woman before him, whom he had come to respect and admire.

'I know it's an issue, and to compound matters, The Ripper knows both of us by sight. He realises we are onto him; he's left enough notes as crumbs for us to follow.'

'You think he wants us to find him?'

'I think he loves the chase it's a game to him, his wit and skill against ours, but sooner or later, he will make a mistake, they all do, and when he does, I will be there to put an end to this and him.'

Elsbeth agreed. 'But the rage within him spilling out in the violence he perpetrates is getting worse. He seems to be getting more and more confident since Brighton. It's as if he's building to something, but I can't see it, at least not yet anyway.'

Abberline took a sip of his drink. 'I accept that, but one can only guess what this is all about, and I don't like guessing, but we are not dealing with a normal human here. He is insane in ways that have yet to be documented and understood. It's almost as if he has different personalities and switches between them to get what he needs. It's a bit like a chameleon changes colour to camouflage itself from being attacked. He cloaks his true nature in the characteristics of another.'

'How many people could be locked up inside his head?'

'Who knows, multiple personalities, one for each occasion. But his original may be lost or buried deep, for reason or reasons we will never know. One thing is for sure: the hate and obsession with violence are gaining momentum, and this is a tragedy that is not going to go away, so we have to get inside the asylum, find him, and destroy him.'

'Do you think the Governor suspects? He's much younger than the real Doctor Patterson would have been.'

Abberline paused. 'Yes, he must be less than half his age, I would think, but the Governor and his sister have never met him, having only corresponded by letter. The Ripper is compelling, and he will no doubt spin them a yarn of a young, gifted professional taking on a medical residency to expand his resume. He has taken on the identity of Patterson, becoming him in every way, copying every detail. However, for those who have come face to face with him, as we both have, the one thing you can't mask is the eyes.

One look into those cold, black stones, which seemed to hold no light at all, would reveal the monster he is. One thing our killer will not be expecting is for us to come inside the asylum to hunt him down, so we have the advantage, and we need to play to that strength. The element of surprise is a good tactic to have in such a predicament.'

Elsbeth picked her glass up, drank half the contents, and then placed it back on the table as Abberline looked on. 'Remind me not to get into a drinking competition with you.'

'I spent some time in Russia, and they drink vodka like water, so I learned from the best.'

'There is clearly a lot more to learn about you, Miss Hargreaves. I think I have only scratched the surface of your talents.'

Elsbeth smiled. 'And what of you, Inspector Abberline? Your dear poor wife, how does she cope with all those little idiosyncrasies you appear to have? Like everything has its place, and your obsession with neatness and tidiness.'

Abberline looked almost offended by her remarks. 'Well, my wife, I'll have you know, is a warm-hearted, loving person who has the patience of a saint.'

'She needs to have', Elsbeth smiled.

'When I met Martha, my first wife, we were young when we married, we were both twenty-five years old. I thought I had the girl of my dreams, the one person with whom I would walk this life hand in hand through the good and the bad, my soul mate, if you like. Martha was kind, considerate, and loving. No man could ask for more. I proposed to her on London Heath, a summer's evening, the sky was clear and a beautiful moon hung in the sky like a silver button, just for us.

As we lay on our backs just gazing up at the heavens, I took my chance, placed a ring I had saved up for months in her hand, and asked her to marry me. I remember she wept with happiness, I think we both did. Then she took my hand and said yes, and at that precise moment, a shooting star flew across the night sky as if the Gods had sent a message.

Two months later after our wedding, Martha became very ill with tuberculosis, and I lost her shortly afterwards. I grieved for days and nights, unable to understand why she had been taken away from me. I was beset with grief. I went to the heath where I had proposed that summer evening, I suppose in my way to feel close to her, and as I lay there on the wet grass looking up, a star sailed across the sky and in that moment I knew it was my Martha and she was at peace. It was some years until I married again, and in truth, I never expected to, so I was surprised to be so lucky.' Abberline laughed a little to himself, then looked over to Elsbeth. 'I've never told anyone this, not even Emma, my wife.'

Elsbeth reached over and placed her hand on top of his. 'Thank you for entrusting me with your story, it means a great deal to me that you shared it with me. Maybe for you, death is better left alone, as there are too many memories that will always be too painful. All I can tell you is she will always be there with you, and all you have to do is look up at the sky to feel that.'

'I would like to think that. I remember—when we first met at Brighton Police Station, you told me that someone close to me, maybe my wife, had died of a chest infection. I still find that hard to reconcile with, if I'm honest. But I am trying to keep an open mind about your psychic abilities.'

'Well, that's all I can ask of you, inspector.' She smiled. 'What's the next move to get me committed?'

'I know of a judge, Titus Voss, who owes me a favour. He will sign the document.'

'And don't we need a doctor?' Elsbeth asked, astonished.

'Yes, we will, and I have in mind one I can ask. He works at Scotland Yard, which means I will have to go past my boss, Monro, first, and that means I have to tell him everything that has happened. I'll keep your name out of it. If he even suspects your involvement, it'll make matters even worse. I've already gone against his orders, so it's going to be an uncomfortable meeting, but one that needs to happen for lots of reasons. I'll leave for London at first light.'

The reality of what they were embarking on started to take hold of both of them. 'What do you want me to do while you're away?' Elsbeth asked.

Abberline got up from the table to go and collect their room keys from the landlord. 'Start thinking about how you will disguise yourself and see what else you can find out about the asylum. The poacher should bring me his old guard's uniform if he wants the rest of his money; hopefully, it will fit. Otherwise, we're in trouble.'

Before Abberline could say anything else, the landlord, appeared distressed in front of him carrying a parcel tied up with string.

'Inspector, this just came for you,' Jonas said, passing over the parcel wrapped in brown paper with '*Police*' roughly written on the outside.

Abberline wondered if it could be his uniform and took it while questioning why the poacher hadn't delivered it himself and collected what was owed. 'Where is the poacher? Why didn't he come himself?' Abberline asked.

Jonas looked down at the floor, shaking his head. 'They found him in a ditch not far from here, had his tongue torn out and throat cut.'

CHAPTER 29

Abberline had left for London to obtain the necessary paperwork to access the asylum, and Elsbeth had agreed to stay at the inn until his return. She understood the importance of both being inside the institution together, as one could not do this without the other. If The Ripper was within the walls, it would be imperative that they communicate with each other as it would be a difficult and dangerous journey into a dark and foreboding place with a horrific reputation. She knew there would be little margin for error.

She felt tired from the day, so she removed her boots and stockings and hung her dress up in the wardrobe provided. She untied her corset, removed her petticoat, and then turned her attention to her ritual of preparing for bed. She sat at an old pine dressing table that had seen better days, adjusting the light from the lamp in front of the mirror. Elsbeth was lucky that she had inherited not only her mother's looks, but also her perfect skin, which had a slight Mediterranean glow to it, free of freckles and blemishes. As a young girl, her mother had taught her how to make natural products using traditional recipes from her home country of Italy, which would always keep her complexion looking fresh and young.

First, she washed her face with water and gently dried it

with a towel. She then took a small glass bottle containing a tincture she had prepared before leaving her home in Brighton. It consisted of distilled camomile water, which she applied to her face using a small sponge. After this, she finally applied some homemade cold cream from a small jar made from a mixture of Italian olive oil, beeswax and rose water. She also slowly massaged some on her arms, chest, palms, and the back of her hands.

Finally, she removed a small tortoiseshell hair grip and let her long, raven black curly locks fall past her shoulders, resting on her back and brushing them until they were free of any knots and felt silky to her touch. She placed the silver-backed brush down on the table and went towards the single bed. She usually slept naked, but as she was away and the room was colder than usual, she kept her cotton chemise on and climbed under the sheets.

She let herself forget the dark days that lay ahead and drifted back to her childhood, to her mother's home in a small village near Sorrento, Italy. Her father died from an illness when she was young, but while he was alive, the family would always visit. She recalled the happy times laughing, playing hide and seek among the olive trees with her mother, and Nonna, the salt air catching the breeze and kissing her skin.

She remembered never wanting to leave and wishing they could all stay together in that house by the sea forever. The love of her family, the sun shining like a jewel, set into a clear blue sky, she knew life could not have been more perfect. Elsbeth rested her head on the pillow and smiled as she was once more in that special place, carefree and young, feeling the warmth of summer on her face and the sounds of the ocean. She slowly fell asleep.

CHAPTER 30

Ignatius Crane sat in his office chair, discussing the intake of new patients with his sister while working out how best to manage the current population, ensuring they maximised profit. Each individual who entered the facility was paid for by private funds from a family member, spouse, or distant relative and, in some cases, the state. Either way, money was at the forefront of any decision, and the simple arithmetic was that there was not enough room for the number of people being sent to Lidgate Manor. The asylum was generating good revenue, but there was insufficient space to accommodate more inmates without significantly overcrowding a ward. Which was precisely the strategy Maude and her brother had decided upon.

'What about those government-appointed inspectors who show up when they like, snooping about the place with their rules and regulations? They could shut us down you know that brother,' Maude said.

'Yes, yes, well, we won't be moving the inmates all at once, we'll be taking a more gradual approach. However, I have it on good authority that one of them, a Dr Arthur Lawson, is in the area and is going to drop in unannounced to carry out an inspection. I don't know when, but we can assume it will happen. If he questions anything, we just say we are moving the inmates about to carry out urgent maintenance. They never send the same one twice, so everything will appear normal, especially with your idea of using some of them for gardening duties. This is excellent and gives the illusion that we care about their rehabilitation, which, of course we don't.' Ignatius, happy with his solution, licked his thin lips, his tongue flicking in and out like a lizard.

Maude snorted as she paced back and forth in the office. 'Hmm, there's always one that can be turned at the smell of extra cash, like those judges and doctors on the payroll. I'm sure we can work it to our advantage, and the board of investors doesn't care, all they want is to see a profit.' Maude sauntered behind her brother's back, finally resting her hands on his temples, slowly massaging them. 'No, you're right, brother, you always seem to know what's best for us, so strong and steady and, once more, you've put my mind at ease. It's business as usual. What of the new Doctor Patterson? What do you make of him?'

'I think he's saying all the right things. However, we should keep an eye on him, but my initial thoughts are that he's going to fit in well. He certainly seems to have an appetite for the position and shares our values, so we can say he is far better than we could have expected. And let's not forget he may be young, but he is very experienced.'

Maude agreed with what her brother was saying, feeling vindicated that together they had given the job to the right person, especially after the last doctor, who had not worked out as they had wanted and had been found dead from a terrible injury.

'I'll go and check on him, brother, see how he's settling in, then maybe I'll show him around the place.'

'That's a good idea, Maude, and I think you can start explaining to him our plans for redistributing the inmates. He could prove helpful in the process. No doubt, some of them will be more challenging than others and will require a more pragmatic and blunt approach.' Ignatius Crane's mood suddenly switched, and his look darkened like a gathering storm. 'I will not tolerate any dissension from them. This is to be carried out with utmost efficacy. Any inmate refusing to be relocated will find themselves at the sharp end of my patience, and we know where that road leads, don't we, sister?' Crane's eyes narrowed as he let out a deranged, repellent laugh.

'Yes, brother, we most certainly do.' Maude left the office for the surgery, where the doctor had his consulting rooms. When she got there, he was nowhere to be seen, so she went through a set of doors into the main ward to find him bent over one of the patients.

'Doctor, I've come to give you a brief tour of the premises. Is there something wrong?' She noticed the withered, frail arm of a bedridden inmate behind him.

'Thank you, Miss Crane. That would be most agreeable.'

'I would like to see and indeed meet some of the patients I may be called upon to treat in some way, and I must say it does seem a bit of a warren of passageways, one could easily get lost.'

'You can address me as "Maude" if you so wish, Doctor, seeing we will be working closely together.' She moved within touching distance of him, intrigued by his calm manner. Standing at six feet, he was a good deal taller than she was, and although she was many years his senior, she was attracted by his youth and pleasing features. 'It's a welcome change to have someone of your calibre and professionalism, and one so young to have already formed such a reputation. My brother and I are making some changes, and we feel you will greatly help during this transition.'

'Of course, Miss Crane, how forgetful, I mean, Maude, I

am at your service night and day.' He smiled, concentrating on her reaction, looking for the slightest sign of interest.

'So I think I will show you the two wings or wards we currently have at present. However, as I have mentioned, that is possibly due to change. But we will come back to that later. It will allow you to see first-hand the type of inmate we have with us here. We don't encourage the word "patient" as it gives the incorrect impression you understand. The human detritus that has been sent to Lidgate is here because they have been deemed to be insane. There is no known cure for what ails them, nor do we care or propose to find one.'

'I agree with your diagnosis. However, with your approval, I would like to continue my private work and conduct further experiments on some of the more distressed inmates. There may well be some financial compensation if I am successful.'

Maude liked the sound of making money and saw no issue with his request, and was slightly excited by what he meant as his *private work*. 'My brother and I will need to be kept informed, however, as long as it doesn't cost us anything or interfere with your daily responsibilities, I see no problem.' Maude again noticed the arm of the bedbound woman hanging limply down behind him and wanted to know what had happened. 'The woman behind you, I saw you attending to her when I came in, what is her difficulty?'

'She was in need of water, so I gave it to her.'

Maude moved around the side of him to see the broken, scrawny body of the old person, her lips blue, bruised, and swollen from death. She wanted to know more.

'Hmm, now I see why you used the past tense to describe her condition. So, upon examination, what action did you propose to take?' She watched for any sign of compassion to see if there was any light behind his black eyes.

'None, she was old, infirm, and useless.'

'So what was the cause of death?'

He turned and looked at the dead woman's face as if he were looking at an inanimate object. 'I killed her.'

Maude said nothing, smiling. Her brother was right, he would fit in here very well, very well indeed.

CHAPTER 31

Abberline took a carriage to Croydon railway station, catching a train on the London and Brighton South Coast Railway to Victoria. From there, it would be a short ride in a cab to Whitehall Place and police headquarters. He enjoyed the travel, giving him time to prepare for the problematic meeting with his boss, James Monro, Head of CID at Scotland Yard.

As the train shunted into Victoria Station, the noise, the smell of the engines and the billowing steam clouds obscured the mass of travellers and staff who swarmed the platforms. Whistles blew and flags waved as the final jolt of the train announced its arrival. Abberline collected his coat and case from the overhead rack, alighted from the carriage onto the platform, and weaved his way through the crowds of people and porters, who were balancing large piles of luggage tied precariously to trolleys.

Making his way out of Victoria Station, he passed the entrance to the underground network, which was still in its early stages. All were constructed using the cut-and-cover design, where shallow trenches were excavated, then track laid, after which the trench would be partly covered by brick or masonry. Abberline didn't like or trust this form of travel, even though the Metropolitan Underground Railway had been open since

1863. He hated the confined space, the lack of ventilation, and the buildup of smog in tunnels, preferring to be in the open air, deciding to walk or take a cab to his destination.

By the time he arrived outside his boss's office at Scotland Yard, he had prepared the speech he would deliver, having practised it repeatedly in his mind; he was ready. James Monro was unlike Abberline in almost every conceivable way, not just in his appearance but also in his mannerisms. Monro had also been a lawyer before joining the police as Head of Criminal Investigations, which gave him his aggressive and razor-like interrogation technique.

He was only answerable to the Chief Commissioner, who tended to interfere with how Monro wanted to run this department, causing a great deal of animosity between the two men. Abberline knew Monro intensely disliked him, as was made clear the last time he was here, and the discussion they were about to have would be tense and confrontational, at the very least. He knew this to be especially so, as he had deliberately disobeyed his command. He knocked on Monro's door and waited for the call to enter.

CHAPTER 32

Monro's office featured as always, an array of files and folders stacked on his desk, some open, some closed with no discernible order to any of it. Abberline often wondered if Monro knew of his irritation with things not being in the correct order or place, and played to this by creating a purposeful mess. The thought came and went as he faced his superior, who, if the rumour was correct, was soon to be promoted to Assistant Chief Constable. It was a move that Abberline found hard to accept, as Monro was mainly, but not solely, responsible for the shambles in Brighton. The only other person who should be held accountable was the Chief Commissioner himself, who was selfishly more concerned about his political ambitions than the lives of three murdered women. It seemed to Abberline that only he had been punished for failing while others were generously rewarded.

Abberline sat opposite his boss, looking about the room, as his boss sat with his head down, reading some papers. The room was stark for his position, with just a picture of Her Majesty and a letter of commendation from the Chief Commissioner on the wall behind his desk. There was little else besides a wall-mounted clock, which reflected Monro's frugal attitude. Abberline clasped his hands together, his palms slightly sweaty with tension, as he awaited the opening salvo that would follow.

Monro put the paper aside, raised his head, and squinted at Abberline. 'Right, inspector, you were sent down to Surrey Hills with very clear instructions, as I recall, to note down any observations of the murder of Annie Crookshank and then report back to me, and *only* me. Now, is there anything about those orders you didn't fully comprehend, inspector?'

'Oh no, sir, they were crystal clear,' Abberline replied. 'But you see, sir, when I got to the scene of the crime, it became clear to me that this was more than just a murder, sir, and I thought—'

Before he could finish the sentence, Monro shouted across his desk, slamming his hands firmly on top of it, making the pens and folders jump off the surface. 'You thought…you thought! We don't pay you to think Abberline, we pay you to follow orders. When I told you to take notes, that meant taking notes and nothing else. Now I have received this letter from Detective Collins at Surrey Police, who has informed me of the situation at Fox Hall, and he assures me that his men are on top of it. It is also very clear that he feels your involvement is no longer required as it falls under Surrey's jurisdiction, or, if you like, *his* authority.' Monro threw the letter across to Abberline, who realised that any preliminary idea to try and explain his actions had now been blown out of the water by the unforeseen correspondence.

Abberline could see a small vein on Monro's forehead enlarge and pulsate with anger, a clear indication that the meeting was deteriorating fast.

'If I can explain, sir.' Abberline tried to get a word in as Monro raised his arms in frustration.

'Please do, inspector I'm all ears as to how you made an ignominious debacle of this, which seems to be your forte.'

Abberline was conscious that there was far more bad news

to come and was thankful that the letter, which he quickly read, did not mention Elsbeth or the other murders, which initially he thought most odd.

'As I said, sir, on visiting the crime scene and discussing the case with both Detective Collins and the Coroner Mr Bates, I thought it prudent, given the extent of her injuries, that I not only see the body, which, as you know was taken to the morgue, but also to inform her employers at Fox Hall. Given that Dr Patterson had passed away some time before, this only left his widow, Camilla and her daughter, Henrietta, at the house. So I thought it incumbent at the time to inform them as soon as possible as they would no doubt be relying on the housemaid and would be concerned that she had not returned to work.'

'So you disobeyed a direct order when I expressly told you Scotland Yard would deal with the employers of the housemaid.' Monro shifted in his seat, irritated and annoyed.

'Inspectors are trained to use their initiative and to take action when necessary. There was not enough time to make the trip back to London and inform you of the situation, and what I went on to discover at Fox Hall only affirmed my decision as the correct choice, even if it contradicted your order, sir.'

Monro leaned forward like a viper ready to strike. 'Patterson was a servant to The Crown, and because of that delicate association, we didn't want there to be a frenzy around these murders. Dragging this whole unfortunate episode onto the front pages of the press who would sensationalise everything wouldn't help anyone. Tarnishing the reputation of a prominent and respected doctor who is no longer with us by spreading misinformation is not a good idea for anyone's career. I'm thinking of yours, inspector.'

'Sir, if you let a local man handle this, it will become a circus. He simply does not have the experience to deal with an incident of this scale. The letter does not fully explain the situation and deliberately omits two essential facts: Detective Collins does not like or want the involvement of Scotland Yard, which he sees as an overbearing autocracy. I have to inform you that Camilla Patterson was murdered in the most heinous way you could imagine. Her body was ripped apart and displayed for all to see. Her daughter Henrietta was just a young girl who was missing, and we later found her buried alive in the tomb of her dead father.'

Monro looked shocked at the disclosure and extremely annoyed at the revelation, recording the information on a separate paper. 'The Chief Commissioner will have to be immediately informed of these developments, and I am sure he will have strong words with the Surrey Police Commissioner about the intentional withholding of information in a murder enquiry and the indifference one of their officers has clearly exhibited towards Scotland Yard.

Given the circumstances, and I have to say against my better judgment, it may be better if you keep control and contain this at least for the time being. Don't concern yourself about Detective Collins, he will be dealt with, I can assure you. So, for the time being, this is yours. But don't mess it up again like you did in Brighton, is that understood?'

'Yes, sir. There is nothing more to be done for Mrs Patterson or her daughter, but there is a more pressing matter at hand. May I be frank with you, sir?'

Monro waved his hand for Abberline to continue.

'I understand you sent me down to Surrey Hills in the first instance because you were worried that the injuries sustained by Annie Crookshank were not dissimilar from those The Ripper inflicted on his victims in Brighton. With the additional murders of Camilla and her daughter, there can be no question this is the same hand, the knife marks bear the same jagged edge, and the manner in which they were killed leaves me in no doubt that The Ripper is back and hell-bent on continuing his reign of terror.'

Monro looked decidedly uncomfortable at the proposition. 'Is there any other proof of this? I have to be sure before I take this to the commissioner.'

Abberline showed the note left by the killer at the tomb where Henrietta Patterson was killed and the blood-stained drawing that was placed under his door at the inn.

'I believe these are evidence enough to confirm what I am saying is true, sir.'

'Earlier, you said the word '*we*' during the conversation, and seeing your ability to remember things, such as orders, appears to evade you, I will quote your words verbatim. '*We later found her buried alive.*' Who is the 'we' in that statement, inspector?'

Abberline was fairly sure Monro knew who the other person was, having caught wind of this slip. It was an old police interrogation trick. So he had to deal with it quickly.

'Let me make it a hundred per cent clear, sir. I did not invite Elsbeth Hargreaves to be involved on any level; I have not communicated with her since Brighton. Camilla Patterson had corresponded with Miss Hargreaves, asking for her advice about a man she had become involved with and had foolishly taken into her home. A man we now know to be The Ripper and responsible for the murders of Camilla Patterson, her daughter and their housemaid. Miss Hargreaves arrived at Fox Hall at the same time I did. I had no prior knowledge of her plan to visit.'

Monro sat back, twisting his large handlebar moustache in his fingers. His anger at the very mention of her name was evident in his expression 'How very convenient for you, inspector. You know how I feel about these so-called psychics, circus freaks, the lot of them, and they have no place in our world. Especially that Hargreaves woman, I don't want her anywhere near this, is that understood?'

Abberline knew it was better not to inflame the situation further and instead took another approach. 'I know where he is, sir; The Ripper, where he's hiding out.'

Monro suddenly took a more conciliatory tone. 'Where exactly is he?'

'He took the identity of Dr Patterson and forged a letter for an appointment to be the Resident Physician at Lidgate Manor Asylum in Surrey. That's where he is pretending to be the doctor. I can get him this time. I need to gain access inside. It's privately run, tighter than a drum, and impossible for outsiders to access, and I don't want to prewarn him by going in heavy-handed. I also have suspicions about the people running the place.'

'So what do you suggest, inspector?'

'I have a way in, but I need to get some authentic paper-work to get me through the gates, a doctor's certificate, and a judge's order, to be precise. With your permission, I can see the doctor here at The Yard, who can supply the documentation to be committed. Then Judge Titus Voss owes me a favour or two, and with his signature of committal, the process is complete. Once inside, I will track The Ripper down, reveal him as an impostor, and either bring him back to face justice or justice will be served there and then. Either way is fine with me,' Abberline said, rubbing his arm where he received a wound from The Ripper's knife.

'You know you were transferred to your present posting because you let this maniac escape. If this were to be repeated, there would be no place for you to hide. Your career, what there is of it, will be over for good. Are we clear on that, inspector?'

'Crystal clear, sir.'

'Alright, take this note to the doctor and get him to give you whatever you need. As for Judge Voss, he has a reputation, so you're on your own there.'

Abberline got up from his seat, still feeling the urge to

straighten out the piles of sporadic folders on Monro's desk, but he managed to refrain from doing so.

Just as Abberline was leaving the office feeling quite smug with himself, Monro shouted across at him.

'I do not want to hear the name Elsbeth Hargreaves ever again. She is not to be part of this operation under any circumstances. Don't forget I have to sell this idea to the Commissioner, who also deeply dislikes you, so do not add to the fire here, Abberline. She stays well away from this.'

Abberline acknowledged Monro, closing the door to his office, knowing it was already too late. Elsbeth was the one to be committed, and the next phase was getting Judge Titus Voss to sign the warrant.

CHAPTER 33

Elsbeth woke from her deep sleep at the inn, weary but rested. As she stretched out her arms, followed by a deep sigh, she got out of bed and concerned herself with how Abberline was getting on in London, and the task of convincing his boss to give him the necessary paperwork for them to gain access to Lidgate Manor. She knew that time was running short, and The Ripper would not hesitate to disappear if he thought the net was closing in on him. She stepped onto the deep, patterned carpet and went over to a wooden side table where a china pitcher jug containing water, a towel, and soap had been left.

It was a long way from her Brighton home with running water and the choice to have a hot bath, but she was not a prissy or demanding person. Having been brought up with down-to-earth values by both her parents, she would always be thankful for what was provided. After cleaning her body, she washed her hair in the basin using the soap to massage it into her scalp. She didn't like or agree with using diluted ammonia on her head, as this seemed harsh, even if many women did to encourage hair growth and reduce dirt, she preferred a more natural approach, as she did in everything in life.

After dressing, she thought about asking the landlord if he

had received any news from Abberline, so she left the room and started to walk down the narrow passage and towards the stairs that would take her down to the reception, where she was most likely to find him.

About a third of the way down, she heard the raised voices of a man and a woman. It was hard for her to hear what they were saying, so she stopped leaning slightly over the bannister to see if she could make out any of the discussion. She recognised the man's voice as the landlord's but not the woman's, who appeared to be older but spoke in an unpleasant and threatening manner. She crept down another few steps, lifting her dress, and gently sat down on a step, noticing that the woman's voice had become more aggressive, but what they were arguing about had now become transparent.

'Let that be a lesson to you, landlord, and anyone else who chooses to meddle in our business. We don't take kindly to people poking their noses about, is that clear? Now my brother and I want to know what the poacher was doing in your pub, and who he was talking to, and don't deny it. I have ears everywhere, I know that thief was here, and don't even think about lying to me...I came with a couple of men outside, just waiting on my word if you decide not to tell the truth.' The woman paused and grinned. 'Make no mistake they'll be only too happy to show you first-hand what it's like having broken glass pushed into that face of yours. You've seen how the poacher looks, haven't you? That's what you get if you cross me.'

Elsbeth listened intently, trying to take her mind off how uncomfortable she was squatting down. It had now become clear that the mystery woman was Maude, the sister of Ignatius Crane. The poacher and the landlord had described Maude to Elsbeth and Abberline, which now turned out not only true but dangerously accurate. There was a moment of pause before Jonas answered.

'No one said nothin about that place, alright, Miss Crane, you 'ave my word. Yeah, I admit the poacher used to come in 'ere to get pissed, and he says a lot of stuff. He's still, angry at you for what you did to him. I'm not lying to you, tell your brother he has no complaint with me.'

Elsbeth could sense the fear in the landlord as his speech stuttered. He didn't want to admit to anything. She moved cautiously a bit further down the stairs, leaning her body forward as far as she could. She wanted to try and get a look at Maude Crane as she would soon be an inmate of Lidgate Asylum, provided Abberline was successful.

'Do not take me for a fool, landlord? *Your word!* Don't make me laugh, that means nothing. I have been well informed that this poacher was conversing for some time with two strangers in your pub, a gentleman and a well-dressed woman. And from what I've been told, money changed hands, and he was only too happy to give out information about Lidgate, talking to them about things he knew were best left private.'

Jonas again went silent, he realised he was in dangerous territory. If he admitted he knew the poacher had been giving out details about the asylum, he was done for. If he told Maude that an inspector from Scotland Yard and a woman were asking how to access the asylum, he would face dire consequences. Either way, he was in an impossible position. It was either face serious personal injury or have his business closed down by the police.

'Why do I get the feeling you're not telling me something, Jonas? Eh, why is it I'm feeling you're holding out on me? Your time is almost up. Then I will have no other option but to pass you over to my two colleagues who will utilise their particular talents to make you more cooperative.' Maude clawed her long, yellow fingernails across the top of the reception desk, scarring the surface.

Before Jonas could answer Maude, a loud creak came from

the stairs, interrupting them. Elsbeth held her breath, sliding backwards, hoping they didn't hear. Maude's eyes glistened with suspicion as she leaned her body sideways and bent her neck to be able to see up to the first part of the stairwell.

'Seems you have an infestation problem, Jonas.' Maude said, resuming her position.

'It's an old place, Miss Crane makes all manner of noises, suppose I just got used to it,' Jonas replied. As Elsbeth retreated further up the stairs which slightly doglegged round to the right, it allowed her a brief side profile of Maude. A spindly woman with short grey hair and a pale complexion, who was wearing a shapeless, plain, muted grey dress, like a governess might wear. Buttoned up the front to the neck, it hung straight down to the floor, with just a pair of black leather boots protruding from the hem. Her dress seemed to mirror the person, cold and without feeling.

'Do you know the name Christine Carpenter?'

'Ah, no, can't say I do, Miss Crane. Does the woman live in the village, here in Shere?'

'She did, sometime ago. She died in the fourteenth century, a horrible death by all accounts. Christine Carpenter was walled up in the church and left to die as penance for her bad behaviour. So, think about what that would be like, with no one knowing where you are, alone in the dark with only your nightmares to keep you company, slowly going insane until the air runs out and you suffocate. I have to say, *Jonas*, I'm finding it hard to believe you, maybe you have these visitors tucked away in one of your rooms, eh?'

'If *any* strangers come by here again asking questions I want to know about it, don't make me come and ask again.'

Elsbeth waited for Maude Crane to leave while every fibre in her body told her not to move. If she were seen, it would be over, and all this would be for nothing. She could hear a low muttering of voices, then a thud. *Probably the door,* she thought. She waited a couple of minutes, then slowly descended back down to the reception, where the landlord stood, his face ashen white, his body shaking with horror.

'She…she left this as a warning, said she ripped it out of the poacher's mouth herself. Listen, you can't stay here no longer, I don't want no trouble, you understand. If they find you here, they'll kill me, you understand.'

Elsbeth looked down to see, in front of Jonas, a blood-stained piece of sackcloth spread out in front of him, and in the middle, the remains of a human tongue. Its pale discolouration and congealed blood sent a clear message. '*Keep away from Lidgate Manor Asylum if you know what's good for you!*'

CHAPTER 34

Titus Voss was known as the 'Hanging Judge', a title he re-
vered and revelled in. It was a testament to his years in the
justice system, meting out punishment to those who deserved
it. Anyone unfortunate enough, man, woman, or minor, who
appeared before the judge was most likely to receive the harshest punishment available. He took great pleasure in wearing
his black cap, which was a square piece of fabric worn on top
of his wig when handing down a death sentence, which was
more often than not in his court. He was known to keep the
cap on his person, saying that he considered himself always on
duty to her majesty's courts and that he would dispense justice
whenever and wherever he saw fit.

Abberline arrived at The Old Bailey, which was not far
from St Paul's Cathedral, to be shown through to the private
chambers where judges would hold consultations. Titus Voss
was a man who loved his food and wine, which was reflected
in his morbidly obese frame. His reputation for living life to
excess was well known in court circles, a powerful, wealthy and
feared individual. His dependency on opium and prostitutes
of all ages and sexual persuasions was well known, especially
after a lengthy trial.

He sat behind his desk wearing his formal attire of a black

silk gown, a short wig covering his red hair, and a court coat, his head buried within a document. He bellowed across the room to Abberline to take a seat in a low gruff tone, the sound rebounding off the gilt wallpaper that adorned the walls of the room. Abberline walked across the well-worn rug and sat silently in front of the judge in one of the high-backed chairs provided and waited for him to finish what he was doing. He knew the judge had a short fuse, having crossed paths with him some time ago, but had probably forgotten the encounter.

Abberline took the time to look about the chamber and it was, to his surprise minimalistic in its order, having only a desk in which the judge was seated and a couple of chairs for clients. Behind the desk along the back wall sat a large bookcase with sliding glass doors. Each shelf was crammed with books covering all aspects of English law. To his right were two large sash windows with drapes matching the wallpaper, and on his left a fireplace with a painting above it of himself in all his refineries posed like a king. The fire provided much-needed heat given that the room was of good proportion with high ceilings.

Titus Voss put aside the document he was working on and peered over his gold-framed glasses towards Abberline. 'So, inspector, what can I do for you. I'm a busy man, so make it quick.'

Abberline could immediately sense the hostility in the room, so he chose his words wisely. 'First of all, Judge Voss, thank you for seeing me on such short notice, and I can assure you I will not take up any more of your time than is necessary. I need you to please countersign an order for committal.'

'On what grounds are you seeking this order, inspector?'

'It's a police matter that requires us to carry out a covert investigation, that's all I can tell you at this time.'

Titus Voss shifted in his chair, clearly annoyed at the answer and Abberline's apparent reluctance to divulge all the details. 'You do know where you are, inspector, and to whom you are addressing, don't you?' Do I look like I have just come out of law school? Well do I?' Voss's voice was now raised and getting louder. 'Do you know what this is inspector?' Voss grabbed the document he was working on earlier and waved it in the air. 'It is the death warrant for an eleven-year-old boy, a habitual criminal who has not learnt his lesson, so now he will experience what the end of a rope feels like. So don't take me for a fool, inspector, I will not be told by Scotland Yard to sign a document I have no prior knowledge of, or the circumstances surrounding it.'

'If I may try and explain, your honour,' Abberline interrupted.

'No, you may not, inspector,' Voss snapped back. 'You say you want this because of some secret operation, but I have no idea what you are talking about. No, this is all highly irregular. You must present the person you require to be committed in court to me at my discretion, is that clear? I am a high court judge, not some boot boy of The Yard. Now get out!' Voss slammed the top of his desk with his fist in anger and frustration at the lack of respect.

Abberline stayed calm. He could see why this judge had gained his reputation, and it was clear that he was not going to cooperate, so Abberline would have to resort to a more direct approach.

'You don't remember me do you my lord?'

Judge Voss sat upright in his chair, taken aback by such insolence. 'Only if you have been before me in court giving a testimony. I see your lot every day, how am I supposed to remember each and every one of you?'

'No, your honour, it wasn't in court. It was in Whitechapel in a house run by a woman called Barrington, she ran what you might call an open house for gentlemen who pay well for sexual favours for clients with a particular taste, and of course with no questions asked.'

'I don't think you would ever find me in a place of such ill repute, and I resent the fact that you should even suggest it, sir. If this continues, I will contact The Commissioner, a good friend of mine, who will be less than happy to hear such a complaint, and you, inspector, will find yourself directing traffic.'

'I attended the house, your lordship, on the night in question, as the alarm was raised by the madam herself. A client had locked himself in a room with one of her— shall we say, "employees", a young man of foreign persuasion, and there appeared to be terrible screaming and pleading coming from inside the room, so much so that the police were sent for. I was nearby and so went to the incident, and upon arriving was taken upstairs where I had to break the locked door down to gain access.' Titus Voss was beginning to look increasingly uncomfortable as the tale unfolded.

'As I have already made abundantly clear, I have no recollection and can assure you I do not make a habit of frequenting whore houses, inspector.'

'If I may continue, upon entering the room I found a young man face down on the bed, dead. The young lad had been stripped naked, his arms tied behind his back with some wire so tightly it had cut through both wrists. From the injuries on his back, legs and genital area, it seemed that a whip was taken to him so viciously it had taken most of the skin away and there were clear signs that the victim had suffered a brutal sexual attack. There was so much blood it looked like a slaughterhouse, and slouched in a chair was a man down to his undergarments, passed out from drink and opium. It's a sight I will never forget and that man was you, Judge Voss.'

'Prove it, your word against mine, a High Court Judge.'

'Not quite Your Honour. I recognised who you were from

giving evidence at The Bailey so I knew it would be covered up by your friends in high places. So I arranged for some pictures to be taken for insurance purposes.'

'That's blackmail, inspector, and I will have you hanged for it, mark my words.'

'Oh I doubt that, before that happens your standing in the legal community will be destroyed as I will make sure every newspaper in London puts them on the front page and believe me they will, and sales will go through the roof.'

Voss's face went puce with rage, 'What do you want, inspector?'

'What I came for my Lord, the paper signed for this person, Elsbeth Hargreaves, to be committed into Lidgate Manor Asylum on the grounds of insanity. Then I will ensure you get all the pictures and no one will ever be the wiser.'

'Lidgate Manor? That's a privately run institution. Who is paying for the woman's incarceration?'

'It should be noted that the public purse will cover her costs in this instance, my Lord.'

Judge Voss huffed and snatched the paper from the hand of Abberline and duly scribbled his signature. 'I couldn't care less who foots the bill and you know it makes no odds what you call her on this paper, she'll be given a number on a badge just like all the rest when she gets there, they don't use names.'

'Oh, and one last thing. Please record the guard's name who will be escorting her as 'Baines' if you don't mind?' Abberline realised that Elsbeth's identity would be hidden, but he had to make sure his was as well.

Judge Voss added the name to the document, then threw it back at him across the desk.

Abberline took the paper, checked the details, folded it, and placed it inside his jacket pocket.

'Thank you, my Lord, for your understanding in this matter.'

Voss pushed his immense weight up from the desk in a threatening posture like a bear standing on his hind legs.

'Inspector, make sure I get those pictures, and you had better pray our paths never cross again.'

Abberline closed the door to the judge's quarters, pulled his collar up, and went out into the bustling London streets. He now had what he had come for. He had one last quick stop to make on the way back, and then he would return as quickly as possible to Elsbeth and put their plan into action.

CHAPTER 35

The Ripper had melted into the lunatic asylum with ease. Ignatius Crane and his sister, Maude, had welcomed him, it seemed, with open arms, not questioning his qualifications or, more importantly, his identity. He had fooled them as much as he had Camilla Patterson and her interfering daughter. He had fed the demon within him with their blood and that of Annie Crookshank; things could not have turned out better, and now he was thrilled once more at the prospect of continuing his work. Madness reigned over the narrow, dim corridors of Lidgate Manor. There was no mercy, no reprieve for anyone sent here; it was hell on earth, and he revelled in it. Clutching the small black bag that had followed him on his journey, he held the handle tight, his footsteps echoing down the corridor as his pace quickened. He felt alive and exhilarated.

He headed towards the area that initially caught his attention, where the more troublesome inmates were kept down on the lower floor. It didn't take him long to trace back his steps and go down a flight of stairs, unlocking a pair of black iron gates. He first noticed the intense cold that bit his skin, then the dark, oppressive conditions with just two wall-mounted gas lamps on low flame to light the way to the single cells.

The walls and floor were soaking wet, rainwater having

found its natural course, staining the bricks. There were eight solitary chambers, four on each side, with men and women within. All had solid metal doors with a hatch halfway down for food to be passed through, and towards the top, a small sliding peephole for guards to check if a fatality had occurred. If it had, the body would be dragged out and disposed of.

He went along each door, waiting and listening outside before opening one of the small peepholes to see inside. He became excited and aroused as he observed the deprivation and sordid environment the inmates had been placed in. Each cell had been provided with some light, enough for him to see a withering sliding presence of movement across the floor, some so weakened by their incarceration that they couldn't even stand. Wet, soiled straw covered much of the flooring and had not been changed for some time. The foul stink was overwhelming. He spoke quietly through the hole like a boy in a zoo trying to get the attention of a wild animal.

'Here, come over here, I have something for you, some food, yes, you would like something to eat, wouldn't you?'

He waited for the bait to be taken, pressing his eye against the metal opening to get a better look. Then, from nowhere, like an eel darting from a rock, an eye from within the cell appeared in front of him. Small, beady, and dirty with cuts to the skin and the look of desperation in it. He shot back, taken by surprise, watching it twitching, moving up and down, then side to side. To his amazement, it went as quickly as it had come, maybe unsure, sensing danger. He continued to lure whatever it was back. 'Hmm, you must be starving. How many are crammed inside, I wonder, eh? How badly would you fight for a crumb? Kill for it, I have no doubt.' Then came a response, not a human sound but a low growl. 'Come closer, come, I won't bite.' As the eye appeared again, he noticed it was wet as if it had been crying, then, without warning, he slammed the peephole shut, shrieking like a hyena.

The Ripper's curiosity heightened. He moved along to another door and inserted one of the keys on the bunch given to him when he arrived, slowly sliding it into one of the doors. He could hear the shuffling of bodies, and leather and metal chains brushing against the stone floor, followed by whispering voices. He waited momentarily, letting the uncertainty and fear gain momentum, then gradually pushed open the solid metal door. The smell of human excrement was so acrid that, it made his eyes smart. He reached inside his trouser pocket, taking out a cotton handkerchief, placing it across his nose and mouth, masking out the stink as much as he could, as he stepped into the abyss.

He saw them watching, too scared to raise their voices, he thought they must have learnt the hard way as he walked around the cell observing them. Once they would have looked very different, but this was of little interest to him; now they were just skin and bones, their faces thin, gaunt, and cadaverous. They were the walking dead. Both men and women were confined in this room, all secured somehow, restricted in their movement. He knew there would be easy pickings and he could continue his work unabated. He placed his trusted black bag on the floor and opened it up, taking out a thin, jagged-edged knife, the type a surgeon would use.

One of the inmates, about thirty years of age, caught his attention. She was on top of the bed, wearing a canvas jacket with sleeves far longer than her arms, pulled tight around her body and tied firmly at the back. An open wicker mask covered her head, it was as if she had a bird cage put over her with leather straps wrapped around the circumference and over the top of it and secured by rivets to the jacket by a strip of leather sewn into the canvas, making it impossible for her to eat or drink.

The Ripper drew closer to this living skeleton, noticing the woman's clothes were ripped and soiled. He leaned over to one side to get a better view. He had not seen anything like this before but appreciated its artistry. It was quite remarkable in its design and purpose, a thing of beauty, he thought, as he got closer and closer. He watched her struggle, excited by her fear. She had little fight in her, but what she had soon expired, leaving her breathless on her back, her eyes wide, darting back and forth as sweat poured from her brow.

The Ripper stopped and stood at the side of the bed, lowering his face until it touched the outside of the wicker structure. He could smell the fear, it was overwhelming. The woman tried to speak, to beg, but the words couldn't come out of her mouth, her lips dry and stuck together. He drew his knife up and ran it across the face of the mask. Teasing, he slowly moved it in and out between one of the openings, then stopped, resting it against the bottom of one of her eyelids.

He watched, smiling, as she forced her mouth open, her skin tearing. 'Please, sir, ave pity, please, don't hurt me, I'm just a working woman, me name's Masie. They put me in ere cos I was with child from a very *important gentleman*. Handsome and wealthy from the royal palace said he was a Prince, my Albie, he ain't lying none I saw the picture with me own eyes I did. When baby is born, he promised he would take us all away somewhere safe, so we can be together like, be a family.'

'Tell me, where are you from? I seem to recognise that accent.'

Masie tried to get more comfortable, moving her body as best she could.

'London, sir, Whitechapel, that's where I work, where I met me prince.'

'You said you saw the picture with your own eyes. What do you mean?'

'On his carriage was a big painting on the side of the door, you know, like what the Queen has.'

'You mean a crest.'

'Dunno, just was the same. But then some men came and took my Albie away from me—put me in here, hurt me.'

'Where is the child, Masie? Your baby, where is the little bastard?'

'They took it. Men came here, the Governor gave it to them, and they stole it away. Please, sir, help me get out of here. My Albie, he will pay you, he's a Prince, please. I beg of you, have mercy.'

'You are in the wrong place for that.' The Ripper wasn't sure what she had said held any merit, but in every lie there was a grain of truth, so he would save this information for another day when he most needed it. He turned his attention back to Masie and smiled. The woman's body stiffened and arched, petrified with fear. She trembled as The Ripper thrust the blade deeper into her eye, hearing it pop, watching her writhe in agony. He felt the intoxicating rush racing through his veins. Then, raising the knife above her, clasping it with both hands, it glinted briefly as he brought it down, slamming into her chest. He was euphoric; he had satisfied the need within him, and he feasted.

CHAPTER 36

Abberline reached the outskirts of the village of Shere as soon as he could, passing the church of St James as he made his way back to the inn and Elsbeth. He had travelled back by train, completing the final leg of the journey by carriage. The night had been calm and clear, giving way for a mist to form in the early hours, which hung low on the grounds as he neared the village square. Trees stripped of their leaves and bark blackened by the cold and the kiss of winter stood masked by the fog, their outline smudged like a watercolour painting. The village lay sleeping as if in a dream, just a dog barking somewhere in the distance broke the spell as he alighted from his ride, paid the driver, and went into the inn.

Elsbeth was already up, her bag packed, conversing with the Jonas Shutterwitch, who stood behind the reception desk, gesticulating with his arms like a windmill in some kind of protest. Abberline knew Elsbeth was a person not to mince her words, so the confrontation was clearly heated. Jonas looked past Elsbeth, acknowledging the welcome arrival of the inspector, as a look of relief washed over his expression.

'I'm sorry sir, but she's going to ave to go. I've had Maude Crane from that lunatic asylum down here, and if this lady don't go, it's me livelihood you see…Me life, even if she gets wind of it. No doubt about it, I'll end up like the poacher, dead, inspector sir. Maude Crane and her brother Ignatius are evil, they have no conscience at all, and would have me killed without batting an eye so they would. The things I've heard about that place and what goes on there.'

Elsbeth looked as if she were breathing fire. 'I have a name, landlord, as you well know, so if you are to refer to me, then I expect at the very minimum for you to have the good manners to use it. Is that understood?'

'I don't mean no disrespect, Miss Hargreaves, but you know the score here. I'm sorry, but I can't have you staying here, neither of you, it's just too dangerous.'

Abberline could see their discovery could blow their plans out of the water, so it was in their best interest to vacate the premises and consider their options.

Abberline drew nearer alongside Elsbeth resting his hand gently on her arm. 'It's alright, Elsbeth, the landlord is correct. We don't want to bring any unnecessary attention to ourselves which would highlight our presence here. We need to keep a low profile. Maude Crane obviously suspects something is awry and people are asking questions, so let's not add fuel to the fire and give her any answers. We have to think of the bigger picture.'

Elsbeth nodded in agreement and collecting her belongings, made ready to leave as Abberline asked the landlord one last favour.

'Look, it's still very early so there is little chance of anyone from Lidgate coming back until later. I need a room for a couple of hours. I'll pay you handsomely, then we will be gone, and I can assure you no one will ever know of our stay here.'

Jonas Shutterwitch tussled with the dilemma, really preferring them to go now, but the allure of earning additional funds was too much. He agreed to Abberline's terms giving them two hours maximum for what they needed to do, then they had to depart and never return.

Abberline and Elsbeth retired to his room. With the short time they had, it was important to cover as much ground as possible. Abberline explained how the meeting went with his boss Monro at Scotland Yard and his encounter with Judge Titus Voss.

'I have all the necessary legal documentation for your committal into Lidgate Manor Asylum and we have the guard's uniform care of the poacher, so at least he did one good thing before his demise. I took the opportunity to call into a theatre before leaving London and was able to obtain some face paint and costume clothing which should fit and match the part you have to play.' Abberline held up a dress that was dirty and torn and also a wig made from human hair to add further to the disguise. Elsbeth smiled, it took her back to when she was a child dressing up for fun.

'You have exceeded yourself, inspector, give me a short while and not even you will recognise me.'

'He won't be expecting us so soon, maybe not at all. It was by chance that we found that letter to the asylum for the position of physician, but we have to be careful. Don't forget he's seen me as well, and we can't take any chances.'

'Can we really pull this off? We know his work and the brutality he is capable of, and he's smart and knows we're on to him, so he'll be extra vigilant, and there's one other thing. He possesses an instinct not unlike mine and that worries me.'

Abberline didn't agree that The Ripper had any supernatural powers. 'He was and is just a man, albeit a sadistic sick, and very a dangerous one. We do have something on our side however, that gives us an edge.'

Elsbeth looked curious. 'What's that, then?'

'The element of surprise. The last thing I believe he will

expect is for us to infiltrate the place, so we need to play that to our advantage.'

Elsbeth nodded, took the rags and wig, and left the room as Abberline changed out of his suit and into the guard's uniform. Sometime later, Elsbeth arrived back at the room, with a theatrical facepaint applied to make her skin pale and old. She had drawn fine pencil lines around her forehead and put dark pigment under the eyes, giving the impression she was sick. Red paint mixed with rouge had been skilfully built up around the nose and corner of the mouth to look like open sores. Lastly, her head was covered by a light blond wig which resembled a bird's nest and a stark contrast to her natural dark tone. This, along with her garment, had completely altered her appearance.

Abberline stood in his uniform, with a peaked cap in the traditional kepi style in black Melton wool pulled down to cover his face as much as possible and applied a dark stain to his blond hair. He placed their belongings in a neat and tidy bundle on top of the table for the landlord to conceal as agreed while they were away. He then turned and spoke to Elsbeth. 'We are as ready as we will ever be. The next stop is Lidgate Manor to hunt down this maniac.'

They collected the few belongings they brought and returned to the reception, going out the front door to await their ride. She knew only too well from past experiences just how formidable the foe was, and it made a shiver run down her spine.

'What are our chances of getting him this time, of bringing this monster to justice for the crimes he has committed? I can't get the face of that poor young innocent child buried alive in that tomb out of my mind, the torture she must have gone through; he has to pay, one way or another.'

'We have a good chance, Elsbeth, I firmly believe it. We know where he is, and even though he probably knows we are onto him, I doubt very much he thinks we will find him this quickly.' Abberline hailed the cab as it slowed and came to a halt in front of the inn, the driver jumping down from his back seat and opening the door for them to climb inside. Elsbeth watched the landlord from the window of the carriage, as he stood outside, his grim and worried look reflecting her deep concerns as the driver whipped the reins and the cab lurched forward, and they began the journey to the asylum and the gates of Hell.

CHAPTER 37

Abberline and Elsbeth reached the outer perimeter of Lidgate Manor Asylum, having changed cabs a couple of times to keep their anonymity. The main gate loomed out of a storm which had followed them, bringing freezing rain that poured from angry black skies that rumbled above. Gale-force winds whipped across the land, howling through the trees that bowed over in submission, void of any life. Even Mother Nature had given up on this place.

The carriage came to an abrupt halt, the horse neighing, scraping its hooves against the mud and water, which quickly turned into a quagmire. Abberline turned to Elsbeth. 'This is it. Remember you're here for committal, so don't give them any eye contact. Provided they don't suspect anything. We should be let through soon.' Elsbeth nodded silently in agreement. 'If anything goes wrong, I have my gun, we might need it at some point.'

Abberline then jumped out of the carriage, drawing his coat closer around his body, keeping his head lower to his chest to fight off the worst of the weather. The guardhouse was a small but dry hut with an angled slate roof, a single door, and a window. Sat inside, huddled over a paraffin heater, were two men dressed in black uniforms, with their hands over the heat to keep warm. Abberline knocked on the door with his fist until one of the guards reluctantly stood up and walked over to open it. Standing in the doorway, he purposely prevented Abberline's entry, the rain reaching inside to the other guard's annoyance. The squall was so loud they could barely hear each other's words, so both men had to raise their voices.

'What business do you hav ere?' the guard shouted at Abberline.

'I have someone here for committal, who needs to be taken in tonight.'

'Tonight, you say…we don't take them in after dark, they always come early on special transport, few at a time like. They let us know in advance so we can make room for em.'

Abberline stalled a bit but continued. 'Look, sorry mate, but I don't know about all that, all I know is I was ordered to bring this lunatic here tonight.'

The guard looked at Abberline. The rain had started to seep through his jacket, turning his face red from the persistent lashing of water. 'You best come in, and make sure you shut that bloody door behind you.'

Abberline stepped inside, stamping his feet to get warm, while giving a slight nod to the other guard, who was sitting at a table looking miserable and cold.

'Let me see the paperwork.' The guard gestured to Abberline to show him the documentation.

Abberline handed him the paperwork and hoped he didn't question it. 'Don't worry, she's secured to the seat, she's not going anywhere.'

The guard read it through, shaking his head. 'We get all types in ere. You'd better hope that nutter can't get out of the cab, or you'll be the one tracking them down in this, cos it ain't going to be us, mate. The Governor ain't going to like it. I'll have to come with you. He'll want to see you, him and his sister. They don't like surprises.'

Abberline waited for the guard to inform the other what he was doing, then picked up a storm lantern from the shelf and made his way outside, opening the large set of gates to let the driver through into the courtyard. Abberline and the guard climbed inside, sitting opposite Elsbeth as the cab continued along a path to the main entrance.

'So this is her, is it?' The guard asked. 'She don't look like she could stab her master and his wife fifty times in some fit of uncontrollable rage. Looks a scrawny thing to me.'

Abberline looked towards Elsbeth, who had her head turned away, resting on the glass window. 'Looks can be deceptive, and I can assure you she's as mad as a box of frogs, and given the chance would have your eye out in a second, most likely eat it an all.' Abberline chuckled to keep up the pretence.

'Bloody waste of time, I'd hang all of them, if it were up to me. Still, gives me a job, I suppose.'

The carriage came to a halt, and they all alighted. Abberline helped Elsbeth down, and together they rushed up a flight of stone steps as the weather worsened, Elsbeth keeping her head bowed from the rain to stop it ruining her disguise. The guard pulled a metal lever by the front set of doors, which were shortly opened by a staff member.

As Abberline escorted Elsbeth into the dark inner sanctum of the asylum, a deafening crash of thunder boomed out, followed by a streak of lightning that lit up the entire sky and building, illuminating a man standing in the hallway with white hair, pale skin, and pink eyes. He moved towards Elsbeth, his face right up against hers, skin almost touching skin, his breath so foul she turned her head to one side, trying to avoid it.

'Welcome to Lidgate Manor,' he snarled, turning and walking briskly down a long corridor. 'Follow me and bring the lunatic with you…I intend to give her a personal introduction.'

CHAPTER 38

Ignatius Crane was already sitting at his desk impatiently drumming his fingers on the top, as Abberline guided Elsbeth into the inner sanctum. Elsbeth kept her head low to her chest, not wanting to make eye contact with the governor and not wanting to attract any more of his unwanted attention. Ignatius Crane sat back in his chair and read through the documentation.

'You've been told at the gatehouse this is most irregular to arrive with a committal at this time of night, we need time to prepare, there are rules, and rules are there for a reason.'

'I apologise for the inconvenience, Governor, but there is always an exception to the rule and on his occasion, the need outweighed following protocol. She killed her employer and his wife in such a manner that only an insane person could commit such an abomination. Therefore, it was deemed by the police, and you will note a doctor and a judge, that she should be taken into an asylum as a matter of urgency. As it happens, the judge in question personally recommended your institution as the most preferable one.'

Ignatius Crane huffed and grunted as he mulled over the document, examining the signatures closer. Abberline glanced at Elsbeth, who was standing still, keeping to the plan.

'Ah well, there it is, why didn't you say so in the first place? Judge Titus Voss, a man whom I greatly admire, a man who has no place for sentiment, you know what they call him, eh?' Crane looked directly at Abberline, his eyes wide with excitement. 'They call him the 'Hanging Judge', and I hear they have permanent gallows always on hand just for him as he sends so many to feel the end of the rope. He once told me he loves to attend an execution, just to see the absolute fear in the eyes of the condemned as the noose tightens, observing their last few seconds of life, as they pray to God for redemption. He told me the best part is when the hangman pulls the lever and the body drops and you hear the snap of the neck.' Crane let out a shriek of laughter and then abruptly stopped.

'So it would seem we have to accommodate this…this thing into the system at great inconvenience to all. She will be processed with a number and badge in the morning.' He looked over at Abberline. 'Whoever they were before, they cease to exist once inside here.' His gaze then shifted towards Elsbeth. 'You're trouble, I can sense that…there's something about you I…' Just at that moment, the door to Crane's office opened and his sister, Maude, entered the room.

'Brother, since when did we start taking *them* in at this time of night?' Maude asked, raising her arms in annoyance.

'We have no option, my dear, the guard has all the documentation and Judge Titus Voss has signed the order and we don't want to turn them away and cause any unnecessary attention do we?'

Maude knew what he was alluding to, the last thing they needed was any investigation by outsiders poking their noses into their business, telling them how to run the place. Maude didn't follow up on her question but walked around to the front of Elsbeth who had kept silent the whole time she had been in the office.

'So this is the mad whore who has caused us so much

bother. Hmm, seems like she wouldn't say boo to a goose she's so small and frail, won't last long in here that's for sure.' Maude lifted Elsbeth's head up from her chin to get a better look at her face.

'She killed two people for no good reason; ripped them apart from what I understand,' Ignatius intervened.

Maude stroked the side of Elsbeth's cheek softly with her fingers, then whispered in her ear. 'I think my brother and I are going to take a very close interest in you, my dear.' Maude then slowly moved around the back of Elsbeth as Abberline stood firm, not knowing what to expect.

Maude grabbed Elsbeth by both arms, squeezing them tighter and tighter, 'Anything to say now, eh?'

Abberline wanted to help, but knew he couldn't lift a finger. Ignatius grinned, thrilled to see the pain inflicted upon another.

'Get off me, you bitch,' Elsbeth bellowed out in a gruff low voice, keeping in character while struggling to get free.

'Oh my, my, don't we have a feisty one here, Maude cackled, pushing Elsbeth hard in the small of her back, propelling her forward.

Abberline watched helplessly as Elsbeth's body slammed into the side of the desk, her ribs taking the main impact, her face wincing with pain as Maude laughed. Abberline's first instinct was to go to her aid, to help her, but he knew in reality no guard would do that. To show any compassion now would undoubtedly give the game away.

Elsbeth tried to right herself, the agony so acute she found it hard to breathe. Her legs collapsed under her as she slumped to the floor, the side of her face resting on the wood of the unit. Suddenly, she was transported away, standing in front of a large tree and a woman hanging from one of the thick branches, twisting back and forth, the bark creaking with each turn. The ground seemed to rise, arms then hands breaking through the surface, grabbing at the air, trying to dig their way out of shallow graves, hundreds of them, men, women, young and old, all clambering out of the cold, worm-infested earth. Then, without notice, Maude Crane yanked her up from the office floor. 'Oh dear, brother, looks like she's seen a ghost.'

'Well, this desk is supposed to be haunted. I had it made from the tree that originally stood in the grounds. Don't you recall they found some woman hanging from it? I couldn't care less why she did it, so I had it removed and sawn up. Waste not, want not, as they say, my dear.' Maude smiled at her brother.

'It's you and your sister who should be in here,' Elsbeth said to Ignatius Crane, her words slurred and broken.

Maude grabbed Elsbeth firmly by the arms and marched her towards the exit.

'Take her to the ward, let her sweat there for a while, then make sure our new doctor knows, I'm sure he'll enjoy giving her an *extensive* examination,' Ignatius Crane barked, getting up from his chair as his sister and Elsbeth disappeared into the corridor.

Abberline had to know. 'You have a new doctor, sir?'

'Yes, we had to replace the previous one… let's just say we didn't see eye to eye, so he left us. Then as luck would have it, I get this letter from Doctor Patterson applying for the position. Attended Queen Victoria, don't you know, so, not wanting to look a gift horse in the mouth, we took him on, and so far, things are working out nicely. He has the right attitude to this type of work, you might say.'

Abberline's mouth went dry as he realised the plan was working. The Ripper was in the building, disguising himself as the asylum physician.

'I was going to ask if I may, sir, if you are currently looking for additional guards. I have little desire to return to my present employer, finding his new methods at odds with how I prefer to perform my duties. In short, to my mind there is no room for sentiment in this job. The only thing these *people,* if we can refer to them like that, understand is a rod of iron across their backs, and if that fails drag them outside give them shovel and tell them to dig their own grave…sir.'

There was an awkward silence. 'Well, we are always on the lookout for the right calibre of person to come and work here. I tell you what, I'll give you a month's trial if, after that, things work out, you can consider yourself permanent. Go to the central office just up the next corridor, someone will be on duty. They will give you the necessary paperwork to get you on the books with immediate effect. Oh, one more thing, do not wander about. When you're new here, the layout can be confusing, and there are other areas that are strictly off bounds, as they can be dangerous. We wouldn't want anything to happen to you, so stick to the main walkways, is that understood? 'What's your name?' Crane barked.

'My name. My name is Baines, Governor.'

Abberline acknowledged his instructions, noting the comments came across as more of a threat than advice. He then left Ignatius Crane alone as his thoughts quickly changed to Elsbeth, who was being dragged along, handcuffed, to meet with the most heinous monster that ever walked the earth, an evil so repugnant, so savage, her chances of survival were next to zero. He had to get to her, before the good doctor or, as he was really known, The Ripper did. But he was in a strange building with a labyrinth of dimly lit passageways with no idea which one to take. A terrible gut-wrenching scream echoed in the distance making his decision for him.

CHAPTER 39

The doors to the women's ward were always kept securely locked, and entry was only permissible with the appropriate key to gain access. Maude Crane had a chain hanging from her work belt with her own set of keys for every room and cell in the institution. There was nowhere she couldn't go. There were even places only she knew, secret spaces for her alone to retreat to with what she called her *family*.

Elsbeth could smell the filth, and hear the mayhem coming through the doors, shrieks, screams, agonising sounds, and some even barking like dogs. Maude roughly grabbed Elsbeth and forcibly shoved her into the ward. The room instantly fell silent, all eyes fixed not on the new inmate but on the formidable presence of Maude Crane. She stood without any emotion, her expression one of disdain and repulsion as the bedridden inmates cowered petrified back under the sheets that shook with fear, hiding as best they could.

Rows of single bunks lined both sides of the large room. A few women had been restrained to the frame with chains while others sat rocking on top of their mattresses, talking to themselves. Others were strapped to chairs or placed in the corners with leather collars with wide brims to restrict movement. A line of windows was on both sides of the high walls and had been purposely positioned near the ceiling. They were small by design, allowing a little light to pass through with iron bars across them.

The wardens were not concerned about the inmates trying to escape because the windows were too difficult to reach. However, they would attempt to throw knotted bed linen in between the iron bars so they could hang themselves, their only way of ending the never-ending cycle of misery and violence. There had been a number of suicides this way, but Maude Crane dismissed them as natural wastage.

Maude took Elsbeth to one of the vacant beds on the right-hand side of the room and manacled her to the frame. 'You can have this one, the old dear who used to have it came to a sudden end in the hospital wing. Oh, how you might ask? Well, our new doctor tried to save her, but in the end, he decided she was better off dead. Don't you worry none, you will be meeting him soon enough. Can't have you passing out again like you did in my brother's office, can we?' Maude tightened the handcuffs until Elsbeth cried out in pain, then smiled, wiping her forehead like a mother would a child's.

Elsbeth opened her eyes, looking directly at Maude. 'You're going to pay for this one day with your life, I see it.'

'What are you talking about?'

Elsbeth shifted her body as best she could. 'All the pain and misery you have brought.'

Maude put her face right up against Elsbeth's and placed her hands tightly around her throat. Maude's eyes, soulless and stormy, were filled with hate and anger. 'You listen to me, I can make your life a living hell here. You understand, I can make you disappear in the middle of the night, have you buried alive with rats to chew on you, and no one will ever know. So you watch that filthy tongue of yours or I'll rip it out and feed it to you.' Spit followed her words, covering Elsbeth's face.

Elsbeth knew she meant it, she had done the same to the

poacher back in Shere for just suspecting he was talking about the asylum with strangers. Maude stood glaring at Elsbeth, her fury still evident, then slowly took her hands away leaving bruises around Elsbeth's neck.

'Say that again, go on, say that again…Please,' Maude hissed, goading her.

Elsbeth stayed silent as Maude regained her composure and started walking towards the exit. Before she reached it, she stopped and stood absolutely still with her back to the room. Elsbeth thought for one awful moment that she was just going to come back and kill her. The moment seemed to last an eternity, the room thick with fear, no one moved, not a murmur passed from the lips of the mad, the wait was agonising. Then Maude, without a word, left the ward. Only the sound of the doors being locked and her footsteps on the stone floor broke the silence, dissipating as she got further away.

After it was clear that Maude had gone there was a sigh of relief with some of the women sobbing while others hugged each other. One screamed out hysterically, 'I can't take this anymore,' then collapsed in a heap on the floor biting her hands and wrists like a starved dog with a bone. An older woman next to her stared at Elsbeth, someone new in the ward had created interest. Elsbeth smiled back at the woman, who held her hand up close to her mouth to hide her words.

'They'll be back—they always come back. Her brother comes at night, takes us to a room, some return, others don't. You're young he likes em like that, he took my daughter. Stole her away from me he did, I heard her, she begged him, she screamed so much, but I couldn't get to her, no one could. Now she doesn't even know who I am, and she has lost her mind completely after what he did. But she still holds the small doggy toy she had as a child; she used to take it everywhere. I made it for her, and she still has it now. She can't sleep without it, clings to it like life itself. Even more since what the governor did to her.'

Elsbeth felt sick to her stomach. She hated Ignatius Crane as soon as she met him and his vile sister. To violate vulnerable women was so depraved it beggared belief. She leaned over as far as she could towards the poor wretch. 'Your name, what's your name?' she asked. The woman didn't reply at first, her hand still covering her mouth.

'They give us numbers, we don't use names, not allowed.'

'Yes, they also gave me a number. Elsbeth pointed to her badge, but do you remember your name before you arrived here with your daughter?'

The old woman stared blankly at the floor for some time, her forehead screwed up, searching her memory as she tried to recall. 'Lilly, that's my name…Yes, Lilly', a tear formed in the corner of her eye as if she had received a Christmas present she had always longed for.

'I'm Elsbeth, Lilly. What is your daughter's name? Do you remember hers?' Elsbeth knew she had to remain patient if she wanted to get anywhere with Lilly, and it was clear Lilly had been deeply traumatised by her time in Lidgate.

'Err…I think, yes, she's my Rose, that's her name, Rose, such a kind sweet girl, so helpful, so loving'. The woman took her hand away from her mouth and stroked her cheek, something that maybe she used to do to her daughter, Elsbeth guessed.

'Do you remember how you came to be here? Why were you and Rose sent to this place?'

'So long ago now,' the woman replied, placing her hand back on her mouth.

'Try thinking back, Lilly, try remembering.' Elsbeth knew it was good for them to try to recall the past; it gave them some dignity if they knew who they were and why they were there in this god-forsaken place.

'He told us we had to go, said we no longer lived there, threw us out onto the street, he did. Had nothing to—we walked and walked around London, sleeping in—my Rose, a good girl she is.' Elsbeth could see that Lilly's attention span seemed to go in and out of concentration.

'Who was *He?*' Elsbeth pressed.

—'My husband John said he had a new family, wanted us gone. I went back, begged him, but he called the police, and they locked us up. John made up lies, said we were both mad and witches and had put a spell on him. Next thing I know, we end up ere.'

Elsbeth knew this was common practice as the man had all the marital rights and the wife none; he could do what he wanted and get away with it, which both disgusted and infuriated her.

'I'm so sorry, Lilly.' Elsbeth wanted to comfort her, put her arms around her feeble body to show her that compassion still existed, even in this nightmare.

'You have the gift, don't you, dear?' Lilly blurted out. 'The gift to see, I know I can feel it. You do, don't you? Tell me I ain't wrong.'

Elsbeth was surprised to find someone who recognised she was psychic; it was so rare, and of all places, it was here that she had met a like-minded spirit. Elsbeth felt a sense of trust between them and wanted to tell Lilly why she was there, to give her some hope that maybe she and her daughter could be free one day. But she didn't know if Lilly would even understand, and she had to be careful; one slipped word, and it could be over for her and Abberline.

'I want you to promise me something, dear, please.' Lilly's voice sounded desperate.' 'When I'm gone, I want you to look after Rose for me. Don't let her die here, alone, please. I couldn't stand that—she's all I got left, you understand?'

Elsbeth didn't argue. She knew it would mean the world to

Lilly if she agreed, and how could she not? It was the very least she could do under the circumstances, and maybe, if all went well, she could persuade Abberline to get them out.

'Of course I will, Lilly. Where is Rose? Your daughter, where is she now?'

'There, next to you.' Lilly pointed past Elsbeth to the next bed along.

Elsbeth looked across where a young woman next to her lay, quivering, her body rigid with fear.

She turned her head towards Elsbeth, her eyes had big black rings around them from lack of sleep and were bloodshot from crying. She mumbled as quietly as she could through the sheet she had pulled over her mouth. 'He's…he's the fallen angel.'

Elsbeth looked over at the fragile, thin body of the young woman, shaking her head as if to say she didn't understand.

'Lucifer,' Rose whispered, then turned her back on Elsbeth as she knew the punishment for talking.

Elsbeth sat motionless, terrified after what Lilly and Rose had told her, realising that The Ripper was not the only monster within these walls. She suddenly felt very alone, worried, and forgotten. *What if Abberline couldn't find her?* Shaking, she tried to hide herself under the bed sheet and wondered how long it would be until the doors of the ward opened once more and the devil came calling.

CHAPTER 40

Maude appeared at the doorway of the consulting room, watching him as he moved about. He was tall, lean, and young, yet he had an air of authority and confidence that usually came with years of experience. There was something else she sensed, a detached and unfeeling nature about him. Even though she had only just met him, she recognised the trait. He was one of those people who could pause a busy room with his presence alone. She continued to observe him as he checked a cabinet full of medicine vials, then proceeded to the equipment, paying particular attention to the surgical knives, holding them up and examining both sides of the blade as if it were an old friend. She moved across the threshold, her steps light, yet her scent alerted him as he turned to greet her.

'Miss Crane, how can I be of service?' His voice was educated, calm, but tinged with irritation.

'My brother has been informed that we are to undergo an inspection. This is a tiresome but unfortunately necessary requirement to ensure we adhere to specific laws pertaining to private institutions such as ours. His name is Dr Arthur Lawson, but we have no idea when the visit will be, only that he will be in attendance.'

The Ripper's blood ran cold. The mere mention of the man's

name cast a black mood over him. His fists tightened as he was momentarily taken back to an earlier time in his life, and to a person for whom he held such hate, it was hard to contain his rage. But he knew he had to, for this was not the moment.

Maude noticed a slight change in his demeanour. 'I do hope everything is alright, you look as if you have seen an apparition.'

The Ripper remained outwardly calm, even though an inferno was raging inside.

'Yes, I'm quite fine, thank you, Miss Crane. I am just familiarising myself with the facilities.'

'Oh, now, I must insist that you call me Maude. After all, you are now a senior member here at Lidgate. As you have undoubtedly observed, we employ few people as my brother prefers to keep staff levels low. He feels it creates a more immersive and private environment, allowing us to be more liberal with the treatments.' Maude moved further into the room, resting her hand on the desk next to a small black bag.

'Well, your brother's methodology is, of course, correct, you don't need high levels of staff, and as most of the inmates at Lidgate are kept tightly restricted to certain areas, the business model becomes easy to maintain. Medication and rigid discipline will keep those who are more troublesome in line, making it a far more cost-effective way of proceeding. And of course, there will inevitably be, shall we say—natural depletion to keep the numbers manageable.'

Maude smiled. She knew precisely what he meant by that remark and wanted to know more about this enigmatic young doctor. 'I'm curious why a young, gifted physician like yourself, who has been referred to the royal household, wants to come and work in a mental asylum in the middle of nowhere? Why aren't you offering your skills in a London hospital or private practice? Did you always want to go into medicine? Was your father perhaps a doctor? I'm sorry, so many questions, you must think me rude and intrusive,' Maude chuckled, and turned her head away, embarrassed, not wanting him to see her blushing.

'My father was a medical man and a successful surgeon, but we had little in common, you understand. Unlike him, I'm not motivated by money, title, or the pleasures of the flesh. I am driven by knowledge, to learn more, to understand the human body and, more importantly, the mind's inner workings and complex mechanics. To me, the brain is the engine of the whole, without which nothing functions, and where better to learn the idiosyncrasies of the brain than here in an asylum, where I can see firsthand the defects and damage caused by mental disease.'

Maude listened to him, liking more and more what she was hearing.' So, do you have any preferential treatment?'

'Well, I'm not of the school of sitting for hours examining behavioural techniques, trying to patiently understand the root of the madness as some of my peers seem to be adopting. No, I intend to concentrate my studies on the more pragmatic side of research. I believe short, sharp shock treatment has proven to be successful, such as submerging the patient under water, sleep deprivation, and hot irons applied to sensitive parts of the body.

All are interesting methods that I intend to explore. I have concluded these techniques force a reset of the mind, clearing it of preconceived patterns or illnesses. The human mind remains a mystery to the medical profession, and I intend to take a step forward in understanding it and answering the many questions. If my hypothesis is correct, I will have found a cure for this debilitating sickness that blights society. I heard a rumour, to go no further than this room, that even a close relative of Her Majesty suffers from such afflictions.'

Maude looked intrigued by the revelation. 'Well, you have to forgive me if I hope you are not too successful, doctor, or you'll put my brother and me out of business.'

'You do not need to concern yourself, Miss Crane; I'm sorry, Maude, it will take some significant time to prove my theory, but the good news is we have many subjects on which to experiment.'

'You mentioned that there could be some form of financial recompense if you were successful, Doctor?'

'I worked for a while in Brighton with a mortician, and he had a profitable line in supplying cadavers to certain people in medical science who had pioneering ways to help improve our understanding of the human form and possible treatments for the most stringent of ailments. They, in turn, would pay me and the mortician a sum, which was starting to prove beneficial to both parties.'

'Does this agreement still exist between you and the mortician?'

The Ripper thought back to Brighton and the body of Cripps twisting in agony after being set on fire, courtesy of Inspector Abberline and Elsbeth Hargreaves. 'No…no, he's, what you might say, burnt himself out, so this will be a completely new and exclusive venture.'

Maude considered the proposal. 'I'm not sure my brother would feel comfortable deviating too far from our present plan. He's what you might call a traditionalist and doesn't like change, but it's an interesting idea and one I would like to think on if I may. Rest assured, I will speak with my brother. We have a fair amount of what we call *dead material* leaving the establishment, so there may be some merit to what you're suggesting. If there is money to be earned with no risk to us, it may be worth further consideration. After all, the bodies would normally be just dumped in a ditch, so as I said, let me talk to Ignatius about your idea, but I can't promise anything.'

'I understand your position. You and your brother have developed a system, but if you can think on it then that's all I can ask. I'm not going anywhere.'

Maude hoped he would stay for a long time, admired his entrepreneurship, and wanted to get to know him better. He was an enigma with many sides, some darker than others. But she was confused. On the one hand, she felt compelled to know more about this man, but on the other, she thought in some way that she couldn't explain, she was betraying her brother. It had only been her and Ignatius. She had not been exposed to other men, she had never needed anyone else. He had always been there for her they shared everything, he had been her teacher, protector: and so much more.

Maude prepared to leave the doctor and return to the office to see her brother. She knew things were never black and white and would revisit him soon to discuss the ideas for Lidgate in more detail. 'Oh, before I forget, my brother informs me that we have a new inmate. He said she's a difficult one, and you might like to look in on her when you have the time.'

'Of course, I would be delighted.' At that very moment, he felt the presence of someone he hadn't seen for a while, and it intrigued him.

'You let me know when you're ready; I would like to attend. I've never seen how holding someone underwater can help cure an illness; it sounds exciting. Send Harker, the guard I assigned you, when the time is right.'

'Thank you, I think you will benefit from a demonstration of my procedures. Perhaps your brother would also like to attend? I'm sure he will find my approach fascinating,' he said, stroking, then picking up, a metal pair of pliers, opening and snapping them shut.

CHAPTER 4|

Abberline made his way along the corridor, guessing it was the direction that Elsbeth had been taken. This was a new world where the normal rules didn't apply, light didn't follow day, but danger and evil waited in every corner and passageway. *Lidgate Manor must have been constructed from the stone of Sodom and Gomorrah, the place seems to be cursed.* His logic and straight rule-of-thumb approach seemed to melt into shades of grey, the lines blurred, unclear, his obsession with order, where everything had its place, was called into question, and what was real and what was not morphed into one.

He questioned his plan to track and dispatch The Ripper. He wanted to kill this monster not just for the crime he had committed here but for mutilating three women in Brighton. For having to tell a wife that her husband, a colleague and fellow policeman, was not coming home. Watching the tears well up in her face, seeing the children hang onto her skirt bottom burying their heads into their mother's side not wanting to hear the truth that daddy is dead. Killed in the line of duty, for doing his job for no other reason than that. He remembered his words meant nothing to the family, for in that moment they had died too, their hopes, their dreams, their future gone like the snuffing out of a flame, their lives torn apart, irrevocably changed forever.

Abberline stood above a flight of stairs that seemed to lead down to another level. Crane had told Maude to take Elsbeth to the ward, so he hoped his choice was right, as there were no signs pointing the way. There was no plan without her, and they had come too far for this not to be seen through to the end. He had to find her. He descended further until he reached a set of iron gates, one side appeared open. Slowly, he pushed it forward; it creaked on its hinges, and he held his breath. Two oil-mounted lamps on the wall set on low flame gave some illumination, so he pushed forward, having made the decision, feeling vulnerable, he glanced behind just for a second, as every fibre in his body was telling him, *this was a bad idea.*

Each step echoed in the damp darkness as he hoped with all his might that he would not find Elsbeth in this pit, but he had to be sure. He was certain of one thing: whatever it was, it wouldn't be anything good. He noticed what appeared to be four solid doors on both sides. The doors were all shut tight but each had a peephole and some other opening halfway down which he surmised was for food or water to be passed through. This area was not a ward as he had imagined it to be. It was something else entirely more like a solitary-confinement block. Similar ones at Scotland Yard had prisoners for a short stay, held on remand, but certainly not in these disgusting conditions.

The furthest door on the right looked open, where a crack of yellow light shone out as he walked cautiously towards it. He wanted to call out Elsbeth's name, he wanted her to know he was here, he wanted to feel better in locating her and less guilt for watching her be dragged away. The closer he got, the more he started to sweat. He put his back against the wall, the wet grit scraping against the fabric of his jacket whilst sliding inch by inch towards the opening. His heart felt like it was going to jump out of his chest. His hand slipped inside his coat pocket, putting his finger on the trigger of his gun, he was not going to take any chances. He had surprise on his side, but the creaking of the gate may have already given him away.

The smell was the first thing to hit him, starting to confirm his worst fears, for this was a scent he knew well, as any animal knows the sweet odour of decaying flesh carries well on the air. The door was now within touching distance. Placing one foot gingerly inside across the threshold, preparing for anything or anyone to attack, his back stiffened, and he closed his right hand as tightly as he could into a fist, he would not be taken without a fight.

The light inside the cell revealed itself as a small oil lamp sitting on a ledge in the wall. It was not bright enough to see the whole room, but it was sufficient to see that the floor seemed to slither in the dark as if it were alive. The smell got deeper and richer the more he moved into the centre of the small stone room, and then he realised that people were crawling on their stomachs across the floor, trying their best to get away from him. Even in this most terrible of places, the basic instinct to survive took hold. He swallowed. He had always put his faith not in a religion or superstition, only in The Police Act, evidence, and facts, but now, in this moment, he questioned that.

Towards the back in a corner, there seemed to be a small bed and upon that a mound that, looked like a mass of dishevelled clothes, but it was a blanket hiding something, and this was where the foul smell was emanating from. He advanced towards it, his heart in his mouth, his lips dry. He slowly put his hand out and grabbed a bit of the cloth, quickly pulling it away, revealing the abomination underneath. A woman in a restraint that covered her entire head, a mask made of wicker, imprisoning her like a bird in a cage. Both eyes were missing, cut out with precision using a knife with a serrated edge, the type a surgeon might use.

Abberline had seen this work before, and he knew the perpetrator who was responsible for this without any doubt. In one way, he was greatly relieved that it was not Elsbeth lying here, butchered. It confirmed The Ripper was alive and somewhere within the walls of this madhouse, deep within its network of passageways and rooms. The dichotomy was, so was Elsbeth. He knew he had to locate her, as without her, the plan would fail. As he went towards the way out he felt a presence behind him. Had the killer been waiting, watching from a dark corner? Was he going to die? Terrible images took hold of him as flashes of his life went racing through his mind, he had no option and swung round.

'What are you doing down here Baines?' Crane shouted, his expression red with rage and suspicion.

Abberline jumped back. The last person he thought he would see was the governor accompanied by one of the guards, but there he was standing right in front of him.

'I must apologise, Governor Crane.' Abberline slowly removed his hand from the gun. 'I confess I did become lost on the way to the main office. There is little to guide you, and I didn't see anyone to ask, and the next thing I know, I find myself down here. So I thought instead I would try to find the ward where your sister took the new inmate I had brought here. That lunatic stole something valuable from me, a gold watch worth a pretty penny, which I need to get back. It has great sentimental value, you see.' Abberline hoped he had said enough to convince a man who didn't trust anyone, and then there was the elephant in the room, the dead woman not two feet behind him.

'I thought I had made it abundantly clear not to wander about, there are areas in the asylum that are strictly off bounds, this being one of them. The confinement block is only to be accessed by me, my sister, our new resident physician, Dr Patterson, and no one else. What you should have done is find your way back to my office. Not to take it upon yourself to go on a walkabout looking for some mad women you brought in here, because you were too stupid to allow her to steal from you. Hmm, maybe I am at fault in hiring you if you can't even follow simple instructions, could be you're just a busybody who has no place here.'

Abberline had to try again, he could not be thrown out now with Elsbeth missing and most likely in evident danger. He knew vain narcissists like Crane had high opinions of themselves and an overinflated ego. 'Governor Crane, you are a highly respected and successful man who rightly does not suffer fools gladly. I have made a schoolboy error, but I assure you, your judgment about me is sound, and I will not disappoint you again. I implore you to give me another chance, to show you what a valuable member of staff and asset I can become under your expert guidance.'

'This will be your last chance, Baines. You're new here, but understand there will be no margin for error in the future. This place is successful because I run a tight ship, and my staff follow my rules. Is that clear?'

Abberline was pleased at the pardon he had received. His strategy had worked this time, but he knew Crane was now watching him, which could complicate things. He now needed to demonstrate his loyalty in more practical terms. 'It appears that one of the inmates in this cell has met with a violent end,' Abberline pointed over to where the woman lay, her body torn and brutalised beyond recognition, as if a wild beast had been unleashed.

Crane didn't bother to go and observe. 'It's to be expected. These...these vermin are nothing short of animals and will turn on each other instantly. The ones locked in solitary away from the main population are the worst of the worst, so mad that I've known them to turn to cannibalism. That is why I said it was a dangerous environment.'

Abberline could now see why people were so frightened of Crane. He had no empathy at all for these poor souls, and if they were driven to eat each other, it was because of how they had been starved into it. He also knew the injuries inflicted on the murdered woman were by the hand of a far worse monster who was still at large to commit more atrocities, which appeared to be with Crane's blessing.

'Thank you, Governor, for explaining this to me. I will never venture here again unless it is with your express permission. Would you like me to dispose of the body, sir?'

'No, leave it for the rats to feed off.'

Abberline tried not to show his utter disgust for the man. 'Yes, of course, sir, as you command. Eh, the matter of my stolen watch, with your permission, sir?'

'Yes, yes, all right. Guard Harker will escort you out of here. Make your way to my sister's office. She has a set of keys so you can access the ward where this common little thief is. Next time, be more vigilant with your personal belongings.'

Harker stood waiting as Abberline removed himself from a potentially dangerous situation. He had to make sure Crane thought of him as an idiot and nothing more.

'Thank you, sir, most understanding.' Abberline continued to pander to the man's self-importance. But Crane wasn't done just yet.'

'If you find the lunatic is guilty of stealing your property, make sure you inform my sister.'

'To have her locked up in one of these cells?' Abberline asked.

'No, to hang her.'

189

CHAPTER 42

Abberline wasted no time finding his way to Maude's office, which was not that far from her brother's. He not only needed the keys to the ward where Elsbeth was being held, but a map to work out how to escape from the asylum, which was crucial given it was built like a maze, and Maude was the way to solving both of those dilemmas.

He knocked a couple of times on the office door, but there was no reply, so he had a decision to make. He had just been caught in a restricted area, and he should wait for Maude; however, time was running out. So far he and Elsbeth had been lucky they had avoided being discovered by The Ripper, the only reason they were in this hellhole in the first place. He knocked again, the silence in the corridor was eerie and strange. He couldn't wait any longer, he twisted the knob and pushed the door open.

The room was quite large and square with a chair and a desk in the middle, a rich, patterned carpet on the floor, and a cabinet with an odd collection of doll heads. A large sash window with deep red drapes half pulled across was at the far end next to an open grate fireplace, which was simple but doubtless effective in providing sufficient heat. In front of this was a medium-sized rocking chair. The entire room was packed with glass boxes containing stuffed animals of the strangest kind. Lizards, toads, snakes, and ravens leered out from behind their glass prisons, watching, waiting; their glass stare seemed to come alive as they followed Abberline around. The bizarre collection matched the room's aroma and atmosphere, which was dank and oppressive, with a strong scent of embalming fluid, a sickly sweet smell with hints of lemon and musk.

Abberline had noticed Maude wore a set of keys hanging off her belt on a chain, and was hoping there was a skeleton or spare set, which most places like this would have. He kept searching under the ever-watchful eyes of the dead animals, tracing his every move. First, he checked on top of her desk, then through each drawer, carefully moving the contents to avoid missing anything. He found an old map at the back of one of them showing the layout of the asylum and how to navigate to the various passageways, offices and wards; essentially, it also gave him the ways out. But no keys were found. He started to feel deflated but concerned that at any time, Maude or her brother could come through that door, and there would be no excuse this time. Next time, it would be fatal.

He foraged everywhere for a spare set, like a mole leaving no stone unturned, putting his hand inside the glass cabinets, thinking it would be a good place to conceal something you didn't want found. The smell of bone and decayed skin was repulsive, and unsettled him even though he knew none of the stuffed prey were alive; yet his base instinct still saw them as a threat. There was nothing to find, and after a while, almost relieved, he stopped searching the glazed tombs. *Maybe there was only ever one set of keys which Maude guarded at all times*; if so, the plan was in serious jeopardy, and so was the entire operation. He sat by the desk, rechecking the room before planning to leave, realising he couldn't be here much longer. *I'm missing something here, I must be.* Out of the corner of his eye he saw a small rail and a curtain pulled across it, hiding something. He got up, walked over, and moved the drape back, finding another door. He tried the handle, but it was locked. Then, using his fingers, he felt carefully along the top of the door frame until the cold metal of a key rewarded him. He took it and quickly placed it into the lock, turned it, and entered.

It was about the same size as the previous room, with one notable exception: there were no windows. Light came from two wall-mounted gas lamps. There was what appeared to be a large rectangular table in front of him, reminiscent of a dining table. A white linen sheet mostly covered it, but on each side, he could see the tops of at least ten chairs. He walked around the table, noticing a large, typical glass-fronted cabinet with beautifully painted china displayed at the back of the room: dinner and side plates, teapots, cups, and saucers, all with stunning hand-painted fauna and flora, and edged with gold. It was a set of the highest quality, and no expense had been spared in the making of it.

He thought it strange to find such a room, which was at odds with Maude's frugal values. However, to his frustration, there didn't seem to be any indication that the keys were in here. Before he left, his policeman's gut told him to look under the sheet. After all, the table was hidden from view, so maybe she had been cunning and slipped a spare set of keys under the cover. He took one side of the sheet in his hand and slowly walked back, removing it gradually so as not to break anything underneath it. Bit by bit, the setting was revealed.

Two silver candlesticks sat at either end of the table, and each place had been set with the correct tableware and cutlery. Silver knives, forks, and spoons all in the proper position, even place names for each person, not with their names but sets of numbers in the same format allocated to inmates. Ten people sat around the table, five on each side, with an empty chair at the top, all embalmed, their skin looking pale and waxy, stuffed like the animals next door. It was a nauseating sight. Each person, male and female, had been dressed for dinner. The men, their thinning hair swept back neat and tidy, in black tuxedos, black bow ties, and pressed white shirts, the women in fine, delicate long dresses, their hair held up with pins, strings of pearls hung around their necks with beautiful costume jewellery for earrings.

Even more disturbing, makeup had been applied to their grotesque, bloated faces, their lips painted a thick red like a clown's. Each person had been positioned as if they were attending a real event, some leaning into the person next to them, pretending to share a secret or private joke. Others were situated leaning back in their chairs, as if in the midst of laughter. Their eyes, replaced with glass ones, offered no warmth or humility but a coldness and emptiness that death brings. It was surreal and deeply sickening, a supper by the mad, for the mad. It made little sense to Abberline as he stood unable to process the twisted and distorted reality of what he had discovered. He went to the one empty chair at the top of the table, and there, lying on the plate, was a set of keys; his high-risk strategy had paid off. He snatched them up, put them in his pocket, but something caught his attention. The place name was different from the rest. There were no numbers; this one had a name written in big capital letters.

MAUDE

CHAPTER 43

Elsbeth noticed her arm had little feeling in it, being shackled to the bed, restricting her movement, which had taken its toll. Sleeping was impossible, and eating the slop she had been given made her feel sick. It was night, and the ward was still; any motion seemed confined to coughs and the odd squeal coming from somewhere in the room. Elsbeth's thoughts went back to Abberline and their plan to capture The Ripper, which, for the moment, was a distant mirage. Her frustration grew, rattling the side of the frame, trying to free herself. She grunted and lay back down, unable to make any difference to her situation if anything, it was making matters worse, as the metal handcuffs sliced into her wrist.

Lilly and her daughter Rose appeared to be asleep, and Elsbeth took some comfort that they had found peace for a while. She thought back to what Lilly had told her the night before and how sometimes the Governor would come into the ward and take one of them away, but they didn't always return, and nobody ever saw them again. She knew she was like a trapped rat, going nowhere he could do anything he wanted, he had the power and control, and she hated that. In reality, like The Ripper, both men were nothing but cowards, freaks of nature that should be wiped off the earth, and if she got the opportunity, she would do it willingly, and that thought, that ember of retribution gave her fuel to survive and fight back any way she could.

She closed her eyes briefly. It had taken some time, but the ward was silent as she waited for the morning to arrive. Sounds carried at this time: taps dripping, the wind knocking on the windows, and the hoot of an owl outside gliding high above, bathed in the silver of the moon's light, hunting for its prey. Other sounds created more worrying feelings: the creak of a door, followed by footsteps.

Someone had entered the room, standing by the door, watching as their deep, rasping breathing filled the tense air. Elsbeth peeped a little, trying to see who it was, yet all she could see was the dark silhouette of a person, a man. She knew if she moved or made the slightest noise, there was a good chance he would hear her. She stayed as still as she was able to, then slowly turned her head as far as she could, to get a better angle. Even so, every time she even slightly changed her position, the pain from her wrist became so bad she had to bite down onto her lip so as not to scream.

The man moved to the centre of the room, then stood turning, she thought, searching maybe for someone in particular. A feeling washed over her, a strong perception, that sixth sense she had relied on since a child, going off like alarm bells in her head. She tried to move further down the bed, worrying even this might signal attention. Squinting, she saw him move to the other side of the room and stand at the edge of a woman's bed, then reach out and touch her face, not in a caring way but in a manner that was unsettling and troubling. His motive was not one of compassion but evil. Then, like a ghost, he seemed to disappear from view, just the sound of his shoes on the floor as he walked further up the room, the pattern changing, pausing, and starting again.

A faint murmuring came from the bed next to her, 'It's him

I tell you, the Dark Angel. Don't let him see you...He'll do terrible things to you, hurt you bad...in that chair.'

Elsbeth didn't understand the reference to the chair but knew that if her voice got any louder, they were both in real danger of being discovered. 'Shhh, now, Rose, he'll hear us. Stay quiet, you understand, don't say another word.' Elsbeth put a finger up to her closed lips to accentuate the request. Rose smiled at Elsbeth and tucked herself under the sheet. Elsbeth noticed that the footsteps had stopped, she sighed deeply. *Maybe he's gone, perhaps he slipped out another way.*

Then from nowhere: 'Did you think I didn't see you?' Now he was over the top of her, she recognised his foul breath and flash of white hair. 'I was merely playing with you,' Ignatius Crane said in a child's voice. 'Now it's our time to play together, pretty please.' Elsbeth slid her body away, slipping off the side of the bed, only her handcuff prevented her from falling further. She let out an agonising yell as her skin tore again, opening up the wound, twisting her body. She slumped back, exhausted, petrified, and bleeding. Crane removed a key from his waistcoat pocket and inserted it into the lock of her handcuff, it sprang open, and she fell onto the cold stone floor, her ribs still sore, throbbing with pain.

He pulled Elsbeth up by her arms as she let out another scream, her whole body aching. 'Now you're coming with me, I'll show you what we do to people who steal. Oh, I know all about it, I know everything that goes on in here. You're going to tell me what you did with the watch you took from that dumb guard that brought you here. Then after business we can have some private time, just you and me, eh.' He licked the side of her face. Elsbeth was too weak to run, too weak to even stand on her own.

As Crane dragged Elsbeth towards the exit, Rose emerged from beneath her sheet, shouting. 'Take her sir, she is wicked, she told me things she did, she needs to be punished,' pointing at Elsbeth, who looked back in shock, too weak and confused to respond. Rose started to laugh uncontrollably, screaming out her name, thumping the mattress like a wild baboon. 'Elsbeth, Elsbeth, you're going to die.'

Crane got Elsbeth into the doctor's consulting room, just next to the ward, and strapped her into a large dentist-like chair that swivelled around and could be set to various positions, even completely horizontal if required. She felt a small pinprick in her arm and almost instantly fell into a drowsy state.

'There, that will keep you quiet,' she heard him say—then watched him go over to a trolley with a good selection of medical tools, scalpels, pinchers, saws, and several serrated knives. He picked up a medium-sized saw, the type they used for amputation, and held it against Elsbeth's damaged wrist, the metal teeth sinking into her skin.

'Now, how about you tell me where you hid that watch, eh, and you won't have to lose one of those pretty little hands.'

Elsbeth felt herself slipping in and out of consciousness. 'I...I don't know what you're talking about...I didn't steal anything.'

'I see. So you're a liar and a thief, then, are we? Oh dear, well, it looks like our you-and-me time will have to wait.' Raising the saw above her head, he waved it in front of her face, taunting her before lowering it onto her wrist. He drew his arm back, licked his lips, his piggy red eyes gleaming excitedly as the saw bit down into her.

'Stop that, brother. I need you *now*. *We* have that Inspector Lawson here, and he's demanding we meet him immediately in your office. You know what they are like, they have the power to shut us down. You can come back for *her*, she's not going anywhere.'

Ignatius snapped his jaw like a dog at his sister's untimely interruption, slamming the saw back down on the trolley.

'Hmm, what a shame. I was so looking forward to getting to know you better. Don't worry, dear, I won't forget about you,' he snarled and hissed at Elsbeth, reluctantly leaving and following Maude.

Elsbeth sat back in the chair, unable to move, unable to scream, and passed out. When she came round out of her blurred vision, a face peered down at hers. Her heart missed a beat, she couldn't take any more, she was done. Abberline reached across her and untied her straps. Picking her up, he quickly moved out into the corridor and vanished into the shadows.

CHAPTER 44

Abberline found a large room containing a supply of bed linen and towels; it had a long bench to one side, which he carefully placed Elsbeth down on. Abberline could see that Elsbeth was not doing well, and this place was far more dangerous than he or Elsbeth could have imagined. He waited for her to feel better, but it was clear she had been drugged her speech was slurred, and he knew it was going to take a while before she was able to comprehend where she was.

Abberline took the time to think about what they needed to do next. Now that he had taken Elsbeth, there was no telling how long Ignatius Crane was going to be or where The Ripper was, and it would not be long until one of them realised Elsbeth was gone and raised the alarm. Elsbeth started to come around slowly, her wrist still bloody from the cut of the handcuff and the teeth of the saw Crane was going to use on her.

'It's alright, Elsbeth. I was outside the room. I heard everything.'

'So you know he's gone off with his sister, back to his office?'

'Yes, I know, he has other, more urgent things on his mind now, so we have a little time. I'm sorry, Elsbeth, I feel this is my fault. I told Crane you stole my watch. That's the only way

I could get away with him finding me in a restricted area. But I found something else in that cell, a woman butchered in the same way as the others. We were right. The Ripper is here, hiding within these walls.'

'Look, Abberline, Crane is going to come back for me sooner or later, and I don't want to be still tied to that chair when he does.'

'Don't worry, he knows I've come to find you. If asked, I will say I saw you in the consulting room and took you back to the ward myself to carry out a proper search for my property.'

'There were other drugs in that room, other than the one Crane used on me, in another cabinet., Everything was marked with a skull, crossbones, and the word '*Poison*'. I have a feeling The Ripper will be paying me a visit soon, and if I can get close enough to him, I can kill him.'

Abberline looked at Elsbeth 'No, I can't let that happen. It's too dangerous.'

'This *can* work, and it's my decision, so just give me a chance to explain. We go back to the room. I'll take a vial of the poison and a syringe and hide them about my person. Then you get me back to the ward. He's pretending to be a doctor, so carrying out his rounds isn't going to seem out of place. The Ripper will know I'm in the room, trust me on this. When he picks up on that, it will lure him over, and when curiosity gets the better of him, I will stick the needle hard into his neck.'

'You better hope you are right, Elsbeth, because you won't get *any* second chance. He won't hesitate, you know that.'

'It's the best opportunity we have to end this. Nothing would give me greater pleasure than looking into those dead eyes of his as he descends back to where he came from. Afterwards, we will need a way out of here, and fast.'

Abberline looked far from convinced. The last time Elsbeth put herself in danger, she nearly lost her life, however, he also knew Elsbeth wasn't going to back down; and deep inside, he also knew she was right, even if he didn't like it. 'I have a map of the place, found it along with a set of spare keys in Maude's *secret room*. I will mark a route out for us, so leave that to me.'

'Secret room?' Elsbeth remarked.

'Yes, a room behind her office, which was hidden. She is as deranged as the people in here. She has dead animals mounted in glass display cabinets, and a dinner table laid out with dead people in chairs who have been embalmed, made to look as if they were alive and attending supper.'

'I could feel it from both of them when I was in her brother's office they are both insane, but there was something else. I picked up on a connection between them, and one seemed to know what the other was thinking. A bond that had come out of years of being unnaturally confined together like Siamese twins.'

'At the moment, Elsbeth, I have to admit I'm more concerned about the matter at hand and how, in reality, this will work out.'

'Abberline. You have to trust me. We knew when we started this plan would have to be fluid and open to change at the last minute, and I, for one, had no idea what to expect until we got inside.'

Elsbeth could see he was worried, but she wanted to proceed. She was the only one who could get near enough. 'His confidence is growing, and his ability to move about seemingly undetected like a phantom is worrying. We have no idea what he looks like because anyone who has met him and seen his face is dead. So he feels invincible. We have to put a stop to this now. We can't let this monster get out again, we simply can't.' Elsbeth felt that familiar dread she had sensed before, back when she and Abberline first worked together.

'I know Elsbeth, he's on a reckoning and he's going to keep on coming, and coming until he is stopped. That's why it's imperative you realise what's at stake here and you don't falter, don't think about it, and strike as soon as you get the chance, because if you don't, you're dead, it's that simple!'

CHAPTER 45

Abberline passed the glass vial containing the poison and syringe to Elsbeth who then carefully placed the needle into the top of the vial and pulled back on the plunger, filling it to the maximum mark.

'Be careful, Elsbeth, only take the chance to inject him if you get a clear shot. You need to try to get the needle inserted into his neck or hand, anywhere where you conclude the skin is exposed to attack.'

Elsbeth wrapped the needle point in cloth to help prevent an accident and then placed it in a side pocket of her dark, heavy dress, which had additional stitching. This was the garment she had been given after being processed into the institution. She hated the rough, uncomfortable textile, which rubbed against her skin, causing irritation and a large rash on her chest and back.

'I'm as ready as I will ever be,' Elsbeth said to Abberline, striding out of the consulting room. 'After this is done, I will need to change out of these clothes, if you can call them that. Can I see the map for a moment?'

'Just in case this goes badly, I'll be close by, but don't worry, I'll be hidden out of view.' Abberline didn't want his deep-seated concerns to be too obvious. 'When it's done, roll the body under the bed, it will be a while until anyone goes looking for him. Ensure none of the inmates observe what you're doing, or all there will be a riot.'

'No,' replied Elsbeth, 'you can't be anywhere near, *he will* know if he gets a whiff that something isn't right, we will have lost our advantage. He will kill me and then hunt you down. No, everything has to appear normal, if you can get normal in an insane asylum. We both know the dangers and risks, but it's the only way. As you said, we will only get one go at this, and I don't want this creature free to butcher one more defenceless woman. He dies, and he dies tonight, for everyone's sake. Don't worry, I'm comfortable with that. You concentrate on finding how to get us out of this place. Now show me the map, please. I have an idea.'

Abberline brought the crumpled paper out, smoothed it in his hands, and then passed it to Elsbeth. She studied it carefully. 'Yes, there it is, the nurse's dormitory. I'll head there after he's dead and take a uniform out of one of the closets. I'll keep my head low, no one will question me, and if the alarm is raised, they will be searching for a patient in asylum clothing, not a member of staff going about her business. It will buy me enough time to come and find you and make good our escape.'

'It's too risky, Elsbeth. There will be guards everywhere once they realise what's happened. The Ripper must know we're onto him, he knows we won't give up. I must confess I find this difficult to ask, but do you sense anything from this madman?'

Elsbeth reflected for a moment. 'Last time in Brighton, I had this strong premonition that *he* could feel me in his thoughts, but this time—this time I'm not so sure. Maybe it's the location, or perhaps he is deliberately not allowing it to happen. The most likely scenario is that he is blocking me because if he knows we've found him, he has only two choices, run or kill us, and either way, we are forcing his hand, which he will not want. He has to be in control, not us, of that I'm certain.'

Abberline still couldn't understand Elsbeth's psychic skills, even though he had witnessed events that defied all logic, yet he still struggled with it. 'I'm not happy about this plan, not happy at all. Just keep alert and a tight grip on that syringe.'

'Abberline, I don't work for you. I am an adult who is fully proficient in making my own decisions. Remember, I have seen with my own eyes what he is capable of, and I have to do this for the women he killed. I was in his grip once before, so this is my time to turn the tables on him. He won't get the better of me again. So you do your job, and I'll do mine.'

He reluctantly unlocked the doors of the ward and let Elsbeth back in, watching her until she got to her bunk and crawled under the covers. Thankfully, most of the other inmates appeared to be resting. Heavy breathing and the odd moan were all that could be heard. He felt a shiver run down his spine as he locked the doors back up. However strongly Elsbeth felt, they both understood the danger they were in and the homicidal maniac they were going up against. The Ripper was not just a killer, he was far more than that, he was an entity, a vessel of evil consumed with hate and rage. He could never let Elsbeth face that on her own, whatever she wanted. He had decided to stay outside the ward, concealed within the shadows, and wait for the Devil.

CHAPTER 46

The Ripper paced up and down in his quarters, a small living area off the main consulting room. It was comprised of a single bed, wash basin, mirror, and a small pine desk for correspondence. It was minimal, but more than enough for his purposes, as he didn't intend to spend long here. His mood changed, voices flooding his mind, doubt creeping in. *Arthur Lawson was here in the asylum as an Inspector. How could that be? How was this possible?* A man who had come to his parents' house all those years ago and altered his life forever.

He remembered back to that time being incarcerated as a boy for years, spending days isolated in a padded cell, with no company, no other contact, just him and Lawson sitting across a table, and the relentless questions: *why did he enjoy inflicting pain and torture on animals, what triggered or motivated him to disfigure the girl?* He had no idea; all he knew was that it felt natural and good. Lawson had considered him so dangerous that he had him shackled to the leg of the table during interviews, so worried he was for his own insignificant and meaningless little life. Yet fate had now brought them together once more, as The Ripper dreamed of a million things he wanted to do to *Dr Arthur Lawson*, silently playing them out in his mind.

Escape had consumed his thoughts back then, and he

knew it would take some time. The hospital's wing for the criminally insane was said to be impossible to break out of, the last person to try was recaptured within an hour. The patients were watched all the time, day and night, and the only way he was ever going to get out was through someone who worked there, someone he could fool into trusting him, that would be his ticket out.

He remembered planning, searching for that one person and then, there he was—a guard in his late forties, disillusioned with the job and his life, who became easy prey for him to apply his particular talents. Months turned to years, and soon The Ripper had him eating out of his hand. He had him obtain medical books, journals, and banned substances, as a test to see how far he could abuse the relationship. The Ripper was building up a history, a pattern of the guard breaking the regulations, crossing the line between patient and staff and becoming vulnerable.

The Ripper knew the man had commitments, a family, and five children to feed, so coming from wealth and a trust fund, he teased the promise of enough money to change his life, making the transition to accomplice easy. Then, when he decided, he would turn on him as was his nature. He would select the time when few staff were on duty, and the weather was howling a storm. Then he would provide the guard with a stark choice: get him out of this place or go home to discover his wife and family slaughtered at the hands of someone he had paid. He knew the poor unsuspecting idiot, of course, had no option but to agree terms. Yet by doing so, he had signed his death warrant; there would be no witnesses.

The Ripper praised himself for how far he had come since he had bludgeoned his parents relentlessly, so much so that it was hard to distinguish who was who after the event.

He recalled his pathological hatred for them and his excitement at watching them crawl on their bellies, hands reaching out begging for his mercy. They were like trapped animals after the hunt, when the fox is cornered, exhausted, unable to continue, and it is then that all hope has expired for the animal, the command is given, and the pack of baying dogs, barking, growling, and snapping, proceeds to tear the prey apart. Blood from the fox would be smeared onto the child's face or forehead, which is all part of the ancient ritual of celebrating their first kill and being accepted.

He remembered standing in front of a large mirror in the sitting room after the murder, inducting himself with the blood of his parents across *his* face. Their broken bodies splayed out on the floor behind him like mangled marionettes, the injuries inflicted on them so severe that it made them almost unrecognisable as human beings. He discovered in that moment, looking at himself when all was silent, and the evidence of what he had done could not be undone, he felt no burden of guilt, no remorse for his actions. The only sensation that raced through his veins like a thundering river was one of complete and utter exhilaration. He was finally home.

He allowed himself some margin of error in the execution of his mother and father, but not now. Going forward, there would be only the constant striving for perfection in his art and the sanctity of his identity, adding to the myth and legend he was destined to become. He was special, he had always known it, and lesser mortals could only look in wonder at what he was about to achieve. For they were asleep and living like sheep, ignorant, unable, or unwilling to open their minds to the beauty and majesty of his work. He would take his rightful place in history, and feed the desire within those who truly understood and one day might dare to follow.

He would not allow anyone to prevent his transformation, this metamorphosis from chrysalis to the man he was to become. Dr Lawson, the man other than his parents he held personally responsible for his years locked away in an institution, was a short distance away from him. He was suddenly aware of a rage burning inside, engulfing and consuming him with hate. The feeling was so strong, he found it hard to breathe, his chest tightened. He felt like he was drowning, being dragged down into black, icy waters, looking up towards the surface and the shimmering face of Arthur Lawson looking back at him. His eyes rolled over black grabbing his small surgical bag, he made his way to the office and a rendezvous with the past.

CHAPTER 47

As The Ripper waited outside the office of Ignatius Crane, he could hear the muffled voices of Crane, his sister, and the unmistakable accent of Dr Arthur Lawson, with whom he had daily meetings from the age of twelve to the age of twenty before his escape from the lunatic asylum to Europe. It had been a few years since he had last seen Lawson, and his appearance had changed naturally over time, so it was unlikely he would be recognised.

If there were a slight *déjà vu* about the situation, the good Dr Lawson would never contemplate for a second that his old patient would have become a respected member of the medical profession and a registered physician at Lidgate Manor Asylum. He sniggered, speaking to himself, *Can't keep* away, *can we?* But this time, the tables had turned, he was in control, and this time, Dr Lawson had made the wrong house call. He knocked and entered the office.

Maude Crane was standing over to one side of the office while her brother Ignatius was at his desk, retelling the story of how the wife of the original owners of Lidgate Manor came to hang herself. Doctor Lawson looked suitably horrified at the disclosure of how Crane's office furniture came about, The Ripper noticing how the subject was quickly changed.

He waited to be introduced, the moment of truth had arrived. He thought of how, when, and where he would visit the doctor. Maybe one night when he was at home, sitting by the fire, feeling warm, safe, and smug with himself, he would be concealed in the room, waiting for the perfect time to attack. But none of those thoughts mattered anymore because the opportunity had presented itself impromptu and on the proverbial silver platter. Ignatius Crane motioned him to come forward like an emperor would for a patron on the steps of Rome. *Would he recognise me? Will he even have a fleeting moment of recollection, a sense of knowing me in some way from somewhere, but unable to put his finger on where?* The Ripper mused to himself, he was so close now he could reach out and touch him.

'Ah, what a feat, two doctors in the same room, must be a record, I would wonder.' Ignatius said, letting out a high-pitched laugh that only he appeared to find amusing. He sat up in his chair, leaning forward, as his sister moved behind him, watching. 'Dr Lawson, correct me if I'm wrong, but I don't believe you two have met before. This is our new resident physician, Doctor James Patterson, and we are very fortunate to have him. I'm led to believe Her Majesty has occasionally called upon his services.'

The Ripper waited, carefully studying his adversary's expression, as if they were in a duel, looking for the twitch of the mouth, the blink in the eye, the giveaway that the other principal was about to discharge their weapon. Or, in this case, the equally fatal wound of Lawson announcing that he was a fraud and an impostor. His concerns proved to be prejudged as Lawson walked towards him, and before a word was said he put his hand out to formally greet him.

'Doctor Patterson, it's a great pleasure to meet a fellow medical man and one who is so well connected,' Lawson said.

The Ripper felt euphoric. He had fooled the one person

in the world who could expose him for who he really was. Now, standing not a few inches away from his lined and old face, Doctor Arthur Lawson displayed no sign of recollection at all. This was a time to rejoice, and it was all he could do to stop himself from screaming in his face. *Look, Doctor Lawson, don't you know me? Don't you remember who this is?* But Lawson stood shaking his hand, grinning like the fool he was.

Maude Crane moved away from behind her brother and towards The Ripper and Lawson.

'Dr Lawson is here in an official capacity. He is part of a group of professionals who have the remit to arrive unannounced, night or day, and carry out a full inspection of our protocols and facilities that cater for the mentally sick. They have the power to close an institution like ours down if it does not meet with expectations within the independent regulatory body they represent.'

The Ripper calmly smiled, nodding his head. 'Yes, I have seen such inspections before, and I can only state that Lidgate Manor Asylum is run with the utmost efficiency by Ignatius and his sister. In fact, I would go as far as to say this establishment should be a benchmark for all those institutions wishing to reach the same high standard. You, Dr Lawson, should have no concerns or questions over their passion and commitment towards the care they show the inmates on a daily basis.'

Lawson appeared somewhat relieved, almost as if his task were complete. 'Well, such high praise indeed. I must say it makes my job a lot easier when I hear such a testimonial to how an institution such as this is administered.'

Maude wasted no time in making the suggestion, 'perhaps you will let Dr Patterson take you to his medical room, where he can explain the approach he takes on the inmates to study and alleviate their symptoms. I'm sure the two of you have much to discuss. I will join you later if that's agreeable, Dr Lawson, to give you a full, uninterrupted tour of Lidgate.'

Dr Lawson turned to face The Ripper. 'That's a capital idea, I'm always very interested in any new techniques you may apply in this area. I have specialised in matters of the mind and, in particular, mental illness, as it fascinates me. You, of course, will not know this, but before I became an inspector, I was employed for many years at a high-security hospital for the criminally insane. Then, after that, I was often asked to consult on cases of lunacy.'

The Ripper's fist clenched when he heard Lawson's self-congratulatory remarks about his career and took him back to those days when he was under his care. It made him want to hurt him—make him scream.

Dr Lawson followed The Ripper out of the office, leaving Maude and Ignatius to discuss how the rest of the inspection might go. There were a number of known issues with Lidgate that they both knew would not pass on closer examination, so discretion and avoidance were now a prerequisite.

The walk to the medical room was not that long, and he was slowly becoming accustomed to the winding passageways that made up the labyrinth. Dr Lawson followed just behind, and The Ripper noticed his mood was quiet and slightly more subdued than before in the office. He decided to say little at this juncture, preferring to leave any discussion until they were inside his domain. On reaching the consulting room, The Ripper looked at the large swivelling chair in the centre of the room, and thought how much fun he could have if he strapped Arthur Lawson to it and extracted his teeth with some pliers. He hesitated and instead offered up one of the seats near his desk. Dr Lawson politely accepted and sat down while looking about his surroundings.

'So, Dr Lawson, is there anything that I can help you with, anything at all?' He wanted with all his might to pick up one of the many surgical tools and drive it into Arthur Lawson's head, make him suffer as Lawson had made him suffer. But he knew he had to stay calm, the game was afoot, and the deception he was enacting was proving all too intoxicating to relinquish just at this moment. Lawson fixed his eyes on The Ripper, who was leaning back on the side of his desk.

'How have you found working with the mad? Certainly not the high standard of patient you would normally attend to, I would wager.'

The Ripper noticed a slight change in Lawson's tone. It was almost as if he were ridiculing him, as if his position and work at the asylum were somehow unimportant. He chose not to rise to the bait for the time being, if indeed he was correct in his assumption.

'No, not at all, doctor. I find the work here most interesting, and let's be honest, you, as you mentioned, were fascinated by the makings of the human mind, and I, too, have found myself drawn to such an enigma of the medical profession. We know little about the brain, yet it controls all our physical and mental functions. This establishment has been good enough to offer me *carte blanche* to use all and any of the facilities so I can try and gain an understanding of those poor souls who, at present, are lost to any cure.'

'I admire such an endeavour, and you are indeed right, this is a most important area of science that we have little grasp on. It would be good to resolve the age-old question: Is a person born mad or made mad by circumstances? Something I unfortunately was unable to find an answer to. Maybe you can now pick up the baton where I left off.' Lawson got up from his seat, walked around, and looked at the various surgical instruments on the trolley.

'Well, obviously, Dr Lawson, I'm younger, and hopefully, my work will attract other like-minded people to this field.' The Ripper spoke while keeping a close eye on him. He was feeling good, this pathetic little man had no idea who he was. He had succeeded, and it had taught him a valuable lesson that confidence and belief in yourself are as good as any disguise, and he was living proof. But he was in turmoil as he wondered how long he could keep up the pretence of being someone he wasn't. Every fibre in his body wanted to tell Lawson who he really was. All concerns about the consequences of such an action seemed to fade the more he thought about the one thing that mattered: revenge. Lawson continued to look about the room, still talking, however, his words seemed to fall away as if in a dream.

The Ripper had waited years for this moment, and here it was, slitting his throat was all he wanted, all he desired, and the pull of it became irresistible. The anger began to grow within him, a dark storm building up inside his head like a wind across the ocean, monstrous waves of hate engulfing him. The addiction to kill was now so intense and overwhelming that he was dizzy with anticipation. He approached the trolley, sweat forming on his brow, his heart pumping like a steam engine. He grabbed a knife, knocking some of the others to the floor; gripping it tightly, he turned around, ready to strike.

CHAPTER 48

The Ripper was ready to plunge the scalpel deep into Arthur Lawson's ageing, frail body. The pleasure of twisting the blade and watching the agony on his face excited him, but even more was the time it was going to take to kill him; he didn't want this to be over quickly. *No, that simply won't do. I have other delights in store for you, Dr Lawson.* Before he could turn, a sharp blade rested against his neck from behind. The cold, razor-sharp steel felt familiar.

'Did you think for one minute I didn't recognise you? Did you? Do you think me a fool, sir? I knew exactly who and what you were as soon as I saw your empty, lifeless eyes, eh? Calling yourself a Doctor, how long did you think you could get away with that, eh? Evil is burnt into your very soul; it is who you are. It follows you wherever you go, and once you know it, it's something you always recognise. I could never...never forget,' Lawson adjusted the blade slightly, scoring The Ripper's flesh.

The Ripper stood as still as he could, he knew any movement would result in Lawson cutting his throat without any hesitation.

'Well, I'm flattered after all these years, Arthur, you remember me.' He weighed up how long he would have to wait to get the better of this situation, to have that perfect moment.

'Don't even think about it, or I will remove your head believe me, it will bring me the greatest pleasure. I know you. I've known you since you were just a boy. You were just twelve years old when we first met. I knew the very day I arrived at your parents' house and heard how you tortured animals for fun, then sliced a young girl's face and eye out for what?'

'To see what it felt like, of course,' The Ripper replied, shuffling his feet slightly. It was, I suppose, a turning point for me, and in that moment, I knew I was meant for greater things, so she served a purpose.'

'You disgust me. That poor girl still can't go out of her home, so afraid, so traumatised by what you did to her. Her mother killed herself, couldn't bear to look at her own daughter after…after what you did to her. And how many others have you mutilated, eh? I know about Brighton and Fox Hall and what you did to Camilla Patterson and her daughter Henrietta.' Arthur tightened his grip he wasn't going to give this maniac an inch.

'I have an admirer in you then Arthur, after all this time.' The Ripper said sarcastically.

'I've been tracking you for years after your escape, the best I could, and then I saw an article in a local paper in Brighton about three women murdered in such a way that it could only have been at your hand. Then you disappeared again, and I worried for a while that I had lost you. I didn't give up, I was on your trail and one day, while on other business nearby, I heard people talking about a servant girl who had been found in Surrey Woods, bound to a tree, her body defiled as if by a wild animal.'

'But you couldn't get to me in time to save her employer and daughter, could you? You have to live with that, and all the others. Let's not spoil our reunion. I want to say how much I miss our little chats we used to have in my cell in that institution to which you persuaded my useless parents to have me committed to.'

'You belonged there. Now you should be on the end of a rope, and that's where I'm taking you, to face justice, to meet the demon that made you. We're going for a little walk, you and me, we're going to see Crane and his sister, who I feel might have a problem finding out that they are harbouring not only an impostor but also a killer. No good for their inspection report.'

Just out of sight, Maude Crane stood at the doorway of the consulting room listening to the conversation before announcing her presence. 'I can't thank you enough, Doctor Lawson, for apprehending this...this fraud. Please accept my deepest apologies my brother and I had no idea this man was impersonating Doctor Patterson. We employed him based on correspondence sent and received, and in good faith. To think he has betrayed that trust…it sickens me to be honest, and you say he's also a killer?'

'He is a wanted man,' Arthur said firmly, 'I intend to take him back to a court of law and stand him before a jury where he will be held answerable for his crimes by his peers, and God. I will not go into details, it would only serve to worsen your condition, increasing your worry and the tension you doubtless feel after such a discovery. But I would be grateful for the help of a couple of guards to assist me in removing him from the premises and into my carriage, ready for transportation back to London.'

Maude Crane walked around The Ripper, who had stayed strangely silent. She eyed him up and down, then looked at the knife being pressed against his neck, a small amount of blood having seeped into his crisp white shirt collar. Passing the trolley of surgical implements, she stopped in front of him, and leaned into his face. 'I would pay to see him drop through the gallows door. It beggars belief that he came here under false pretences, lied, and cheated his way, and had unfettered access to the patients. Of course, I will send for some guards immediately and inform my brother of this outrage. The sooner you take this…this fraud away from us, the better.'

The Ripper felt Arthur Lawson's grip lighten. He was beginning to tire and The Ripper assumed some cramping in the muscle was also causing discomfort. 'Thank you, Miss Crane, for your understanding. Of course, this will reflect well on my report, you and your brother do not need to be concerned about my continued support and recommendation of Lidgate Manor to the relevant authorities. Now, if you don't mind the guards, please, Miss Crane?'

'Of course, Dr Lawson, I shall fetch them this instant.' As Maude passed behind Arthur, The Ripper felt his grip suddenly loosen and the knife drop away from his throat, followed by a faint whimper and the sound of a body hitting the floor. Arthur Lawson was lying on his back with an expression of total disbelief, gasping for air.

The Ripper stood next to Maude, both looking down at their victim. Maude held a large knife by her side with a serrated edge, its blade smeared and dripping small crimson pools onto the stone floor.

The Ripper turned to Maude, wanting to frame this moment, seeing *that* look in her eyes. 'How do you feel?'

She dropped the weapon, the metal clanging as it hit the hard surface. She watched the last few seconds as Doctor Arthur Lawson slipped away into the darkness, his fight for life over.

'Magnificent,' she replied, smiling.

CHAPTER 49

Elsbeth stayed secluded beneath the cover of her bedsheets, Lilly on one side, and her daughter Rose on the other. Both were in a deep, induced sleep; most likely, a triple dose of morphine had been administered to keep them quiet. Those inmates known to be troublesome were subdued one way or another. However, increased dosages were often asked for as chronic addiction soon took hold, but it was not something the governor agreed to and would prefer restraining the inmate to the bed frame. If they created too much vocal resistance, a gag would be inserted and secured at the back of their heads with a strap and left on for days, preventing any food or water from being taken until they had learnt not to cause a fuss. Some would be taken to the solitary confinement cells and left on their own for weeks at a time in pitch black, freezing cold conditions, sleeping in their own filth with only hungry rats to keep them company.

The ward was uncommonly quiet, just the rhythmic breathing of the inmates, like an ocean, moving silently through the dappled waters of the asylum. Her thoughts went back to the predator within these walls, a rogue killer, dangerous and unpredictable, she sensed his dark energy. She felt for the security of the syringe in her hand. Gripping it tightly, she knew he would be here soon. It was time for him to hunt, to feed off the pain and suffering of others in his relentless addiction to death. Elsbeth turned her head left, then right, checking that her neighbours were still asleep, which they were. She felt alone and scared, and in hindsight, wished that Abberline had been close by, yet her fierce independence often took precedence over putting her own safety first.

A tiny creak towards the back of the room broke the stalemate of silence, not a loud noise to announce a presence, but enough to gain her attention, to alert her instinct for self-preservation. She froze, not moving a muscle, not changing position, her face barely above the sheet; she didn't even turn her head towards the direction of the sound. She had to be patient, she had to wait. Very slowly, she lowered her grip on the syringe towards the needle end, and with her fingers, teased the cloth off so it was primed and ready for the chance. *Where are you?*

The main doors were at the bottom of the room, but they had to be locked, making it obvious if anyone entered from that direction. The sound she heard was from the opposite end, yet as far as she knew, there was only one way in other than a small exit to a room Lilly had called 'The Steam Room', not a place you wanted to go by all accounts.

She listened intently. Still nothing stirred, then, something caught her eye moving from out of the shadows, a person gradually working their way down, traversing the centre of the room towards her, randomly stopping, staring obsessively at the women sleeping. It was difficult for Elsbeth to establish much as she was engulfed in darkness, only the small windows near the ceiling allowed any light in. The Moon was resting, with only charcoal-smudged clouds drifting past, they had created a perfect cover for anyone wanting to remain unseen.

As the figure approached, she could see that the outline was of a tall man—*The Ripper.*

He stopped next to her bed, halfway between hers and Lilly's, and sniffed the air. Had he picked up her smell like a wolf? Did he know she was here? Did he always know? Had he sensed her here? She moved the syringe up the side of her body, turning it around so the needle pointed upwards. Her heart raced. She had to remain as still as possible to reel him in and make himself vulnerable. Everything now rested on her, this was it, do or die, to fail was no option. She kept her eyes half closed, she could feel the sweat on her back sticking to her gown. His breathing was erratic and rasping; he was aroused, as he got closer.

He stopped, with his back to her, looking over Lilly. He then turned and touched the top of Elsbeth's head, stroking her hair softly, almost with care as if it were a child's. Elsbeth moved the syringe up to her chest. The Ripper was so near that all she needed was for him to get a bit closer, then, as quick as a moray eel, she would strike. Instead, her mind flooded with self-doubt, almost crippling her. After all this time, and all the awful things she had seen this maniac do to women, her body froze.

He bent over the top of her, moved his head towards hers and whispered. 'You know stealing is a crime, and criminals have to be punished. So now you have to pay.' The edge of a blade kissed her cheek as she felt his other free hand slide under the sheet, slithering slowly towards her breasts.

The disgust and hatred for him made her want to wretch. Finding her strength, she pulled and raised her arm up and out from under the sheet, and just at the point before pushing the needle into his neck, a hammering at the main doors made them both stop and look. There was a man's voice shouting her name. Abberline banged for all his might, trying to warn her while frantically unlocking the door. Elsbeth slammed the needle into his neck and pushed the plunger down as far as it could go. He ripped it out, throwing it to the floor as

Elsbeth watched him stagger back. It was too late: the eel had delivered its killer bite. It seemed longer, hazy like in a dream, but the combination of Abberline coming through the doors and the man, almost in slow motion, collapsing to the ground dead happened at the same time.

'Elsbeth, are you all right? Are you hurt at all?'

'I'm fine.'

'I couldn't leave you here on your own, facing this monster. How could I? Despite what you wanted? But I had no idea there was another way in, and by the time I realised what was happening—he was standing right over you.'

Elsbeth climbed out of the bed and stood over the man, turning him by pulling at his shoulder so she could see the monster they had been hunting for so long now finally dead. The last time in Brighton, his identity was hidden by a mask, so nobody knew how he really looked until now. 'Funny how different people appear when you eventually see them for who they are. But now we have Ignatius Crane and his equally insane sister to deal with while trying to get out of here in one piece.'

Abberline walked round to view the body. 'We have a bigger problem than that.'

'What do you mean?'

'This can't be The Ripper, you killed the wrong man.'

CHAPTER 50

Elsbeth could not believe what she was hearing. 'What do you mean, I've killed the wrong man? It can only be him. It has to be!'

'I know this man, Elsbeth. His name is Harker. He's out of uniform, but he's one of the guards here. I met him when Ignatius Crane caught me in a restricted area, which I came across by accident while trying to find where they had taken you. It's a solitary confinement block where they put the more troublesome inmates. I found the body of a woman who had been badly mutilated, it had all the hallmarks of The Ripper. Then Crane discovered me along with Harker. I managed to talk myself out of it by concocting a story that you had stolen a valuable watch from me, and I needed to get it back. It's all I could think of then, but I had to make sure Crane didn't suspect.'

Elsbeth looked back at the body again. His lips had turned blue from the poison. 'And you're confident this is the man you say it is?'

'One hundred percent. He was as close to me as you are. He obviously overheard about the watch, and maybe thought he would find out who I had brought in and fancied his chances of beating me to it, keep it for himself to sell no doubt, for some easy money.'

'And taking advantage of me also at the same time. He put his disgusting hands over my person! How many other women get abused in this way by these animals?'

Abberline shook his head. 'I understand widespread abuse is common in privately run institutions such as this. There are no rules to protect the inmate, and after witnessing the conditions for myself, this just goes to support everything I know to be true. The Ripper will be in his element here, able to carry out his murderous spree, hidden behind the walls of an asylum where nobody cares what happens to the poor souls that are sent here.'

Elsbeth looked angry and sickened. 'I've also seen the treatment towards the people here, this place should be shut down and condemned forever. It's unacceptable and when, or I should say, *if* we get out, I will make sure everyone knows about Lidgate Manor, Ignatius Crane and his sister.'

'We urgently need to get rid of the body before anyone comes looking for him or any of the inmates start waking from whatever drug they have been given. We can't just bundle him under the bed, we need a better solution.'

Elsbeth thought for a moment. 'He must have come in through the steam room, which is concealed at the back of the ward; you wouldn't even know it was there.'

'Steam room, what's that used for?' Abberline asked while picking up Harker's body under the arms.

'I don't know, I just heard about it from Lilly, who's in the next bed from me.' Elsbeth pointed over to where she was sleeping.

'Well, we can't leave him here, help me move him, at least he will be out of the ward if anyone does come poking around.' Abberline continued to pull Harker from under his armpits as Elsbeth took his feet and pushed from her end. The man was heavy, making the going tough as they grappled, trying not to rouse any other inmates. As they arrived at the door to the room, Abberline and Elsbeth carefully rested Harker's body on the floor, pulled the handle, and then entered.

On either side were three wooden box chambers, slightly triangular, with two doors that opened outward at the front, with a round opening at the top. One of the chamber doors had been left open, and inside was a small wooden bench spanning the unit's width. Attached to the bench was an iron hoop with a heavy chain and a leg or wrist manacle attached to the end. Abberline inspected the contraption carefully and noticed a pipe inlet coming in from the back. He leant down and felt the surface of the metal to find it extremely hot, taking his finger away quickly before he got burned.

'What on earth are these for?' Elsbeth asked, walking up beside Abberline and looking inside.

'I don't know, but from their design, they are made for people to sit inside, and there's this hot pipe at the back pro-truding inside. If I can just trace it back...' He went around the other side of the box as Elsbeth stepped inside. She bent over, touched the bench, and sat down. Her body instantly became so hot that she could hardly breathe as the door slammed shut. She felt the skin on her legs blister, the sensation clawing up her body to her chest and neck. She tried to move, but a heavy chain made it impossible, snapping her back.

Her breathing became deeper and deeper, her hair drenched in sweat her body shook with pain and panic. She turned her head as much as she could in the small opening trying to call for help, but her mouth felt as if it were on fire, and her vision blurred as a dense, billowing cloud of scorching steam completely engulfed her. She kicked out with her feet at the doors, but they wouldn't open they had been locked from the outside. She was trapped in a tomb-like cocoon, being cooked alive. The next thing she knew was Abberline's voice calling her name.

'...I know what they do to people...I just felt what...'

Elsbeth bowed her head and coughed, still shaken from the vision.

Abberline moved Elsbeth away from the chamber. 'I know a pipe comes from somewhere else, spurs out to the other chambers, and look what happens.' Abberline went behind the unit and bent down. 'There's a small valve.' Watch when I turn it on.'

As he did, a massive cloud of hot steam came from inside the chamber. 'They secure an inmate in here, probably naked, turn the valve on and…' He stopped short, seeing Elsbeth was still recovering from her ordeal.

'I know, inspector, I felt exactly what it's like to be incarcerated in one of those things. They use them to torture the madness out of people. I'd like to put The Ripper, the governor, and his evil sister in one and leave them all to scream.'

Abberline went over to the body and started to pull it over towards the chamber. 'Help me move him in here, it will buy us some time.'

Elsbeth recovered and went to assist Abberline in moving him to the bench, leaning over so his whole body was concealed inside. Abberline then shut the twin doors, sliding a dead bolt across the chamber, sealing Harker in.

'What now?' Elsbeth asked.

'Now we get you out of here. I studied the map while waiting outside the ward before you were attacked. You mentioned previously about the nurse's dormitory and taking one of their uniforms. Do that, it's a good idea, and as you said, they won't be looking for a nurse. Then make sure you follow this route exactly as I have marked out, it will get you to the outside, then make your way back to Surrey Police. See Detective Collins and no one else. Remember, he's the policeman you met at Fox Hall. Tell him everything, and get him to return with reinforcements urgently.'

'What will you do? It won't be long before they work out

I've gone, and that guard Harker is missing. What will you do?'

'One of us has to stay here. They have no reason to suspect me. I'm still a member of staff. If Crane follows the standard protocol for missing persons in secure units, he will call for a complete lockdown and an immediate search of the whole place.'

'And what about The Ripper? We don't even know where he is, and if he suspects we are in the building, he will flee, and we might never get another opportunity.'

'He has an ego, Elsbeth. Since Brighton, he thinks he is untouchable, and I have a suspicion he will want to stay and see it out. Anyway, if the place is locked down, nobody will be allowed in or out, and that will include The Ripper.'

'And what if you're wrong, what if The Ripper knows what we're up to?' Elsbeth said, looking worried.

Abberline took out the revolver he had brought with him into the asylum. 'Don't worry, Elsbeth, as I told you, he's leaving this place, one way or another .'

CHAPTER 51

Maude took some time to savour the moment, the kill had altered her, had restructured her approach to taking a life. Before, it was simple, she had a reason, they were insane, so no one would miss them, no one cared, it was the same as throwing out the rubbish, but now this was different. Dr Arthur Lawson was a respected member of a team of inspectors whose job was to investigate and report back any recommendations for improvement.

Or in the worst case, any serious breach of ethical and legal laws regarding the treatment and rehabilitation of those committed to the asylum. Most inmates had been sent to Lidgate for an indeterminate period of time by a judge under the Lunacy Act of 1845. The act was corrupted and abused by many, mainly for profit or gain, and The State only had so many places available, so the private asylum became a popular resource to use.

Arthur Lawson represented a new beginning for Maude Crane. She had learnt a valuable lesson, killing had no boundaries if one opened one's mind to the possibilities. There was no right or wrong there was just life and death, and to hold that power, to stand in judgment and wield the sword one way or the other, as the emperors of Rome once did, was exhilarating.

'I want to thank you for allowing me to put an end to this meddling, small-minded bureaucrat. I knew when you took that old woman's life on the ward when you first arrived that you were special. This inspector was here to create issues. His modus operandi was change and control, and my brother and I are not about to alter how we do things for anyone. We have had inspections before, and they usually take a quick tour, tick a few boxes, get some gold sovereigns for their trouble, then disappear. You see, Dr Patterson, we have learnt that greed is by far the most potent of the seven deadly sins when changing a person's agenda. You give a person a way of enriching their life they will take it.'

'But not all, I assume, would succumb to such a provocative offer.' The Ripper looked down at the dead body of Arthur Lawson. 'You do not need to thank me, although it will become clear to you that, given my personal connection with the late Dr Lawson, 'it's of no consequence. For me, it was the look in his eyes at that very point when he knew his life had come to an end. That is something you can't photograph, draw, or paint as it has a uniqueness that captures the soul and can only be appreciated in the moment by a true artist.'

'Can you teach me? Can you show me how to feel what you do so I can become a master?'

'Well, it's not something I have ever undertaken or considered doing. What I can tell you is that the ability lies within. The beast has been inside you, always. You will feel it stir within you when it awakens. I chose at a young age to recognise that, and embrace it, letting it free to do what comes naturally, and when you let that happen, it is truly the most transformative and profound experience you can ever imagine.'

'You say you know this man who has come to inspect our institution. How is that, if I may ask?'

I feel an affinity with you, Maude. There is trust, so I feel at last I can unburden the heavy weight I carry, but to achieve this, I need to tell you how my predicament came about. I did indeed know Dr Arthur Lawson. He was someone who, when I was a child, came to my home and advised my parents to have me committed to a secure mental facility.

I was different from other children of my age, and my interests were confined to experiments in, shall we say, the darker side of human nature. I considered myself a radical and independent thinker, not bound by the rigours of a rule-based society. However, my parents, with the aid of the late Dr Lawson, decided that this was far from normal behaviour and that I required being taken away and put in a cell and scrutinised daily, being asked question after question about how I came to be the way I am.'

'You have indeed gained my attention, and please do not misunderstand my manner; it is not one of anger but one of intrigue. However, this does not sound like the resume of Dr Patterson we employed. So if you are not him, how did you come to take his name, and more importantly, who are you?'

'All in good time, Maude ...all in good time.'

Maude watched him closely as he got up from the chair and walked to the other side of the room in what appeared to be deep thought. She knew he was also holding back on the details.

'I have been hunted down like a dog for crimes I am ac-cused of committing, but without any witnesses or evidence that prove my guilt. These people seem hell-bent on pursuing me to the point of obsession. So I had no option but to borrow the name of a prominent Surrey doctor who died of natural causes. I implore you to understand this was done with the best intentions and not to commit any fraudulent activity, but for one purpose, and one purpose only, that of self-preservation.'

'Who are the people, and what crimes do they accuse you of?'

'One is an Inspector from Scotland Yard, who goes by the name of Abberline, and the other is a so-called psychic, Elsbeth Hargreaves. Both are capable of anything and are relentless in their pursuit of me. They won't rest until they see me on the end of a rope.'

'Well, we can't have that, can we? It would be such a waste of talent,' Maude said, moving over towards him. She felt something stirring within her, a sensation she had not sensed for some time, attraction, the pull was becoming harder to resist. 'Do you think they have followed you here, to Lidgate?'

'Yes, I believe they are already here. Elsbeth Hargreaves is not the only one with skills beyond normal understanding. I have felt her presence she is too close for comfort, and that blundering fool of a policeman will surely follow like her little lapdog.'

Maude, now right behind him, placed her hand on his shoulder. 'I don't care what they say you have done or if you are responsible. I see you for what you truly are. You are emerging, becoming, and I want—no, I need to be there with you to share in the glory of what is to become your legacy.' She waited for his reaction, worried if she had destroyed any chance of him reciprocating her sentiments. She wondered if such a man could have affections for her; she dreamed of such a thing.

He turned, facing her, and placed his hand on her cheek. Maude Crane was a good deal older than he was. Her skin was pale and lined by years of toil and neglect. 'I am forever in your debt, Maude, and deeply honoured that you should give me such a personal account of your emotions, a man you hardly know. And yet I also feel a connection between us. Age does not appear to have any bearing on this we are joined together by something far deeper than that.'

Maude could not have been happier. She felt as if she could fly; her stomach buzzed with anticipation and excitement. She was again a young, free girl in the grips of that first love when everything was possible. Mountains could be climbed and oceans crossed there was nothing they could not do together, and anyone showing the look of disapproval would melt away into the abyss of obscurity, for they could not ever understand the depth of what they shared. She knew above everything else, he had given her something more precious than gold—he had made her complete.

'And what can I call you now that we've been so open and honest with each other?'

'Jack, you can call me Jack, but just between us two, not for anyone else to hear, is that understood? The fewer people who know, the better,' he said, knowing full well this would be a short-term relationship.

'Oh, I completely understand, my love, know that your secret is safe with me forever.'

'And what of your brother? I can't see him approving of our association.'

Maude didn't immediately reply, thinking for a moment. 'It's always been just my brother and me. He has been my rock, and I his. As you have seen, he has a particular physical deficiency in his albinism that attracts negative attention. This has brought us closer for many reasons. And it's fair to say we have indeed shared a bond not many people would be able to understand, and discovered much about ourselves together in ways society might view as abhorrent. Lately, I have felt trapped and unfulfilled, however now, after meeting you, I feel alive once more, and I know these feelings are real, and I want to explore them more. My brother does not need to know anything about you or us, it is better that way.'

'I need to do one last act before we move this body to a more appropriate place.' The Ripper went over to his black bag, retrieved a long serrated knife, and knelt next to Dr Lawson.

'What are you going to do?'

'Removing his eyes and liver—a small memento to remind me of him, when the moment takes me.'

Maude's eyes widened, enthralled, her heart raced.

CHAPTER 52

Maude Crane stood back, still euphoric about the way she had killed Dr Arthur Lawson, while The Ripper moved his dead body over and onto his side. The doctor's eyes and liver, which had been removed, had caused some excess blood that had spilt onto the floor. 'You need to get a mop and bucket to try and get rid of this mess. You can't have him found like this, it will be the end of you, and your brother won't be able to protect you if it ever gets out.' The Ripper had a system to his kills he was always in control, but now he was placed in a situation where he wasn't, and he didn't like sorting out someone else's mess.

Maude suddenly snapped out of her dream state. 'Yes… of course, I'll fetch some cleaning items now. I…didn't know I would do this; it just happened. I heard what he said about you, which made me angry. I just wanted to make him stop, that was all. Yet he kept going on and on at you, and something inside me broke. I felt rage, and it was a good feeling, and… well, I wanted to hurt him, make him go away…I wanted to kill him.'

'Dr Lawson would have had a field day, two of us in the same room.'

Maude looked puzzled by what he meant.

'You're a natural-born killer, Maude, you just didn't know it. There's no stopping you now.'

'I enjoyed every moment, and I will relive it all the time. It's special because you were here with me, think what we could achieve together. We are one, and now that you have shared who you really are with me, nothing can stop us.'

The Ripper sneered inside. He was fuming, but they had to get rid of the body. 'Do you have a furnace in this place?'

'We have a coal-fired one in the cellar, but my brother disagrees with them, says they are an unnecessary expense and that people can generate their own heat by exercising during the day, sleeping together or on the floor at night in the colder months. We could use it, but it would take hours to get hot enough to incinerate the body completely and might bring unwanted attention.'

'So anywhere else?'

'Yes, there is. Let me get the cleaning equipment and I'll tell you about it when I get back. As you said, we can't have anyone finding out about this. I promise, my love, I will get better, I just need more practice. There are plenty in this place I can start with. Nobody will miss them or give a shite if they live or die. I feel like I'm sixteen again.' Maude cackled, then left to bring back the items to clean the blood off the floor.

Feeling nothing but utter contempt for her, The Ripper disregarded Maude and focused on the deceased before him. He walked clockwise around it, his breathing heavy and deep, ranting and shouting at the corpse. 'Now you will see what death is like, now you suffer in eternal hell, as you made me suffer. If I could, I would cut off your head and wear it as a hat for all to see. You think you know about the mind? How I think? You know nothing, you understand *nothing*. You made me sit in that room day after day, talking on and on, trying to change and understand me. *Why did you cut that girl's face up? Why do you like tearing the wings off birds?* Why, because I liked it, it's as simple as that, for no other reason other than it brought me pleasure. You people think with your textbooks and lectures and exchanging of notes with each other, that you will come to know me. No, you're all on a fool's errand.

I am the first of many. I am the fallen angel who came back to this Earth to reap revenge on the filth that walks the streets. You were actually arrogant enough to think you started to help me, didn't you? I saw your notes: *Boy making progress.* Well, you *hadn't,* I tricked you. When I got out with the help of that stupid guard you entrusted me with, I paid my dear parents a visit, and I made certain how I felt. It took me days to clean the blood and brain matter off, and I understand that when they were finally found, they were not even able to recognise them after what I had done with them.'

He sped faster around the body, his words spitting out, unable to contain himself. He had lost all notion of where he was, all he saw in his mind was a red mist and hate. He didn't care who heard, he didn't care about anything other than Dr Arthur Lawson and what he wanted to do to him. He kicked the body in the side repeatedly, each time harder than the last. Almost screaming in a high-pitched voice, he was now consumed with absolute loathing. 'Now you know what pain is, what suffering is, feel this.' He kicked the body again and again, his boots thudding into the torso, legs, arms, stamping on the face and ribs. 'Look up from the cesspit you are in and know that it's me standing over your rotting corpse, and I'll see you at the gates of hell.'

Maude arrived back, hearing his voice down the corridor. 'What on earth are you doing? I could hear you at the end of the passage. You said not to attract attention, to keep quiet while we dispose of him, didn't you?'

The Ripper was slouched back in one corner of the room, his head to one side, his eyes as black as coal, his breathing erratic as small beads of sweat formed on his brow. He said nothing but stared at her in a way she knew it would be wise not to say another word. He had the look of the possessed about him, the face of Satan himself. She promptly got on and wiped the blood up from the floor, washing the mop out a few times until it had all but gone, just a few marks left, which she didn't bother with and then went to empty the bucket. When she returned, The Ripper stood waiting, his composure back to normal as if nothing had happened.

'So, this place you mentioned where we can dump the body, where is it?' The Ripper asked.

'It's some waste ground at the back of the asylum for inmates who have died naturally or unnaturally,' Maude grinned. 'Dig shallow graves, that's the trick, then the animals come at night, feed off the flesh and even take the bones, nice and simple like, no fuss, no mess, nothing left of them.'

The Ripper nodded in agreement.

'But we need to move. I just heard my brother has been told that a guard called Harker has not turned up for his shift and is missing. This and the recent intake of a lunatic, a woman late at night, which caused him more paperwork, has him in one of his rages.'

The Rippers' suspicion was immediately aroused. 'A woman late at night you say, how did she arrive?'

'With a guard just turned up at the gates. They had all the right papers, but something didn't seem right; it was all very irregular. She was a mouthy cow, but I made her pay, threw her into the side of my brother's desk. She didn't have much to say after that.'

'Did you make a record of their names. The woman and the guard? Can you remember what they looked like?'

'I can't recall anything particular about them. He was just a guard, and she was well, just another mad idiot. To be honest, they all look the same to me. My brother allocates a number on a badge to each one when they come in here. But a record of their legal name if they have one, and who brought them here is recorded in a file from the committal documents. It's the law, you see,' she said sarcastically.

The Ripper felt a cold rush over him. *I wonder.* As soon as they disposed of the body, he had to find out if his hunch was correct and find Abberline and Elsbeth before they found him.

CHAPTER 53

Maude and The Ripper carried the late Dr Arthur Lawson out of the consulting room and into the passageway. Maude returned to the cupboard, where she had put away the mops and bucket, and retrieved a folded sheet of sailcloth. 'We use this to wrap around the dead, stops the stench from being too bad. Don't want any potential clients looking to put their nearest and dearest in here being put off by the smell.' Maude laughed caustically.

Maude laid the sheet out on the floor as The Ripper dumped Dr Lawson's body roughly to one side, then together they rolled the sheet around the body until it was completely concealed.

'Now, if anyone comes, they will think just another inmate has passed over, and we are moving the remains to be buried,' Maude said. 'No one will know it's him, and his investigation into Lidgate Manor will be like him, well and truly dead.'

With that, they both took an end and started to walk towards a dimly lit passageway that would eventually get them to a gate that led out to the back of the asylum. As they reached the outside, Maude lowered her end of the body and went to fetch a small wooden wheelbarrow. The ground was covered with a low-lying, ghostly mist that clung to their boots and ankles, seeming to float like a dead sea far out into the distance.

'Put him in this, the ground gets a bit rough from here and we don't want him spilling out all over the place, do we?' Maude said.

The Ripper said nothing, following her lead. It was a wide-open space laid to lawn with high, wild, knotted grass growing out from it, clawing out from the fog. The grass was unkempt and brown in colour and clearly had not been tended to for some time. They steered the wheelbarrow across the ground and towards the centre. A large stump stood hauntingly in the ground, a remnant of the great tree that once stood there.

'Can imagine what this place was like when Lord High and Mighty lived here before his idiot wife took her own life,' Maude shouted across to The Ripper. 'The rich don't know how good they have it.'

'The Ripper ignored the comment and momentarily thought back to his childhood and the money he had inherited from his parents after he had butchered them. He was rich and knew how good that was and what it gave him. He had created a world that fascinated him, a journey of discovery, purpose, and meaning to his existence at the expense of others. He was on a mission and let the path guide him to a place he knew would be his crowning glory, where he would reach his potential and achieve what most can only dream of—immortality. He passed the stump, giving it little attention until they came upon an area that still had the faint outlines of a large rectangle. The grass was also different, richer with a deep hue of green.

'They had a lake built here in the old days, had all sorts of mad parties around it, with even small rowing boats made available. After the place fell into ruin and was purchased years later, they filled the lake in and left it. My brother had the genius idea to use it as a graveyard without any headstones, of course. Just a place to dump the carcasses. The ground has become more fertile over the years, must be all of them decomposing bodies.' Maude let out a high-pitched shriek. 'You can have your own private area if you like, for the ones we can't sell to medical science for a profit, the ones that are too, shall we say, *damaged* to be of any use.'

'Yes, it would be beneficial to my work to have a place to dispose of the dross, which I do not require. The bodies have to be of good condition if they are infected with diseases, they hold no market value and hold no use to me or any paying client.'

Maude loitered as they reached a spot where the ground was broken up into twenty small side-by-side plots, each about six feet long and two to three feet deep. A solitary worker was digging more graves, not far from them, who parked his shovel in the earth as soon as he spotted the visitors. He was an older man, approximately five feet five inches tall, of medium build, and wore clothes that were dirty and torn. As they walked towards him, The Ripper could see he was not one of the guards, observing him closely as he removed his flap cap in an almost reverent manner. He looked slightly away from Maude as he spoke. 'Good to see you, ma'am.'

Maude didn't respond, and instead introduced him to The Ripper. 'This is Steine, been with us for years, does odd jobs about the place, comes from the village, don't you? Well, speak up!' Maude snapped at him.

'Yes, ma'am, sir,' Steine replied, his head bowed.

'Steine is one of those workers who knows his place in life and when to keep his mouth shut, don't you?' Maude said as Steine nodded, 'He knows his wife and kids would end up in one of these holes if he started to talk. Now I don't have time to chat with the likes of you all day, so get rid of this.' Maude pointed to the body in the wheelbarrow. 'Make sure you show enough flesh to scent the animals. Do you understand? I don't want to return in a few weeks and find anything left of him, is that clear? Do your job, and do it well.' Maude had moved within inches of Steine's face, yelling at him.

'Yes, ma'am,' Steine replied, still with his head lowered in a subservient manner.

The Ripper tipped the body of Dr Arthur Lawson as if it were garbage out and onto the ground, and then walked back to the asylum with Maude. Steine, still within earshot, listened to Maude as she continued.

'Tiresome little man, if it weren't for him being so cheap, I would have got rid of him long ago. I suppose at least we have shown good faith in employing the village idiot,' she bellowed with laughter.

'Maude, I need to get access to your brother's office. As I told you before, I have a good reason to suspect that outsiders who mean to do me harm are here, hiding in plain sight. If I'm right, there are two of them, but to be certain, I will need to see the file of admissions and the number assigned to each committed individual over the last month or so.'

'Of course, my dear, my brother will have to be informed about Dr Lawson's untimely demise, and I can let him know of your suspicions about these two impostors at the same time. Above all, my brother admires and rewards loyalty.'

The Ripper thanked her. He knew he couldn't rely on her and would wait for the opportune time to access her brother's office, with or without her help. It was too important not to. However, his immediate attention was drawn to the sound of several dogs barking and howling in the distance. 'They seem agitated,' he remarked to Maude.

'I keep the pack half-starved, keeps them mean and heightens their senses so they can track and kill anything for miles just by a person's scent, far more reliable, and better than any human. Loyal and without mercy, they will rip their prey to pieces. I don't have to give any commands, they know what to do. I raised them myself, and they have a way of smelling the air, they know when a kill is imminent.'

The howling became louder as The Ripper passed close by. The pack had become restless, pacing up and down the cages, snarling and growling, as they sensed a presence. But he knew it was not their natural hostility that had riled them, it was something else—fear.

CHAPTER 54

Abberline and Elsbeth made their way out of the steam room and back through the ward. This was the only way out, and they had to be careful not to wake other inmates. They got about halfway when Rose, Lilly's daughter, stirred, moving about under her covers. She moaned slightly, gasping for air but not opening her eyes. Abberline was ahead of Elsbeth, holding his fingers up to his lips as they slowly made their way to the set of doors leading out. He held the door for Elsbeth to pass through, relieved that at least they were clear of the first obstacle. The next one was to prove more difficult. The medical consulting rooms were next to the women's ward, where Abberline rescued Elsbeth from Crane, who was called away by his sister to attend an inspection.

Elsbeth stopped just outside the door, whispering. 'He could be in there now, and we could just do what needs to be done. As you said, we take him one way or the other. You have a gun, so we have the advantage.'

Abberline vigorously shook his head. 'We need to get you out, it's too risky. If it goes wrong, all hell will be let loose, and we will have nowhere to run to, and you know what will happen then.'

'Sorry, I disagree. If he's in here, what better time is there?'

Before Abberline could stop her, Elsbeth opened the door, and was halfway through before he could do anything. He quickly removed his revolver, cocking the hammer back until it clicked, and followed her in. There was a quietness about the room that was unnerving. Elsbeth pointed to another door, then joined her hands and put them to the side of her head, indicating sleeping. Abberline guessed what she meant and made his way over towards the bedroom. He waited, pressing his ear to the door, but couldn't hear a sound. He held the gun in one hand and, with the other slowly lowered the handle; it creaked, then opened.

The room was empty. Abberline let out a deep sigh of relief. It was a small and rectangular room with white walls and a single bed. A pine dresser with four drawers sat to one side, and on top was a plain, cream-coloured jug and basin for washing and shaving. The bed had a dip in the middle where The Ripper had rested. He placed his hand on it, as a tracker would do to see if it was still warm, but it was cold to the touch. He uncocked the revolver, placed it back in his pocket, and quickly exited the room. 'All clear,' he reported.

'Alright, that's good,' Elsbeth replied, clearly reassured.

'We can't let our guard down, he could be back any second. Anyone could walk in here at any moment, so we need to move quickly and look for something, anything. If Crane or his sister finds us, we tell them everything. We have no choice. We tell them who we are and why we are here, but we need some evidence to prove what we are saying.'

'So that's your plan, to tell the governor of this madhouse, who should be in here himself, *everything*? Don't forget what he was about to do to me when you saved me in this very room. Crane is not nice, Abberline. He is a narcissistic bully, and his sister is even worse. You saw her *private room* with the disgusting dinner party for the dead, and how she treated me in the office when we first arrived, pushing me into the side of the desk, and laughing. She's insane and, to my mind, is no better than her brother.'

'I plan to get you out so you can get help, that's what we have to stick to.'

'You can't trust Crane or his sister.'

'I don't, but remember when I found you in here? Maude told her brother there was an official here to inspect the place. So if we have to, we find this inspector and tell him what's happening, and he will then demand that Crane and his crazy sister explain.'

'That's a lot of assumptions, and I thought you only dealt with logic.'

'I agree. I would prefer to deal with certainties, but with madness, there aren't any. Stay with the plan, use the route on the map to stay hidden and get to Detective Collins as quickly as possible.'

'That leaves you alone in this place with more than one lunatic to contend with.'

'I know, but I will be much happier knowing you're outside getting the help we need. I'm a trained officer. I know how to look after myself, and I will tell the governor all I know if I have to. He may not be trustworthy, but he doesn't want to have this place closed and lose his income. Greed is a powerful motivator, and I'm also armed and won't think twice about using it on *anyone* if I have to.'

Elsbeth reluctantly agreed and continued looking for any scrap of information while Abberline stood watch at the door.

'There's nothing here, he's been too careful,' Elsbeth said. 'But wait a minute. On the floor, there was a stain, a blood stain.' She bent down and touched it. It was dry, and some attempt had been made to clean it up, but it was still clear enough to see that someone had bled out. 'Look, Abberline. Here, blood, and a lot of it,' Elsbeth said, pointing at the mark.

'Yes, remember, a lot goes on in this room and none of it for good.'

Elsbeth stood back up and leaned against the desk in shock. Just opposite her was a shelf with some books and a large glass jar filled with a liquid tinted red. Elsbeth recognised it as a human liver after The Ripper had left one inside her house in Brighton as a gift the last time they had encountered him. Then, above it, two freshly removed eyeballs were suspended, gazing out at her through the glass with a look of horror on them.

'I…I think we've found our evidence,' Elsbeth said quietly, still reeling from the sight before her.

Abberline looked back to where Elsbeth was fixated. It confirmed everything they knew: The Ripper was back to his old ways and collecting trophies.

'Who do they belong to?' Elsbeth asked.

'I don't know, but they are fresh, and whoever they were, that person was utterly despised by The Ripper. He wants to preserve these, keep them, look at them, remind himself who they came from and the agony the victim went through.'

Elsbeth looked sickened as she thought back to the victims who had been mutilated and the parts cut out of them, to be kept as keepsakes, as he had done in Brighton.

'I'll return for this once we have you on your way. Not even Crane and his sister will be able to ignore it. There's nothing more to do we need to move fast, we must get out of this place before it's too late.'

CHAPTER 55

Maude arrived back at her brother's office and went through to find him standing at the window, his arms behind his back, staring at a flint courtyard below.

'Something, sister, is amiss in this place, I can feel it in my bones, and my bones are *never* wrong.' he turned around, his pinky red eyes, smaller than usual, peered out at Maude. 'I am given to understand one of our guards, Harker, has disappeared, vanished into thin air.'

'Brother, not wanting to change the subject, but there is something I need to tell you.'

'I don't need any bad news, sister. I have enough to contend with this inspector snooping about the place. And where the hell is the man? I don't want him left to his own devices to wander freely about. These people like poking their noses into areas that are strictly off-limits. The last time I had eyes on the tiresome man was in this office. Then he went off to the consulting room with Dr Patterson, and since then I have not seen or heard from him.' Crane sat back down behind his desk, his hands tightly clasped together like a vice.

'The inspector, Dr Lawson, is no longer a problem for us. I had to deal with the issue myself, and I can assure you, brother, he will not be telling anyone about our operations.'

Ignatius Crane became enraged. 'What did you do, Maude? What did you do with him? Do you not realise that if he does not report back to the committee, they will wonder why and send another in his place. Did that little fact not enter your thinking?'

Maude sat on one of the chairs opposite her brother to try to calm his temper. 'Brother, Dr Patterson had to check on the ward, some emergency, and I…I was left alone with the inspector…I did not feel comfortable in his company, and my judgment proved to be correct as he tried…he tried to assault me. He made it clear that if I did what he wanted, we need not worry over his report, but he would have us closed if I did not comply with his advances. So you see, brother, I had no option other than to fight back as you taught me, and as I pushed him back, he fell and accidentally knocked his head.'

Ignatius Crane rose from his desk. 'So you're telling me the inspector is dead…you killed him in some act of hysteria. What possessed you, Maude? Why didn't you come to me? Have I not always protected you?'

'You have, brother, of course, forgive me. When Dr Patterson returned from the ward, I told him everything. Well, he will vouch for what occurred, and with his help, we have disposed of the body. I have Steine burying it as we speak.'

'You seemed to have thought of everything, sister, and how fortunate you had Dr Patterson to assist,' Crane's tone had an air of disbelief tinged with jealousy about it. 'I will correspond with the committee myself as to the conduct of Dr Lawson, and in defending your honour, he met his untimely end. If they want the body, they can dig it up themselves, what's left of it after the birds have fed off his decomposing carcass. And Dr Patterson, will concur with this account?'

'Brother, before we trouble Dr Patterson to answer that in full, there is one other matter I need to bring to your attention.

However, I want you to know you need not concern yourself, as I see the matter easily remedied.'

Ignatius Crane sat back in his seat, unconvinced but hoping to receive better news than what he had just been exposed to.

'I am extremely concerned that one or two people in Lidgate have gained access fraudulently. I do not know why they are here, but the mere fact that they are, if I'm right, is concerning enough. They must be dealt with in the harshest manner. The last inmate that arrived here sent by Judge Voss, you remember it was late at night. You said at the time it was strange and then not long after that we had an inspection. Something doesn't ring true, brother, we had better find out what.'

Crane jumped out of his chair, unable to contain his anger further. He went over to a cabinet, removed a buff-coloured folder from the drawer, and opened it. He stood for a moment reading down some columns until he came to the date and information he was looking for. 'Ah, yes, here it is, some little whore called *Hargreaves. E.* The papers were all signed off by Judge Titus Voss, as I recall. Everything looked in order, but it was most odd and caused me *more* work.

The guard who brought her here even dared to ask me for a job. I found him sneaking around the solitary confinement cells when I explicitly told him to go to the office to be put onto the payroll. What was his name? I remember now…Baines. Probably not his real name, another pack of lies. I remember him saying this Hargreaves woman that he had brought into Lidgate had stolen his watch, and he wanted to find her and get it back, but he got lost.'

'You see how odd this all starts to look now,' Maude said.

'We need to find out what is happening here, sister, and return this facility to normality. We'll go and have a little chat with this *so-called* inmate, and that fool guard Baines, who brought her here. And Harker is still missing, have the bell rung. I want him found.'

A short while after Crane and his sister had left the office, The Ripper came out of the shadows where he had been listening to their discussion. He entered the office, and looked at the file on Crane's desk. He had to be sure, he had to see it for himself. As he checked down the list, his eyes widened at the discovery. Right next to a number was the name '*Hargreaves. E*', and the guard who brought her, '*Baines*'. The Ripper smiled. *I have you. Both of you.*

CHAPTER 56

Abberline and Elsbeth got ready to move as they heard footsteps and shouting from Crane and Maude. Abberline slowly opened the door and closed it as a number of guards followed, all rushing into the ward where Elsbeth had been held.

'Shhh, they might return to check in here, so we must move fast.' Abberline opened the door again, slipped into the corridor, and waved for Elsbeth to follow. They could hear raised voices in the ward, and shouting as they proceeded on around a corner and into another passageway. Abberline stopped. 'I just need to check the map before we go any further, before you make the rest of the way by yourself.'

Elsbeth quickly turned her head both ways, making sure no more guards were coming their way. 'I don't like you staying here, it's too dangerous. We have no idea how much Crane and his sister know, and we still have no clue where The Ripper is.'

Abberline folded the map back up. 'Don't worry, I can take care of myself. Let's get you to the nurse's dormitory, where you can change into one of their uniforms. As you said, they will be too busy looking to bother stopping you, especially if you're dressed as one of them. Sooner or later, they will realise you and Harker have gone. If I can get to this Lawson, I have a good chance to persuade him to come with me to see Crane.

I'll tell him and his sister who I am and how he's been aiding a maniac who is responsible for multiple deaths. I will make sure Crane knows I'm here on behalf of Scotland Yard, and if he gets in the way of me doing my job, he will also feel the full force of the law.'

Elsbeth was still concerned. 'I have a bad feeling about this, Abberline, you should be very careful.'

'I realise it's a risk, yet with you bringing Detective Collins back with enough officers in tow, I will feel better knowing help is on the way. But remember, when you get out, run and don't look back. Don't talk or trust anyone until you get to Surrey Police Station, and make sure you tell Collins *everything*.'

'And what about the monster we came here for?'

'I think this will flush him out. I feel he knows we are here and will be on the hunt. He has a score to settle, Elsbeth, with both of us. Last time in Brighton, he wore a mask, but this time I want to look him in the face, and I have to confess there is a large part of me that wants to put my revolver to his head and pull the trigger.'

Abberline followed the route he had worked out to the dormitory on the floor above where the men's ward was also located. There was some commotion in the distance, shouting and people running and dashing about, so speed was of the essence. They went through several narrow corridors lit with gas lamps, with doors on both sides. Some marked 'No Entry' while others were unmarked. A couple of guards rushed past them, muttered and swore, boots with hobnails echoing off the hard floor. Fate was on their side on this occasion, but their luck might run out next time. They reached a wide metal staircase that took them up to the next landing. As they reached the top, they found they had two choices. To the right was the nursing dormitory, and on the left was the male ward.

'I'll be quick,' Elsbeth said, moving fast towards the door to change into a uniform to help make her escape.

'Wait, the door will be locked.' He went with Elsbeth, took out the keys he got from Maude's office, and unlocked the door.

'Now hurry, please, I'll go back and keep watch,' Abberline said, moving back towards the male ward to take a quick look and make sure there were no guards. There was a small window on one of the doors that led into the room. Peeping through, he saw the horrendous conditions of the inmates. Men of all ages, young and old, all mixed together, beds crammed against each other with no space or privacy between them. Some of them were aimlessly wandering around the ward without any clothing, thin, gaunt, starving bodies, screaming and yelling out to anyone who might listen. Others sat on the floor, weeping, rocking from side to side, muttering to invisible people, while a few lay on their beds, staring up at the ceiling, in some form of catatonic shock.

The floor was covered in filth and human excrement. Abberline doubted if anyone had been here for some time. He turned quickly to check if Elsbeth had left the dorm, but there was no sign of her. He turned back to look through the glass in the door again, and just as he did, a face appeared from nowhere. Abberline jumped back in shock as the man's haggard face and hand pressed against the glass. His eyes were red, sore, and bleeding from the corners. He looked old, just skin and bone, his hand on the glass, hardly able to move his mouth to speak. Abberline got closer, trying to understand him, before being interrupted by the familiar voice of Elsbeth.

She was standing on the top of the stairs, adjusting her hat and uniform, which had been hurriedly put on. 'I'm ready, let's go.' Elsbeth said.

As they started descending, Abberline checked back on the man, but he had disappeared, swallowed up by the madness within. They soon reached the bottom of the stairs and returned the way they had come until they reached a passage where Elsbeth would have to go on her own.

'Remember, if anyone stops you, you're a nurse, just say you're doing an urgent errand for the governor,' Abberline said, unfolding the map and pointing out the route he had marked for her to follow. He put his finger on the line. 'We are here, just follow the way, and it should get you to this door that will take you to a gate, and if I was informed correctly, it is always kept unlocked. They use it to bring provisions at all times of the day. Once you're through there, run across the heath and into the woods. From there, keep north. I have marked it until you reach the road. The rest is up to you.'

'I'll be back with reinforcements as soon as I can. If you see The Ripper, don't let him get away again.'

Abberline reached into his coat pocket and handed his revolver over to her. 'Take it, and use it if you have to.' He paused for a moment. 'You do know how to use one of these, right?'

Elsbeth snatched it, flipped the cylinder out, spun the chamber, checked that it was fully loaded, and swiped it shut with her hand. 'I'm part Italian, inspector, my mother taught me to shoot back in the old country when I was six years old. But don't you want this?'

'No, it will be all right, anyway your need is greater than mine, I will make do, don't you worry.' Abberline watched her vanish into the dim light of the passageway and then started his way back to find Ignatius Crane and the inspector as a sound he had not heard before travelled down the corridors and passageways. As he worked his way through the labyrinth, the sound of a bell boomed out from the tower. It was rung for one, and one reason: to sound an alarm.

CHAPTER 57

The Ripper had discovered from the records in Ignatius Crane's office that Elsbeth and Abberline had worked their way inside the asylum. Changing his priorities, he collected his black bag from his room and made his way to the women's ward next to his consulting rooms. Crane and his sister had gone on ahead and taken some guards to find Elsbeth to interrogate her, so he knew he had to act fast. Elsbeth was bound to try and tell Crane her real identity and why she was *really here*. He had told Maude about the two hunting him down, but she was keeping this to herself, for now. If Crane believed Elsbeth even for a moment, his cover could be exposed, and things could become difficult.

When he arrived at the ward, he saw men turning over beds, searching cupboards, and throwing out all the contents. All the women, apart from two who were kept in their beds, were lined up on one side, guards beating them back with batons. Some inmates were half-dressed, others screaming and ranting words over and over again, hollering, tearing at their hair, pinching their skin. A few had been handcuffed to railings secured to the wall and left, too much of a risk to themselves and others to be let loose. It was loud and chaotic madness, and it filled his heart with joy.

The place stank of sweat and urine, with clothes and bed sheets flung over the floor. He scoured the room for Elsbeth, hoping to see her so he could get to her before she said anything, but she was nowhere to be seen. Ignatius Crane was furious, his face puce with rage, shaking his fists at two women he had kept apart from the others. As The Ripper approached, Maude turned to greet him.

'Jack.' She stopped herself, ensuring her brother didn't hear her address him so casually. 'I apologise, I mean, Dr Patterson, the woman we think is an impostor is missing. My brother is questioning these two inbreds, Lilly and her daughter Rose, who slept on either side of this Elsbeth Hargreaves where she went, but it isn't getting very far. I do fear Ignatius will have a heart attack, he is so consumed with anger.'

'Yes, I can see,' replied The Ripper.

'Perhaps you might have an idea of how to extract the information with your many talents.' Maude looked at him with a knowing smile.

The Ripper moved over to Crane, who had his hands wrapped tightly around the throat of Lilly.

'Tell me where the new woman who was in the next bed to you has gone, or I will twist your scrawny neck until it snaps off,' Crane screamed.

'I dunno what you're talking about, Governor, I was asleep, they give us stuff to make us sleep. When we woke, she had gone, she didn't say nothin, not a word to me nor me daughter. God's witness, sir, I would not lie.' Lilly coughed as she spoke, finding it hard to get her words out as she was being half-strangled.

'If I may,' The Ripper interrupted, placing his bag down on the floor. He could smell the scent of Elsbeth in the room.

Crane looked over to him and then reluctantly removed his grip on Lilly's neck and stood breathing heavily. 'I need answers and fast, so if you think you can get the truth out of her, be my guest.'

The Ripper stepped beside the bed, bending slightly over so she could see him, his voice calm, clear, and controlled. 'Now, Lilly, it is important that you tell us the truth. You do not need to worry, nothing will happen if you tell us what we need to know. Now, I realise you are here for your own well-being, but I hope you understand the difference between right and wrong. Hmm, yes?'

'I told the Governor, I told him the truth, please sir, I dunno nothin I don't, honest, neither of us do. We were sleeping like I said. Ain't that right, Rose?' Lilly glanced over towards her daughter who was shivering with fear, nodding nervously in agreement.

The Ripper smiled, collected his bag and stood up, going over to her daughter's bed. He placed the bag on top of the sheets and opened it up. He gently stroked Rose's hair away from her forehead. 'Such a pretty face. Now, Lilly, are you sure what you have relayed to the governor is the truth?'

Lilly watched, afraid for her daughter .'Yes, I told you the truth, please, I beg of you, please believe me, I would tell you if I knew anything.'

'For God's sake, man, this is getting us nowhere.' Ignatius Crane ranted.

The Ripper said nothing, his eyes fixed on Lilly. He gently pulled Rose's head back, and with one movement, her throat opened up. Blood slowly trickled down her neck, then gushed out like a torrent. Rose slumped over like a rag doll as The Ripper threw her roughly backwards onto her bed. Her eyes went still, staring over to her mother as if to say goodbye.

There was an eerie silence for a moment as the world stood still, broken by the guttural cry for a lost child as Lilly screamed, her hands covering her mouth, then her face in complete shock, as she yelled through the tears. 'No, no…not my baby girl, no please God not my baby.'

Crane stood watching as Maude grinned behind him.

'Now, maybe you will tell us the truth. Where is the woman who was put right next to you?'

Lilly collapsed into a bundle, unable to control her grief, her words broken and slurred. She could hardly breathe. 'I told you *I don't* know. I don't know'…' why, why did you have to take my baby from me?'

The Ripper turned to address Ignatius Crane. 'I had to be sure, and I now believe the wretch is telling the truth.'

Before Crane could reply, a young man appeared in uniform in front of them. 'Sorry to interrupt, sir, but we've found Harker. He's dead, looks like poison. Whoever it was then hid the body in one of the steam chambers. '

The Ripper noticed a small glass syringe lying on the floor. He picked it up, inspected it, and then handed it to Crane. 'I think you'll want to see this.'

Crane snatched it out of his hands, turning his head to Maude. 'Well, sister, it appears this *so-called* inmate is not only an impostor but a murderer.'

'What shall we do, brother?'

Crane went over to Elsbeth's bed, ripped a sheet off, and held it tightly to his nose, breathing it in for a second, then threw it across to Maude.

'Set the dogs loose.'

CHAPTER 58

The Ripper followed Maude Crane out of the women's ward and towards the exit to make their way back to the dog compound. His thoughts now focused on Elsbeth and where she could be. The idea of meeting her again after following his trail of destruction aroused him, and he looked forward to that moment when they had time alone. He would tell her how he wooed his way into the affections of Camilla Patterson. Then he would spare no detail of how he killed her and her daughter, what he did to them, how they pleaded for their lives, as did their servant.

'I can't tell you how much I enjoyed the way you cut that girl's throat, it was masterful, I don't think anyone saw that coming.' Maude interrupted his train of thought.

'Well, your brother had given the mother ample chances to come clean about what she knew, and as I said, we have to be sure, these types lie in their sleep. If I'm being honest, the daughter was going to die anyway; they both were. I'll go back later and finish off the mother, I have need of her ears and nose for my collection.'

'You could put them alongside the bits from Dr Lawson,' Maude laughed.

The Ripper didn't respond, she was ignorant of his art and

possessed little imagination to even begin to comprehend its beauty. She had no concept of the loneliness, the voyage of discovery he was on, or the path he had yet to travel. His destiny beckoned him like a Siren on the rocks of a dark landscape. His soul yearned once more to feel the euphoria of the kill, that moment between light and dark, life and death, and that unearthly wisdom that ran through his veins like a drug filling his heart with joy and song; it made him whole.

The lone figure of the gravedigger Steine came into view once again as they neared the compound. As they drew closer, the howling, barking, and snarling broke the silence as before. One of the dogs, a massive beast with black fur, jumped up at the wooden fence, biting bits out, scratching it with its claws, trying to get out, trying to escape.

'They know animals, they know when somthin ain't right,' Steine said as Maude and The Ripper approached.

'I don't pay you to tell me how my dogs do or don't feel, is that understood, Steine? Where have you put that body I gave you?'

'Over there, ma'am.' Steine pointed out a freshly dug grave, the top layer of earth had already been disturbed. 'Birds 'ave already pecked the skin from his face, then the rats. Only been in the ground a while, but they don't take long. The smell of rotting flesh you see, carries on the wind for miles.'

Maude walked the short distance to the grave and leaned over to inspect it. 'Do you want to take a look?' she asked The Ripper.

'No need, he's not going anywhere,' The Ripper replied, his dark humour making her smile.

Maude walked back towards Steine. 'Get the cages open. You had better stay here, they don't take well to strangers,' Maude said to The Ripper.

The Ripper knew the beasts had wind of him and he had no trouble in staying behind. *If they find Elsbeth before me, that will be disappointing, but I'm content she will meet with quite a horrific end.*

Maude entered the pen as eight huge dogs circled her, whining and jumping up at her, trying to lick her skin.

'They see ma'am as the pack leader, they won't let anyone near her rip 'em to pieces if they tried,' Steine shouted across to The Ripper.

Maude bent down and gave the dogs the sheet from Elsbeth's bed. There was a frenzy of barking, howling, and baring of their teeth as they clambered over each other, all wanting to sniff the scent of the prey.

'What if she changes her clothes? Will the dogs lose the trail?' The Ripper asked.

Maude laughed. 'No, how little you understand. They hunt by her smell, not what she's wearing. 'She stood up, got them all to sit and wait, then came the command. 'Find,' Maude shouted at them in a stern and gruff voice.

The dogs dashed out of the compound and towards the asylum, sweeping across the grass, yelping and barking, focused on the hunt.

'When they find her, will they corner or kill her?' The Ripper asked, wanting that final moment for himself.

'They are trained to seek out the prey, and once they have it, I've taught them to let their natural behaviour, their basic instinct, take over, which is—to kill. They are, after all, hunters, so I believe in allowing them the excitement of doing what they are born to do. I have to admit I enjoy watching them attack without mercy or hesitation, tearing into the flesh of a doomed being. The screams and hollering of the victim are delicious.'

'Indeed, but don't forget there are two people on the run, and usually, they would stick together. However, I think this time they have split up. Giving them more of a chance that one would make it out, and if I'm right, she's on her own.

Which leaves her accomplice, the guard who brought her in. So we will have to find him.'

'I wouldn't concern yourself too much on that front, Ignatius will have given the order to put the asylum in lockdown so that all exits will be cut off. This accomplice will soon be caught, and if I know my brother, he will have him strung up like game in one of the solitary cells before too long, where he will no doubt extract a confession out of him. Now let's get back inside and see if my lovies have picked up the scent.'

Steine watched them leave quietly, smiling. *Every dog has its day, ma'am, and yours is comin.'*

CHAPTER 59

Abberline quickly made his way back through winding passageways, the walls stained and stank of damp and stagnant water. He had to find the Asylum Inspector, Lawson, and tell him why he was here. If not, he had no other option but to let Governor Crane know everything. Crane's self-preservation and greed should be enough to get him onside. Abberline knew he couldn't trust Crane, although he knew sometimes you had to take risks, and this was one of those moments. He hoped that once Crane realised that he had employed an insane killer who was wanted for several murders, he would be forced to work with him to save his own neck.

Abberline passed several other guards along the route. They were searching for Elsbeth, shouting out to one another to look everywhere. 'She can't have got far. Keep looking, lads. We need to find her'.

Still in his guard's uniform, he was hurriedly given a description of Elsbeth and asked if he had seen her, to which he replied he hadn't. However, he said he would help join the search as soon as he could, giving them a false hope. He kept looking along the way for the inspector, but he was nowhere to be seen, and it wasn't long until he found himself back outside the office of the governor. He knocked and quickly entered, waiting for Crane to address him as he sat behind his desk. As Crane lifted his head, Abberline noticed he seemed pleased to see him, which worried him.

'Sir, I have been trying to locate the Asylum Inspector Dr Lawson, who, as you are aware, was here to perform his appraisal. Unfortunately, I have been unable to track him down. I wanted him here to bear witness to what I am about to tell you, but given he can't be found, I have no choice but to inform you of who I am and what I am doing here at Lidgate.'

Abberline was oblivious to the fact that Crane already knew about him and Elsbeth, having found out from his sister, who had told him. But Crane didn't know why Lidgate Manor. Or why they were posing as a guard, and an insane woman.

'Please continue, the stage is all yours,' Crane said.

'My name is not Baines and I am not a guard. I am Inspector Frederick Abberline of Scotland Yard, and I have been acting undercover with the woman I brought in here to bring to justice the most prolific killer I have known, who is hiding within these very walls. I must ask you to do the right thing and assist me by instructing your staff to search and detain him until I can arrange transportation back to London for him to stand trial.'

Crane leaned forward, his hands tightly clasped in front of him, realising that if this was true, Abberline could not find out about his sister's crime. He could not lose Maude to the hangman's noose for killing Lawson. Crane needed to know more. 'And who, pray tell, is this prolific killer you speak of? As you have already admitted, you also lied, pretending to be a guard, and then fooled me into employing you at the asylum. How can I believe a word you say? And yet you expect me to accept you are a police officer. Well, if this is the case, then show me proof.'

'I do not have my identification card at present, but I assure you that my position will become clear to you soon. We do not have time to argue about this, Governor. Every second we waste talking about it, the killer has a chance of getting away again.'

'Again, you say you had an opportunity before to catch your man, and you let him escape. And now you want my help and expect me to trust you, which I am finding it very hard to do at this point. So I ask you again, who is this person you make such accusations about?'

'You know him as Dr James Patterson, the resident physician of Lidgate Manor. However, he is known to me and the police as The Ripper. His real name and description remain a mystery to me, as anyone who has seen him has been killed before we can obtain anything.'

Crane became uncomfortable at the revelation. *'Anyone who has seen him has been killed.'* He let Abberline continue for the moment.

'The real Dr Patterson died some time ago from an illness. The Ripper somehow learned about this, probably by reading it in a newspaper obituary, and deliberately infiltrated the family home, Fox Hall in Surrey. Dr Patterson's widow, Camilla, and The Ripper became lovers. He gains the trust of women easily yet harbours a twisted and deep hate for them. Some will mistakenly perceive him as sincere, but he is extremely manipulative and has no sense of compassion or remorse.'

Crane started to feel worried and jealous at the same time. He questioned his sister's time with this man and whether she had fallen for his patter. He listened as Abberline continued.

'Things took a far darker turn as Camilla and her young daughter, Henrietta, noticed a marked change towards them, and they felt threatened and scared of this man who had worked his way into their home and lives. They were right. He killed the housemaid who was sent to get the police. He then went on to murder Camilla, ripping her body to pieces, and suspending it with ropes above her bed, and burying her thirteen-year-old daughter alive.'

Crane got up from the desk and walked over to the window, his hands joined behind his back. 'Earlier, you said *assist us* in finding this…this Ripper. So there is another? The woman you smuggled in here, pretending to be insane and committed to Lidgate. A woman by the name of Hargreaves. How on earth you got Judge Titus Voss to sign off on this preposterous charade is beyond me. We are searching the place for her now. You know she killed a guard? We found his body in one of the steam chambers. I believe, poisoned by the empty syringe she clumsily left behind in a rush to conceal her crime.'

'She had no option it was self-defence, she works under my protection. At the time, she thought it was The Ripper, but it turned out to be Harker, who was about to assault her. Any woman would have done the same, and I wager a few more will come forward with the same story. 'She is…innocent,' he paused, choosing his words carefully. He still didn't want to let Crane know she was trying to get away and return with help.

'This all seems far-fetched to me, inspector, if that is who you are. Why have I not heard of any of these stories about this killer, you call The Ripper, eh?'

'You would not have heard of them because Scotland Yard does not want the press to get hold of them until they are ready. We don't want this maniac warned only to disappear. You want proof? The time you caught me in the restricted area when I first arrived. A woman inmate had been mutilated in one of the cells. You saw it with your own eyes.'

'Nonsense man, I told you at the time that they turn on each other, it's not evidence that this bogeyman you speak of exists,' Crane replied.

'I've seen The Ripper's handiwork, and I can tell you it was him without any doubt. Get the Asylum Inspector, Dr Lawson, here, and let's see what he has to say about all this. If he agrees with me, I will tell him to shut this place down with immediate effect.

Abberline's tone changed. 'You and your sister are the ones who need to be locked up. The way you run this place is worse than the darkest prison. You will have to answer to Dr Lawson, he, in turn, will levy charges against you for the cruel, barbaric acts you have committed against people who need care, not beating and keeping them in appalling conditions.'

'We run a tight ship here and we have to discipline these inmates. Lest you forget, they are mad and would kill us in an instant given half a chance. They need harsh rules to follow, not some cosy fireside chat, or we will have chaos. We had no problems until lately, but I intend to get us back on an even keel before long, *Mr Policeman*. We do here what we need to do, and don't take kindly to outsiders telling us differently.'

Crane was incensed at Abberline's criticism, but he couldn't tell him that Lawson was dead, killed by his sister and dumped in a shallow grave for the animals to eat. Yet there is something else more pressing: if Abberline were telling the truth about Dr Patterson being The Ripper, there was a far greater concern. *'Anyone who has seen him has been killed.'* His thoughts returned to Maude.

'Nothing had better happen to Elsbeth, I'm warning you, Crane, if even a hair on her head is touched. You'll answer to me.'

'Oh really, inspector. Your nosy little Miss Hargreaves will be found very soon, don't you fret none. My sister has released her beauties to seek her out, and trust me, they will find her, and when they do,' he licked his lips sneering.

'What do you mean, Crane?' Abberline asked.

'She'll find out soon enough, inspector. She will hear them before she sees them, a pack of highly trained dogs just right for this occasion, and if she resists...well, let's just say there won't be enough of her left to fill a bucket.'

269

Abberline went to grab him, but Crane moved swiftly to the side, and unknown to him, had picked up an object off the top of his desk and struck Abberline hard on the side of the head. Abberline looked at Crane as he felt warm blood slowly trickling down the side of his face, then fell to the floor.

CHAPTER 60

Elsbeth studied the map according to the route marked out by Abberline. She knew they would seal off any exits, so she had to be fast. She could hear the distant voices of men calling out orders and running along the stone floors, the opening and slamming of doors, shouting, and the piercing noise of whistles blowing when one of them thought they had discovered something of significance. She knew a lot now depended on her. She had to get out and bring Detective Collins and as many police officers back as fast as possible.

She reached the fork where the passageway divided, one going to the boiler room and the other to the kitchens. The route was marked with an arrow indicating that she should head towards the kitchens down a staircase, then towards the back of the room, where some small steps led down to the basement and a door to the outside.

The gate where provisions were brought into the asylum was only a few feet along a gravel path, and then she would be outside the compound. She then needed to run across some open land and into the cover of the trees. Elsbeth crouched into the shadows behind her and slowly moved down the spiral stairs. Holding onto the iron railing, she was led down into the main kitchen area and descended as quietly as she could. She turned her head, looking back up the flight she had traversed, the voices now almost upon her.

'Hurry, lads, she ain't far, hurry before them beasts catch up.'

Elsbeth wondered what they meant as she reached the bottom rung and entered a large square room. In the centre was a substantial rectangular table where food preparation was carried out. To the left was a pine dresser with cupboards below for linen and above shelves containing plates, cups, and saucers on the far wall. To the right was the cooker, a huge black wrought-iron stove fuelled by coal. It had three main ovens, two large ovens on either side, and a medium-sized one in the middle.

On top sat three smaller iron plates for pans and a hot plate for the copper kettle that was sitting ready. Above were two roll-back covers where food for the Governor and his sister was kept warm before serving. A large, deep pan containing a grey, water-like liquid inside was on one side of the stove, made especially for the inmates. It reminded her of a type of gruel she had seen in the workhouses, but this had no substance to it and smelled of rotting meat it made her want to vomit.

She looked around for the set of steps that would take her down to the basement, finding them in the far right-hand corner of the room just next to a dumbwaiter, a small platform inside a housing operated by a system of ropes and pulleys. The shouts of the guards in the background seemed to fade in and out like the waves of an incoming tide, replaced by another sound, something more ominous. Snapping, growling, and barking like thunder came from a pack of animals barrelling down the asylum corridors. *Dogs.*

They were fast, and as soon as she had registered what they were, they were almost upon her. Their biting and gnawing at each other, yelps, and howls became closer and closer. They were hungry for a kill, hungry for her.

She knelt, hiding behind one of the sides of the large

rectangular table in the centre of the kitchen. But the scrambling of paws and snarling seemed to pass overhead by some chance, some card of fortune; she had been given a lifeline, a cloak of invisibility. Until the snarl of a large beast crept down the spiral staircase, sniffing the air as it descended. Its low growl sent a chill through her as she edged her way further round to the top end of the table. Elsbeth sensed the beast stop at the bottom of the stairs, waiting, looking to pick up her scent. She gradually leaned around the corner of the table to take a look. If she knew where the thing was, she might have a chance to make a run for it. She could use the revolver Abberline had given to her, but if she did this, everyone nearby would know where she was, and any chance of escaping would be over.

She first caught sight of its hindquarters, of jet-black matted fur. The dog was huge, its hind legs stood with its paws spread out, with long claws like the talons of a bird of prey, projecting out like razors. She hung her head for a second, not knowing what to do. When she looked back up, she saw that the animal had gone. She quickly slid back round to the side, every fibre of her body alert, listening for it. Just to her right were the steps down to the basement. *Could she make it? Was she quick enough?* Her life depended on it, one false move, one wrong judgment, and she would be dead. *Where was this - this creature?*

As she shuffled her body into position, ready to dash for the steps, she saw a large shadow on the opposite wall, its body low, moving along the side towards her, its breathing now heavy and hard. It was now inches away from where she was hiding. She looked about for anything, but there was nothing. *A kitchen and not even a knife;* she froze as the beast was getting closer and closer, so near she could smell its rancid breath.

She put her arm up and with her hand searched desperately on top of the table one way then another for anything to use.

As the snout of the animal protruded past the corner, its lips folded back, revealing a row of large white teeth dripping with saliva. Frantic, her fingers made contact with something. She took hold of a pan handle and threw it across the room as hard as possible. There was a loud bang as it landed against a shelf full of plates, smashing them on impact. It was enough to instantly divert the dog's attention toward the noise. Elsbeth lunged forward, falling at first, grazing her hands. Pulling herself up off the floor she ran with all her might towards the steps.

The dog quickly realised he had been tricked and turned back on himself, jumping towards her as the rest of the pack hearing the commotion hurried down the spiral staircase, baying for blood. At the very last second, Elsbeth changed her mind and propelled herself into the dumbwaiter, the dog's teeth just missing her face. She pulled at the rope, and the contraption started to move down as the pack tried to pile in, one on top of the other, snapping, snarling, howling in a frenzy, biting at the rope which became frayed, Elsbeth kept pulling faster and faster as the fibres snapped, the dumbwaiter started to wobble then without warning dropped smashing to the bottom, throwing Elsbeth onto the basement floor. Then came a voice: 'Move and you die.'

CHAPTER 61

When Maude and The Ripper returned to the asylum, The Ripper told Maude that he had had to collect his black bag from his consulting room.

'There is no need, my dear. I have your belongings safe in my office. Come, we shall go to retrieve them together. I have some plans I wish to discuss with you, and there is nothing further we can do until my dogs do their job.'

Before they could move towards Maude's office, Ignatius Crane stepped out of the shadows, standing before them, his eyes gleaming with mistrust.

'Ah, sister and Dr Patterson, I do believe, eh? It seems, dear sister, that you were right. The guard who brought the woman in here, Miss Elsbeth Hargreaves, is a fraud, and this Baines is no guard he is an inspector working for Scotland Yard. He told me himself before I knocked him out, and is now languishing in a cell.'

'Yes, brother, I will send word for Steine to round them up and get them back to the pound immediately, but what of the woman, brother?'

'The guards detained her, trying to escape through the kitchens. They should have let the dogs have her, but she could prove useful. She will join Abberline, and now we will have two birds to bake in a pie. I am so looking forward to some quality time with each of them.' Crane could hardly disguise his joy at the prospect.

The Ripper wanted to know how much Abberline had told Crane, if it were too much, then he would have to take evasive action himself. 'So did this Abberline say why he was here with this woman, what was their purpose for fraudulently gaining access to the asylum?'

Crane didn't want to tell The Ripper what Abberline had discussed, he didn't trust him. He knew Abberline was a policeman, and if allowed, he would have his sister arrested for murder, and Lidgate Manor would be closed down for good. He could not allow that to happen and would deal with the impostors and this so-called Ripper himself. So he decided to keep up the pretence for a bit longer.

'No, he did not tell me anything. He said it was official business and demanded to speak with Dr Lawson, and only *he* would be privy to his orders. As we all know, Dr Lawson is no longer alive, thanks to my sister's actions. I have since detained Inspector Abberline, along with the Hargreaves woman, until I have time to deal with them myself. Suffice to say, sister, your error of judgement will then disappear—along with them.'

The Ripper could not let Abberline and Elsbeth talk, the only way was to dispose of them both before Crane got to them. However, for that, he would need his trusted black bag. 'You seem to have everything in hand, Governor, so if you do not mind, I need to take my leave and collect a rather important personal artefact from your sister's office.

Crane noticed how keen The Ripper was to get away and knew that if Abberline had told the truth about him, there would be three people to dispose of, and the sooner he told his sister, the better.

'I just need to have a private word with my sister, so please attend to your urgent matter, I will not keep her long.'

Crane watched to make sure The Ripper had left, then turned to his sister, grabbing her arm tightly, pulling her towards him.

'If Abberline is telling me the truth, he and his sidekick are not the only two impostors in here. It transpires that they have been tracking down a man responsible for multiple murders, a man they call The Ripper. He told me this Ripper apparently killed and butchered three women in Brighton last year, then recently went on to kill a widow, her daughter, and their housemaid in Surrey. He then wrote to me accepting the job as a Resident Physician at Lidgate, the position we had originally offered to her husband before he passed. Do you have any idea who that might be, Maude?'

'No, brother, I don't,' Maude said sheepishly.

'Dr James Patterson, my *dear sister*, the man you have taken to be your fancy man, has come to this place to hide from the police and evade justice, under an assumed identity, and he will bring us down in the process. Everything we have worked for and built up here at Lidgate will be for nothing. And *sister*, the man you killed, when they find his body, you will hang for it, make no mistake, accident or not.'

'Brother, I don't…I don't know what to say, I…I,' Maude tried to implore her brother to hear her.

'Now you listen to me and listen good. You've made a fool of yourself. He's not interested in an old shrivelled-up spinster like you. He's using you, don't you see? I, for one, am not going to sit back and watch all I've worked for all these years and my nest egg go out the window for your stupid dalliances with this maniac. Do you understand? Pull yourself together, and get back to your office. He has no idea we know, I want you to kill him, do you hear, kill him now. I'm going to deal with Abberline and this Hargreaves woman, and I'll make sure it's done properly, then we'll dump the bodies for the pigs to eat.'

'Yes, brother, I understand. I'm sorry for my foolhardy

behaviour. I had no intention of causing you or, indeed, us any harm. I have become blind and have acted as an imbecile. I must apologise. Know that I love you. Please forgive me, brother.' Maude pleaded with her brother, as Crane pushed her away, unconvinced of his sister's sudden guilt and regret.

'There has been trickery at play here, so you have to prove now where your loyalty lies, Maude. You have to dispose of this Ripper, bring a piece of him to me so I can see you have done as I have asked, and let that be the end of it. Meet me back in my office in one hour, is that clear?'

'Yes, brother, one hour.' Maude turned her heart pounding and headed towards her office as Crane's eyes narrowed in rage and suspicion.

CHAPTER 62

Maude arrived at her office and went in to find The Ripper sitting at her desk, looking magnificent, young, handsome, strong, independent, and above all, ruthless, all the qualities she so admired in a person. But he was more than that he represented a way out for her, away from her brother, whom she had become weary of. For the first time in her life, she felt something she didn't think she would ever feel: real love and hope.

'So what was so important that your brother wanted to talk to you privately?' The Ripper asked, picking up a silver letter opener from her desk, placing the point on the blotter.

Maude walked over to the desk and sat down on one of the chairs opposite him, smiling. She rested her hands on her lap.

'Well, Jack, my love, you are intelligent and have probably already deduced that the conversation circled mainly around you. My brother has found out who you are from Abberline. The Inspector from Scotland Yard told Ignatius everything about you, what you have done and why you are here.'

The Ripper pressed down harder on the knife's point, pushing it into the blotting paper.

'Hmm, I see…and of course, you didn't let on that you already knew, and I had told you who I was after you killed Inspector Lawson in my consulting room.'

'No, my love, why on earth should I do such a thing? That I will take to my grave, you have my solemn promise, he will never know what we discussed that day. I have come to despise my brother, and it is only by finding you and discovering real love that I now see him for what he is and…the things he made me do all those years ago.' Maude stood up from the chair and walked behind him, placing her hands on his shoulders.

'I never in my wildest dreams thought that one so hand-some, so powerful would ever look at me, an old woman past her prime, let alone reciprocate the love that I harbour inside for you. It pains me when I am away from you, Jack. We are bound together, you and me. I know we are destined to be one, and to carry on the work you mentioned when you first came here.'

The Ripper leaned back in the chair. 'I doubt your brother will take kindly to your proposals. I think he intends for me to be silenced along with Abberline and Elsbeth, who are now languishing in a cell waiting for your brother.'

Maude took her hands off his shoulders and walked away towards the back of the room. 'I trust you, Jack, and there is nothing I want hidden between us as we move forward. I loathe the way my brother talks to me, belittling me, I can honestly say I hate him. He can never understand what we have, and I know he suspects us, Jack. I know he is jealous of what we have. We must strike before he does, he won't stop at getting rid of Abberline and Elsbeth. He wants…he wants you dead, for me to kill you, and bring a piece of you back to him to prove I am still…still his. I need to show you something, I know you will understand.'

The Ripper got up from his chair and went over to join Maude. He watched her slide a drape across a rail to reveal a door, then feel along the top of the frame, retrieve a small key, place it in the lock, and open it.

The Ripper, standing by her, was greeted by the smell of

death, a sweet almond scent overpowering the room, mixed with a veil of dust. A long table was formally laid out for supper, and seated around it, ten dead embalmed guests were positioned as if they were conversing with one another.

'These are my friends. I come here of an evening and we talk about the day. I tell them how I hate my brother and how, since meeting you, it has changed my life. They don't judge or argue with me, they listen and *only* offer advice if I ask. They have wanted to meet you for a while now, and they are so happy to see you at last, and the *ladies*, hmm, they are saying how handsome you are. Now, ladies, don't make me blush,' Maude told them out loud.

The Ripper looked at the scene before him and wondered how Abberline and Elsbeth would look sitting there—he smiled.

'So where did your *friends* come from, Maude?'

'Why, from here, the asylum, of course. They were inmates, if you can call them that, who were lost, damaged, and useless to anyone. So I merely helped the process along somewhat. After all, who would miss them? I saw a way for them to become valuable members of society once more, to debate, hold conversation on all manner of topics, eat and feast like Gods, then, after, we dance and dance until the early hours of the morning.' Maude took hold of The Ripper's arm.

'Oh, Jack, my love, don't you see what fun we will have? All I need to do is get rid of that brother of mine, and all this is ours.'

The Ripper turned his attention to what he had come here for. 'Where is my bag, Maude? You said you had the black bag here. I need it to finish off Abberline and Elsbeth, they are mine, not your brothers, not anyone else's. We have history, and theirs is about to come to an abrupt end.'

Maude went over to a small pine dresser with a black lace

cover over the top of it. She bent down, pulled out one of the drawers, took out the bag, and handed it to The Ripper.

'Now, my love, go and do your work, then come back to me here, where we will consummate our feelings for one another as couples should.' Maude grinned at the prospect.

The Ripper opened the bag, checking that nothing had been removed. For a brief moment he touched a knife handle with a long, thin, serrated edge, the type a surgeon might use, feeling excited and aroused at reuniting with it.

'Do you think I want anything to do with you? You disgust me. You and your brother are both insignificant cockroaches in my world. You could never understand my journey, my work, or what rises within me.'

Maude looked visibly shocked and hurt at his words, trying to justify why he would be saying such terrible things.

'My love, what are you saying? What has gotten into you? Have you not heard a word I have said? I have laid my heart open to you.'

'You are a sad old woman easily pleased by a smile there and kindness here, and yet you think someone like me would ever be interested. No, looking at you makes me want to retch, and you have outlived your purpose. There was never any *us*, never any future; whatever fantasy you created in your mind was your own.'

'I killed for you, I killed Dr Arthur Lawson! He was going to expose you. I protected you…I helped you.' The gravity of the situation started to dawn on Maude as tears welled up, spilling out over her wrinkled skin.

The Ripper's eyes rolled over black, his rage funnelling through his body.

'Lawson died by your hand, call it a gift if you like, but I took enough of him to be satisfied. You chose to kill him because you thought that I cared?' He laughed out loud. 'I don't care about you, I never have. I see you as a means to an end, and that is all. You are nothing to me, so go back to your dead friends as that's the only offer you'll ever get—poor, pathetic, barren Maude. Or maybe your brother, I'm sure he would be happy to rekindle that flame you alluded to. Keep it in the family.'

Maude's tears quickly turned to anger as she rushed towards The Ripper. The realisation that he had been stringing her along all this time, taking her for a fool, was too much to bear.

'I'll kill you, how could you, how could you…my brother was right about you.' She threw herself at him, landing in his arms, her face changing from one of rage to pain. The Ripper stood back, watching her look down to see the knife he had carefully taken out of his bag protruding from her stomach.

Time seemed to stand still for a moment, then she dropped to the floor like a stone rolling onto her back, still clinging to life. Her look softened towards him as she gazed up at him, raising one arm. She held her hand out, hoping for his, for one last desperate sign of affection. The Ripper bent down, stroked her cheek with his hand, then took the knife out of her. She sighed deeply as the pain sang through her body. He paused briefly, then plunged it back in, cutting deep around the heart. She tried to speak, tried to call his name, but she was choking on her own blood as death wrapped its wings around her.

The Ripper put his hand into the cavity and tore out her beating heart, smiled, and stood back up. 'Don't worry, Maude, I'll make sure your brother gets something to remember you by.' He wiped the knife clean on her dress, put it back in his bag, then picked her body off the floor, dumping it on top of the table, and then left the room. He had unfinished business to take care of.

CHAPTER 63

Ignatius Crane was growing impatient. It had been a while since he sent his sister to take care of The Ripper and put Lidgate's interests first. He collected a small knife, placed it in his coat pocket, and walked the few corridors to Maude's office. He noticed the door to her office was slightly ajar, which was very uncommon, so he proceeded with caution. The room was quiet, there didn't seem to be anyone inside, just the glass cases with stuffed creatures looking out, their eyes wide, their last look frozen in time. He stepped in, pulled the knife from his pocket, and held it tightly. The room was dimly lit, with only one oil lamp flickering away on the wall. He listened for the slightest movement or noise, his senses on full alert as he continued around and behind the desk.

To the right, he noticed a drape had been pulled open across a bar, revealing a smaller door which had also been left slightly ajar. He went towards it, holding the knife out in front of him, weighing up in his mind whether to call for his sister or not. If he said anything and someone else was in here, it would forewarn them. He would have to be careful, he would have to be quick, just thrust, wound or kill.

As he went through to the next room it was not the dining table all laid out complete with dead guests around it that shocked him, but his sister, discarded on top of it. Her arms out to the side of her as if she had been crucified, her face to one side, blood trickling out of her mouth and onto the white lace table cover. Her chest had been ripped open, a large cavity where her heart would have been, now just a gaping bloody hole. The sudden realisation that the person he had known all of his life was now dead before him, butchered and left like garbage. There were no last words of love and affection, nor loyalty, trust, or obedience, just the dark silence that death brings. He stood over her corpse, looking at her mouth stretched open, her scream frozen across her face for all to see.

The feeling of guilt and rage consumed him, for it was he who had sent her to kill The Ripper, now she lay here, a vision he would never forget. And yet she had betrayed him for another. The Ripper, who had come here under a false identity to hide and in doing so had lied to him and his sister, had in turn stolen her affection away from him. This perhaps was a greater crime than the ones he stood accused of. His sister, whom he had known in flesh and blood for all this time, bonded by true love, true desire, now lay in tatters, nothing more than a mutilated carcass of the woman he once adored.

He grabbed one of her hands, her thin, delicate fingers now limp and cold, which gave nothing back, as he fell to his knees, promising revenge. Hate was now the fuel he needed to continue his life, as he vowed they would be united in the next world as they had been in this. But for now, he wanted answers about where this Ripper was and how he could discover him, and he knew exactly where to find this information. He would take his time there and make every tiny little cut last an eternity. Agony and suffering for Abberline and Elsbeth would now reach new heights; he would personally see to it and enjoy every moment. Their pleas for mercy, their cries for help, would fall on deaf ears, only the night air would record their howls of pain as they boomed out of the solitary cell.

Ignatius Crane picked himself up from the floor and glanced at his sister one last time before leaving. He looked down at her and, stroking her forehead, looked around at the embalmed bodies seated at the table and smiled.

'Don't worry, my dear sister, I will be back, and you will live again. You will sit at this table, and you will never age, and never want for anything. Death will not separate us, it will unite us in a new beginning.' He bent down and kissed her gently on her lips. Sleep now, my dear sweet Maude, for tonight we will feast upon the head of the man that took you from this world.'

CHAPTER 64

Abberline had been strung up by his wrists from the metal bar that ran across the width of the cell, the tips of his feet brushing the floor. He had been in one of these before when Governor Crane had caught him snooping around. That seemed some time ago now as he waited for Crane to return. He knew that their next meeting would be far less amiable than their first.

He was on his own in the cell, usually there would be others, all packed in like sardines. People died from the conditions, dead bodies curled up on the floor, undiscovered until the stench began to be too much to bear. Guards would come in, beat the inmates back and then move the deceased to a corner of the room for the rats. There was no mourning, no kind words said and no grave to acknowledge the existence of a human life. It was just a short trip on a wooden trolley to the back of the asylum and a shallow pit covered over with damp, worm-infested earth, and left to rot.

It wasn't long before he heard the gate opening and people coming down the steps towards where he was being held. More than one voice he could make out, as well as a woman's groan as they stopped outside the door. There was a jangle of keys, then the turn of the lock, *click, click*, and the cell door swung open. Two burly men dragged Elsbeth by her feet, one then holding her up under her arms as the other tied a leather strap around her wrists and hauled her up to the same height as Abberline. Her disguise was now gone as her long black hair, now dirty and knotted, hung over her face, and her chin rested on her chest. He noticed the nurse's uniform she had taken was torn, as if something had ripped at the fabric.

One of the men turned to Abberline. 'Guvnor be down here soon. I don't reckon she has much chance of making it out of here in one piece, let alone you. If there is anything left after, we'll be back for seconds. We ain't fussy.' Both men chuckled, slamming the door shut behind them, and then the familiar *click, click* of the lock.

'Elsbeth, are you alright? Can you hear me, Elsbeth?'

'Abberline...Abberline, is that you? Where are we?' Elsbeth said, her voice weak.

'We're in one of the cells. Crane caught me by surprise, knocked me out. Why aren't you halfway to Surrey? What the hell happened?'

'I was going through the kitchen that you had marked on the map. I could hear men shouting...guards, I think... Then, I heard another sound...barking. That bitch sister of the governor had set a pack of dogs to hunt me down. They found me. I was so close to being their next meal, but I jumped into one of those dumbwaiters.

The dogs kept coming, trying to get down the shaft like they were possessed. One of them started biting at the rope holding the contraption. Anyway, it snapped and I fell to the bottom, I got clear, and when I managed to get back to my feet, I found a gun pointing at my head and a voice telling me not to move. The next thing I knew, I'm being dragged into here. And what about you, how come you ended up here as well?' Elsbeth said, blowing away some loose strands of hair away from her face.

'I told him, Governor Crane everything about The Ripper,

the murders he's committed, and myself being a Police Inspector for Scotland Yard. But then out of my view, he smashes an object across my head, and then here I am.' Abberline shook his head to try and stop the flow of blood going into his eye that was still trickling down from the wound.

'Once he knew the truth, and that you were working for me and were smuggled in here under the guise of an insane patient, our fates were sealed. Crane wouldn't let some killer like The Ripper come between him, his sister, and the small fortune, which they have undoubtedly amassed here over the years. Greed, corruption, and untold cruelty on a scale unheard of are enough motives for those two.'

'I'm sorry, Abberline, I didn't get out. I'm sorry for letting you down. Now what? We're going to be sliced up and left to rot in some god-forsaken part of this hellhole.' Elsbeth wept, as the stress fell on her like a dead weight.

'It's fine, Elsbeth, it's not your fault. We knew this would always be difficult inside an asylum; what was I thinking of? If anyone is to blame, it's me, so please don't hold yourself accountable for any of this.'

'It's been good working with you, and I wouldn't change anything. We had a chance of getting this maniac. I hope that if this is the end, someone takes up the fight to catch this monster, so our work has not been in vain.' Elsbeth breathed in and thought back to happier times as a child playing hide and seek with her Nonna amongst the vines in Italy as she waited for the inevitable.

'I'm sure they will, Elsbeth, and thank you for being a colleague and a ...' Before Abberline could finish the sentence, they heard the *click, click* of the key turning in the lock, realising their time was up. The door then swung open, followed by footsteps behind them.

CHAPTER 65

'Look, Crane, it's not too late. You know if you kill us, you will have even more to answer for. I've told you I'm an Inspector with Scotland Yard, and it's not you I'm here for, it's The Ripper we want. Help us now, and I'll talk to the judge when he is considering sentencing for you and your sister.'

The footsteps got closer, an arm reached around Elsbeth's neck, then a flash of steel. She turned her head away, not waiting to see death approach. Then, without warning, she felt herself drop to the floor, quickly followed by Abberline.

'You two need to get out of here fast. Governor Crane won't be long behind me.'

Abberline helped Elsbeth off the floor to her feet as she brushed the dirt off her dress.

'Who the hell are you?' Abberline asked.

'My name is Steine. I work for them. I overheard her, Maude, talking to some gent, called him Jack, about setting the dogs on you ma'am and that they had you, sir, locked up. I've had enough of how she speaks to me, and it's time she and her brother got what was coming to them.'

Elsbeth looked over to the man. 'Where is Crane and his sister now? And the gent, the man Maude called Jack, do you know where he is? It's very important. He's known as The

Ripper, a cold, calculating killing machine, who is extremely dangerous and has butchered, mutilated and tortured a number of women, and we have to stop him.'

Steine looked back at Elsbeth. 'All I know is you need to get out and as far away from this place as you can, and don't ever come back here, not if you value your life.'

'I can't do that, I am afraid. I am Inspector Abberline with Scotland Yard in London, and we came to this place for one reason: to infiltrate it, and bring The Ripper to justice.'

Elsbeth looked behind them quickly, checking no one was coming through the door.

'The inspector is telling you the truth, we have no option but to find this monster and take him back with us before he kills again. Please help us you must have some idea where he might be. If he knows about us and who we really are, he's not going to risk another confrontation, when flight in this case, is easier than fight. He's going to try to get out, so where would he go? Think man, this is important.' Elsbeth snapped at Steine.

Steine rubbed the top of his head with his hand. 'Well, Crane would lock down the asylum exits, so the only other way out would be to make his way towards The Bell Tower. Not many people know, but there is temporary scaffolding on the outside of the tower as they repair the stone. He could access it from the inside, but the stairs are dangerous. If he makes it, there is a small window at the top that he could use to access the scaffolding. Then it's a straight climb down, taking him over the perimeter wall. If he makes it that far, he's in the wind and gone.'

Abberline and Elsbeth got ready to leave, thanking Steine for his help. They ran towards the exit from the cell up the stone steps through the gate and out into the corridor. 'Now all we have to do is stay hidden and try to find a way from inside to where The Bell Tower entrance is. If Steine is right and this is where The Ripper is heading, and we can get to the tower first, we've got him. The problem is I have no idea which way to go, and we can't exactly ask anyone the way.'

'So this might come in useful then?' Elsbeth handed Abberline a crumpled-up bit of paper, which he immediately recognised.

'The map, you kept it,' Abberline said, both grateful and relieved.

'Yes, and also this. Did they think to search me? Probably didn't think that women would know what to do with one of these.' Elsbeth handed over the revolver to Abberline, who smiled, checking the chamber, then held the gun up in front of him. 'I should have known, you never cease to amaze me, Elsbeth. Now let's go and get this monster—*one way or the other.*'

CHAPTER 66

Steine prepared to leave the cell and return to his hut on the asylum grounds. He was done working for such a place and had decided to pack his belongings and leave. He would tell the authorities what had been going on here to clear his name and show them the burial plots. At the very least, this awful, evil place would be shut down, and Crane would be arrested, charged, and hanged for his crimes. Then his conscience would be clear.

He went to walk out and close the door behind him when he felt the razor edge of a knife to his throat.

'No, no, not so quick, Steine, you and I need to have a little chat first.'

Steine knew that harsh voice could only belong to one man, Governor Ignatius Crane. His tone full of hate and anger, he spluttered, spitting on Steine's face as he spoke.

'I want to know what you have done with my two guests, and don't even think to deny it, or this will be the very last thing you hear. Do I make myself clear?' Crane said menacingly. 'I want to know why you let them go, Steine, what pack of lies they told you, and why, after all the years of loyal service, you choose to throw it all away, hmm?'

Steine felt Crane's grip tighten, and the edge of the blade

cut into his flesh, warm blood slowly flowing from the wound. 'I got fed up with being your sister's dogsbody, making me bury those people who done nothing wrong other than being sent here. You two as good as murdered them the way you've been treating people, worse than animals.'

'Oh really, Steine, when did you start having any morals? Don't think your hands are clean of this. As I remember, you did your job willingly, so it won't be just me they come for. And my sister is dead, so you had better start talking.'

'That policeman, Abberline, and the other one, Elsbeth, told me they would help me. They told me you and your mad sister would be held accountable, not me. But she's dead now, ain't she, most likely at the hands of The Ripper—the killer you gave a job to. Look, Governor, I just want to leave and get as far away as possible from this place. Let me go, you'll never hear from me again. I'll get a boat out from the coast, I'll not be back on these shores, just let me go, I'll tell you what you want to know.'

Crane moved the knife down Steine's back, the point now pressing into his spine. 'Oh, that's just like you, trying to save your worthless, pathetic life. Don't worry, I'm not going to kill you, but one slip of this blade and you'll never walk again, instead you'll have a life of sliding across floors like the slimy slug that you are. Now, where is the bastard that killed my sister, he has a dinner date to attend. And I want the other two, I want them all. Where are they?' Crane screamed into Steine's ear.

'I told the inspector and the woman to go to the old Bell Tower. That's where The Ripper will make his escape, it's the best way not to be seen.'

'This had better be the truth. If I let you go, I don't want ever to see your face again is that clear, Steine? If I even get a whiff of you, I'll come for you, make no mistake.'

'I ain't never comin back 'ere. I want rid of it forever. I told you the truth as God is my witness.' He felt the knife being taken away from his back as Crane pulled him around to face him. Crane said nothing, his pink eyes burrowing into him as if he were trying to look into his soul.

'It's alright, I believe you. Now you had better be on your way like a good little dog.'

As Steine went to walk out of the cell, Crane pulled him back around by his arm.

'It's good you told the truth, they say it sets a person free.' Crane smiled, his yellowed and blackened teeth grinning as he slashed the throat of Steine, who stood for a moment, then dropped. Crane watched him take his last breath, then deliberately walked over the body, wiping the soles of his shoes on him like a doormat before leaving and making his way swiftly towards The Bell Tower.

CHAPTER 67

Abberline and Elsbeth followed the map towards their destination, The Bell Tower at the other end of the asylum, as they ran through the various corridors and passages. A wave of voices, loud bangs, screams and yells could be heard from behind in the distance, coming their way. Abberline and Elsbeth stopped briefly to listen.

'What is that, Abberline?' Elsbeth said.

'I'm not sure, it sounds like a lot of them, and they are headed our way.' Abberline knew whatever it wasn't good, and one thing was for sure, they could not go back. 'We need to move fast.'

They turned into another corridor through a set of double doors, then found themselves just outside a large room with a number of tables lined up against each other in rows. Abberline looked at the map to check where they were.

'According to the map, this is a dining area with a small store room at the back.' Abberline pointed to where they were with his finger. 'If we go through this store room, there should be another door, then we should be at the bottom of The Bell Tower.'

'That noise is getting nearer, can't you hear?' Elsbeth said, looking around, trying to see if anything, or anyone was approaching.

'Come on through here,' Abberline unlocked one of the doors, putting the keys back in his pocket, letting Elsbeth pass. At the end of the corridor, there was movement. A large group of people shuffled toward him, a low murmuring coming from them as Abberline waited, wanting to see who they were. He kept one hand on the door as he peered into the dimly lit corridor until the first individual became visible. A tall, thin, gaunt man with long grey hair, wearing a dirty smock that covered his bony body down to the floor, revealed himself. His face was a picture of insanity, his eyes wild and fixed on Abberline, his thin lips stretched back over bleeding teeth that shut and closed, snapping at him.

There was an eerie silence as two women joined the man's side, dressed in the same way, both with an insane stare. One of them started to howl and hoot like an owl scratching at the air with her long yellow fingernails, hissing, turning her head to the side, then up and down, wailing. All were armed with long metal rods and what appeared to be wooden chair legs. The group started to advance towards him, hitting the side of the wall with the weapons, the chatter getting louder and louder as they got closer. Abberline carefully and slowly stepped back into the dining room, where Elsbeth waited.

'What is it, Abberline? Who's out there?' Elsbeth asked.

'He's let some of the inmates out, a load of them armed. Quick, we don't have long, let's move a couple of tables against the door, it might buy us some time.'

'Who let them out? Governor Crane?'

'No, The Ripper, he wants to cause a diversion while he makes good his escape. We need to act fast they are right on top of us.'

'You have your gun.'

'Yes, but there are too many of them, Elsbeth, we won't be able to shoot them all.'

Together, they started to slide two rectangular pine tables

against the doors as the group reached them on the other side. Now screaming and spitting, they hit the outside of the door as hard as they could with their weapons. The door started to groan and splinter as the force of the bodies pushing forward began to breach the barricade Abberline and Elsbeth had hastily built.

Abberline grabbed Elsbeth by the arm as he headed towards the back of the room and the small kitchen. The doors were smashed open revealing a horde of screaming, snarling people baying for their blood.

'Quickly, we need to get through to the other door,' Abberline shouted over the commotion.

Elsbeth slipped, crashing to the floor as the thin, gaunt man reached her, grabbing her hair, yanking it hard, screeching at her as the others caught up behind him. The man raised his arm, carrying a heavy metal pole as it descended towards Elsbeth's head, as a deafening bang rang out. The man's body jerked, then flew backwards into the crowd, his head covered in blood. Abberline fired his revolver into the air as a warning that he would shoot again if he had to, white smoke dancing out of the end of the barrel. Elsbeth scrambled to her feet. Abberline quickly reached into his pocket with his other hand and threw the keys as she ran past him and into the kitchen towards the back door.

The group stopped in their tracks, touching, feeling the man's face, wiping the blood from his wound, chattering, then sniggering to each other. The warning shot had made no difference, as they pushed forward. Abberline ran as fast as he could towards Elsbeth, who waited by the door. He turned and fired into the mass. One of them was hit and instantly dropped like a stone, causing the others to pile over the top.

Abberline and Elsbeth rushed through the exit, slamming the door behind them. He kicked it hard with his foot, wedging it into the frame. 'That will stop them,' he said. But there was no reply. He turned to see Ignatius Crane standing with a knife to Elsbeth's face.

'Drop the gun, inspector, or she's dead.'

CHAPTER 68

Crane shifted Elsbeth into the bottom of The Bell Tower with a firm grip around her neck. The Tower was eighty feet tall, made of stone and was in a great deal of disrepair, with some of the walls having large cracks and areas missing, letting the wind, rain, and leaves blow through. He pushed her roughly up a wooden staircase, which was starting to come away from the wall. It led up to the very top of the tower, where a small platform with a thin wooden guardrail housed the large brass bell inside a wheel with two ropes attached to it, reaching down to the bottom of the tower through a gap in the platform.

The way up to the platform was heavy going, and with no handrail to hang onto, it was a death trap. It was murky and cold as Crane inched his way up, firmly gripping Elsbeth. Every step saw more debris fall from above, as Elsbeth looked down towards Abberline with real fear in her eyes. 'You two are responsible for all of this. My Maude would still be alive if it weren't for you two coming here, lying your way in,' Crane shouted.

'We didn't kill your sister. The Ripper did. She was already dead the moment she met him; she just didn't realise it. Do yourself a favour, Crane, let Miss Hargreaves go, she serves you no purpose, and if you kill her you also die in the process.'

'Oh, boldly said Inspector, without your gun in hand, exactly how are you going to do that?'

'I don't have to do it myself, Crane. The state will hang you for this. I will personally see to it.'

'Well, I don't see any reinforcements. I suppose that was the plan for the little bitch here to get out and raise the alarm, eh? As they say Inspector, best laid plans and all that.' As Crane continued pulling Elsbeth up with him, the stairs groaned under their weight, a couple of boards came loose, falling away, with dust and nails following them to the bottom.

'Crane, I urge you not to go any further, it's a death trap. Come back down, and let's talk about this.'

'Listen to him, Crane. Do you want to die? Listen to what he's saying, the real enemy here is The Ripper, he killed your sister and many others, it's not you who we want,' Elsbeth pleaded.

Crane snorted. 'But there's just one small problem with that. He's not here, *is he*? My sister was a fool to think anyone other than me could love her, she betrayed me and paid the price for it. An eye for an eye, isn't that so, inspector? So someone needs to die, and at the moment, it's your little friend here.'

Crane, ignoring them, kept ascending, holding Elsbeth tighter, one step at a time, as the whole structure started creaking and snapping. The side of the staircase became unstable and shook, beginning to come away from the wall. Chunks of plaster dropped out and fell onto the floor below with a distant thud, as white powder flew up with the impact. Abberline had no choice but to follow, despite the obvious danger. He could see sweat pouring from Crane's pale white forehead as he struggled to take another step towards his goal. 'Crane, this is insane. Come back down, the whole thing's about to collapse.'

'Don't worry about that, Inspector. I would concern myself with this pretty little thing and how she will look if she should fall all broken and busted on the hard stone floor of this tower if you don't stop.' Crane pushed his face into Elsbeth's. 'Hmm, yes, beautiful thing you are, maybe I'll change my mind and keep you all to myself, hmm, I need a new…*partner*, would you like that?' he bellowed, shaking his head with excitement.

'I'd rather kill myself than have you touch me, you disgusting freak,' Elsbeth shouted back, twisting her face as far away from his as she could.

'Ha, we are so strong and rebellious, aren't we, dear? Well, let's see how long that lasts, shall we? If I were you, I would shut up, or you'll meet your maker sooner than planned.' Crane howled with laughter. He turned her around, facing him, then with one hand around her throat, pushed her back, stopping just at the edge of the stairs, her arms dropping to her sides. One more word out of you, and I'll throw you off like a rag doll.'

'Stop, don't do it, Crane, I'll do whatever you want, please.' Abberline was frightened, there was nothing he could do to help her. If Crane let go, she would fall to her death.

'Oh, how sweet he cares about you, dear,' Crane's face turned red with rage. One more problem with you…next time you're gone.' Crane pulled her back, turned her round, and put his arm around her neck like a vice.

Abberline had to keep following them up, whatever happened. Crane had lost his mind and was not going to listen to reason. He wondered if he should have returned for his revolver, but he knew he didn't have the time. 'Look, Crane, we can work this out. You don't get the man who killed your sister, this way.

Think about that. Don't you want him to pay for taking your Maude away from you, for lying and deceiving you? If he hadn't come to Lidgate, in the guise of a dead doctor whose wife and child he murdered, none of this would have happened, and your sister would still be alive.' Abberline watched but found it hard, it had become almost pitch black as Crane reached the top, just a few steps before the platform and the bell.

'Yes, why don't you listen to the inspector Ignatius?' Another voice came from the top, a calm, well-spoken person, his tall silhouette stepping out of the dark.

'You!' Crane growled as he and Elsbeth finally reached the bell platform at the very top.

'Now that's no way to greet a friend, Ignatius. Why don't you let me take care of everything, then you can get back to your sister, as I'm sure you have a lot to catch up on, once, of course, you have stuffed her rotting corpse.'

Elsbeth heard the other voice but couldn't see the speaker as Crane still had her in a neck lock, facing towards Abberline, who was still carefully navigating his way up the stairs, but she knew who it was.

'It's The Ripper, Crane, who killed your sister, he's here right behind you. Do you really think he will let any of us out alive?'

'I told you to keep quiet,' Crane snapped, trying to turn Elsbeth to see him.

'No need to exert yourself, Ignatius, save that for later, hmm. Now, who do we have here, the delightful Elsbeth Hargreaves and the Inspector Abberline of The Yard, no less. Well, we do seem to keep missing each other, don't we, but hey ho. I trust you found the widow Camilla Paterson and her daughter, as I left them. I enjoyed my time with them, particularly at the end, I have to say. Oh, and not forgetting their poor little servant Annie…at least I think that was her name?'

Crane shifted his body round, but it was too dark to see his face, just the outline of his figure, and he was carrying a small bag to one side. Crane reached inside his pocket for his knife and held it at arm's length towards The Ripper. 'If I didn't have her to contend with, I would gut you like a pig for what you did.'

'Would you indeed? You might like to know that your little sister did so beg for her pitiful life, and to think I would be interested in a tired, wrinkled old hag like that. She had served her purpose, and once that expired, she was useless to me. So I killed her.' The Ripper let out a screech from the dark. 'Oh, and by the way, Ignatius, being one who never likes to throw away a keepsake, I have something that belonged to your dear sweet Maude.' The Ripper reached inside his black bag and took out a small, wet object. 'Here, catch, it's her heart. I tore it out of her dying body.'

Crane propelled Elsbeth forward so hard that she fell face down. He jumped up, catching the slimy, wet, and cold organ in his hands. Landing, he stumbled, not quite finding his balance, going too far back, breaking through the flimsy guardrail, teetering on the edge. The Ripper quickly shot out of the dark, holding him by his throat. 'Time to join your whore of a sister.' Then he released him, letting Crane fall silently backwards into the dark abyss until a thundering crash was heard below.

The Ripper quickly went over to Elsbeth before she got to her feet, grabbed her by the hair, and yanked her up. The pain was excruciating as she yelled out. Abberline, now just a foot or two away, scrambled over the last part of the stairs that had given way. He was within touching distance of the platform when he heard the wood splinter and what was left of the stairs give way, leaving him just hanging on by his fingers to the loose boards that made up the deck. There was nothing other than an eighty-foot drop he was now clinging for his life as he watched The Ripper take Elsbeth to the centre, where the wheel holding the bell was.

The Ripper stood behind her, his grip tight and firm. 'Don't struggle, little one, or I will do what I did to Camilla and gut you right here.'

'Just go, leave us,' she implored him. Elsbeth struggled to free herself, but The Ripper's grip was too firm.

'Take me instead of her, if you want a kill, I'm here, all you have to do is let me drop like you did Crane, all you have to do is let her go.' Abberline felt himself slipping.

'No, Abberline,' Elsbeth screamed back.

The Ripper didn't react, the darkness still shielding him. 'Oh, don't worry, inspector, if you haven't already descended to your death, I was considering cutting your fingers off one by one, feeding them to you and then sending your head back to your wife. However, that would spoil the theatre of the short time Elsbeth has left, and we should embrace it and let you share in her last few moments of existence. Don't you worry, I have decided that simply throwing her off the edge is just such a waste. No, this young lady is going to put on a real show for you, so you cling on for a little while longer, because *you* have the best seat in the house.'

Abberline tried to heave himself up. His fingers were now sore and burning from taking his whole weight. He tried swinging his body from side to side, an old mountaineering trick, to gain an advantage, hoping that he might get enough momentum to throw his leg over the top. But it was risky, and time for Elsbeth was fast running out.

Elsbeth pushed back again, trying once more. She was going to die anyway, so what did it matter? She tried to kick his shins, missing. He ripped her head back, wrapped his right hand around her mouth and nostrils, tighter and tighter, she couldn't breathe. She felt as if she was suffocating, her legs buckled, and life was slipping away, then he released her. She fell forward, bending over, and her lungs felt on fire as she gasped for air.

'Now don't go spoiling the finale,' The Ripper said.

Abberline swung his body back and forth again as the boards he clung to started to spring up from the deck, the old nails snapping and coming loose. He had seconds before he fell. He had one last attempt, then with all his might, he swung as hard as he could, just managing to get the heel of his shoe on the top of the deck. It wasn't much, but it was enough to get an advantage and heave the rest of himself over.

'Hurry, if you want to save her.' The Ripper took Elsbeth towards the large wooden wheel with the two bell-ringing ropes that passed through a gap to the bottom of the tower eighty feet below. He lifted one of the ropes, which was frayed and old, wrapped it under her arms, and knotted it tightly. 'Poetic, don't you think, inspector, as her body smashes into the stone floor, the bell will toll, people will hear it for miles.'

Abberline pushed himself up with all his might onto the deck and scrambled to his feet.

The Ripper laughed hysterically as he leaned in, whispering into Elsbeth's ear for the last time. 'Time to join the dead.' With that, he pushed her through the gap and disappeared back into the dark. Elsbeth cried out as she went hurtling towards the bottom. She had just seconds to live.

Abberline ran launching himself onto the rope grabbing it with both hands. It was travelling so fast that it tore his skin off. He held on with all his might, working through the excruciating pain, as he scrambled round on the deck, throwing himself backwards, taking the weight. The rope stretched and strained, dragging him towards the hole, then came to an abrupt halt.

He had stopped her from plunging any further, but the rope had become damaged, and the strands were unravelling quickly. He gritted his teeth, pulling her back up as fast as he could, his hands badly torn. The rope seemed to creak and groan as strands flew apart. Time had run out. He let out a massive cry as he pulled one last time with every ounce of strength he could muster until she was close enough for him to reach out with one hand and grab her.

Once he had hold of her, he released the rope and then, with both hands, hauled her through the gap in the platform and onto her back, quickly untying the knot. She wasn't breathing. Abberline put one hand on top of the other on her chest and pressed down, counting, trying to massage her heart. Nothing happened. He tried again, this time pushing harder and longer. 'Come on, Elsbeth, don't give up, don't let him win.' It seemed like an age, but then she coughed and sputtered, taking in a massive gulp of air before rolling onto her side.

Abberline collapsed back and sighed with relief. 'I thought we had lost you there.'

Elsbeth smiled, looking at his hands. 'You're hurt.'

He looked down at his injuries, getting a handkerchief out from his trouser pocket to wrap around one of them. 'It's nothing, they will heal.' Abberline helped Elsbeth up, and they both sprinted towards the tower's window. Looking down, they could see the scaffolding up against the side of the building and a cloaked figure moving at speed towards the bottom.

'Shall we go after him?' Elsbeth asked.

'It's too late he has too much of a head start on us, and I doubt I could climb with my hands the way they are. We have to accept he's gone, Elsbeth.'

They continued to watch as The Ripper moved away from the bottom of the scaffolding. He stopped for a brief moment to look back up. There was a strange silence in the air, a stillness touched by a cold wind that sent a chilling feeling through them both. Then, in an instant, he had vanished into the night.

'It's not over, you know that. He's on some kind of mission and will kill and keep on killing until we stop him,' Elsbeth said.

'Where do you think he will go next? What does your intuition tell you?'

Elsbeth remained silent for a while before she answered as she looked out over the dark, rolling hills and thick woods in the distance. A strong sense filled her like no other she had known, of blood-stained alleyways and crimes beyond anything they had yet encountered. Then, a vision of Abberline standing over a woman's body on a foggy street in London, as the world woke up to the birth of a monster.

'Well, do you know Elsbeth? Where will we find him?'

'He's going home. He's going to Whitechapel.'

EPILOGUE

LONDON 1887

Edward Hughes, a Lighterman of many years, slipped the oar of his flat-bottom barge into the foggy waters of the River Thames. The vessel silently cut through the black, glassy surface as he made his way over to the docks at Rainham to collect his next cargo. The night was still and the air thick and heavy, making the foul stench of the river even more potent. Edward knew a storm was coming as dark anvil clouds gathered and growled. Drunken laughter, singing, and shouting echoed, breaking the silence, the sound travelling for miles. Trade of all sorts was conducted in secret, hidden within the dirty, dilapidated buildings that lined the wharf.

He was about midway to his destination when there was a low thud as the bow struck an obstacle. He rowed backwards, the water lapping against the wood of the oar, slowing the vessel to a gradual stop. Collecting a small oil lamp from the stern end, he made his way carefully around some crates towards the front.

The object bobbed up and down like a cork as Edward leaned over, shining the lamp closer to get a better look. He picked up a gaff lying next to him and held it out, snaring the object with the hook. He pulled it to the side, then, putting the pole and lamp down, used both hands to haul it up onto the deck. The smell was so putrid that it made him want to retch. The sackcloth that covered it was bound with rope, with patches stained a deep crimson.

Holes had been torn away by hungry eels that had bitten through the material looking for food. He pulled a knife from his belt and cut the rope, then pushed the wrapping away with the tip of the blade. He fell backwards onto the wooden planks of the deck, sickened and shocked, pushing his body backwards with the heels of his shoes away from the horrific sight before him.

The torso of a woman lay before him, wrinkled and bloated; her skin had turned a dark green in colour. But there was something else, one of her breasts was missing. It had been cut away, the rotting flesh left slithering across the exposed bone of her rib cage.

* * *

Whitechapel Road was an impoverished and poorly lit area of London. Yet, it was also a hive of activity, with traders of every description lining the pavement, selling their wares, shouting for customers. The rat-infested slums sat behind where overcrowding, prostitution, and disease were rampant. The Ripper knew it was a perfect place to hide; it was the ideal hunting ground.

The building was unremarkable, it did not advertise itself as a Masonic Lodge or as anything other than a detached house of Georgian construction like many others in the capital. It sat towards the end of the street, alone, with a small flight of steps leading up to a black door and a silver knocker in the shape of a gargoyle. The visitor knocked twice and waited for a few minutes before the door was opened, and he was shown through by a small, balding man in his sixties, dressed in a dark suit and gloves.

The hallway had a black-and-white checkered floor, with several portraits on the walls of men looking down from heavily gilded frames. The man produced a blindfold from his pocket and proceeded to place it about The Ripper's head, after which he slowly guided him forward.

'Sorry, sir, it's protocol, but rest assured the Worshipful Master is expecting you.'

A short while later, they came to a halt. The man removed the blindfold and walked away, his footsteps echoing off the tiled floor.

The Ripper was facing a small confessional booth, where the door on one side had been left open. He stepped inside. It smelled old, stale and musty as he sat on a polished wooden bench. He drew back a black velvet curtain in front of him to reveal a fine mesh that allowed communication with the next compartment.

'I trust you heard about the torso of a woman they fished out of the Thames?' A voice came from behind the screen. 'The surgeon who examined it, a man named Callaway, said she was around twenty-seven to twenty-nine years of age and that the person who dissected the victim was very skilled and, I quote, *"thoroughly acquainted with anatomy"*. I presume you have knowledge of the matter?'

'Yes, you could say I am familiar with the incident. Why do you ask?'

Lord Silas Dydko placed his face close against the lattice, his voice slow but sharp. 'This Lodge is unlike any other. It is far older, with many dark rituals and secrets that society would find abhorrent to say the least.'

'We provide complete anonymity to all who join, along with full protection against any prosecution for past or present deeds. This provides the privileged few within its ranks to live as we wish, to act out our deepest, darkest fantasies without fear or judgment, however depraved. But there are *conditions*. Nothing can ever be traced back to The Lodge, is that clear, sir?

'I realise I have yet to be officially inducted into the brotherhood, but I can assure you I have no intention of ever causing you to regret that decision.'

'Yes, however…and please do not deny it, I know it was you who was responsible for that stump they found floating. It has your signature all over it, we are not fools! We are extremely well-connected all the way up to the very top. The other examples of your work in Brighton and more recently in Lidgate Manor have not gone unnoticed. You need to take care, sir, do I make myself clear?'

'Indeed, I understand, and I can only give you my word that no act will lead back to the brotherhood. I swear it on my life.'

'Oh, yes, your life. Well, you will pay with it if you should ever bring questions to our door, and I promise you, it will not be an easy death. What is it you want from us?'

The Ripper thought carefully for a while before answering. 'I intend to wipe clean the vermin that infects the streets of our great city, and to that end I require to be able to move about at will, and strike whenever I have the need, or opportunity.'

'When you say vermin, what do you speak of?'

'Prostitutes.'

'And what would you have done with them?'

'Kill them. I intend to kill them all, in ways the world will never forget.'

Lord Silas Dydko grinned. 'Welcome to The Black Lodge.'

Book III – The Black Lodge. Coming soon!

Please click "Follow" on Amazon to be kept informed.

If you enjoyed this book, please consider leaving a review.

Acknowledgements

I want to express my heartfelt gratitude to the following individuals for their invaluable help and support in bringing this novel to life.

Jane Dixon-Smith - Book Cover Design and Formatting.

www.jdsmith-design.co.uk

Thank you, Jane, for your incredible cover design and formatting. Your patience and ability to know what I wanted when I didn't were genius.

Scott Nicholson / Snr Editing & Development.

Scott Nicholson. A successful published writer in his own right, Scott has been invaluable. His professional editing skills, wisdom, and insight have made this book the best it can be. He has been a delight to work with, and I look forward to working together on many more projects in the future. Thank you, Scott.

Advanced readers and editorial support

Thank you to the following for their editorial help and assistance in comments and suggestions for improvement

Spencer Britton (USA)

Muriel Bal

Debi, my wife, without whom this book would not have been possible. Thank you for all your support, patience, and unwavering belief.

Printed in Dunstable, United Kingdom